WICKED STOP,
GEORGIA

WICKED STOP,
GEORGIA

ZANE SMITH

WICKED STOP, GEORGIA

Zane Smith

NEW PULP PRESS

Published by New Pulp Press, LLC, 926 Truman Avenue, Key West, Florida 33040, USA.

For information contact:
Publisher@NewPulpPress.com

ISBN-13: 978-1945734212 (New Pulp Press)
ISBN-10: 1945734213

Printed in the United States of America
Visit us on the web at www.newpulppress.com

Dedicated to my daughter Debbie,
who has always stood by my side.

Author's Note: There is no town by the name of Wicked Stop in south Georgia as depicted in this novel nor anywhere else for that matter. Nor are any of the characters in this novel real.

WICKED STOP,
GEORGIA

"If people bring so much courage to this world the world has to kill them to break them, so of course it kills them. The world breaks everyone and afterward many are strong at the broken places. But those that will not break it kills. It kills the very good and the very gentle and the very brave impartially. If you are none of these you can be sure that it will kill you too but there will be no special hurry."

– Ernest Hemingway

"I do not wish to kill nor to be killed, but I can foresee circumstances in which both these things would be by me unavoidable."

– Henry David Thoreau

"Nature has no principles. She furnishes us with no reason to believe that human life is to be respected. Nature in her indifference, makes no distinction between good and evil."

– Anatole France

ONE

Clair

There was something about the motel clerk Clair didn't like. Something that made her shiver. It was nothing she could put her finger on, the feeling was too elusive. It wasn't because the lewd old fool gave her the once-over as soon as she and her family stepped into the motel office first thing in the morning to check out of their rooms. That wasn't it.

Call it instinct, an instinct she inherited from her Japanese-American mother whose own mother and father had been interred by the American government during World War II. A harrowing experience that left them wary of authority and suspicious of white people in general. Or, maybe it came from her father who was half-black and half-white, his black heritage yielding the cautionary forewarning. Part of the black man's DNA, she reasoned.

"All you have to do," the clerk said, leaning over the counter, the map spread out in front of him, "is follow I-75 south until just about here." He pointed a dirty fingernail at a section of the map of Georgia located not far from Jimmy Carter's hometown of Plains, Georgia and the former Civil War prisoner camp of Andersonville.

"That's sort of out in the sticks, isn't it?" Clair's father, Marshall King, asked. "For a first class resort hotel."

"It's a retreat," the clerk said, smirking.

"Resort, retreat, whatever," Marshall snorted.

"Got a four-star restaurant, so I been told."

"What else?"

"You name it, it's there. Hot tubs, cocktail lounges, shows, all the stuff rich people like. Reasonably priced, too."

"What's the name of the place, again?"

"Wicked Stop. The Retreat at Wicked Stop."

"Funny name for a resort."

Helen, Clair's Japanese-American mother, smiled. "Funny name for a town."

"Suppose so," the clerk said. "Way I hear it, the town was named for something that happened during the Civil War."

"What was that?" Marshall said.

"Don't rightly know. Got to ask the folks at the Retreat."

Marshall peered at the clerk. "You get a commission if we stay there?"

"No reason to get uppity ... sir." The clerk came down hard on the "sir."

Helen tugged her husband's sleeve. "We can talk about it later in the car, Marshall."

For a second time, more boldly now, perhaps in response to the challenge issued by Marshall, the clerk's hungry gaze roamed Clair's body, a nose to toes appraisal ranging from her coal black hair and matching dark eyes, depthless and hypnotic, to her ample bosom, out of proportion for a young woman who stood 5'4" tall and weighed 115 pounds. Skin color the lightest shade of cocoa butter. His gaze came to rest on her long, shapely legs that jutted out from a pair of short-shorts.

Clair avoided the motel clerk's gaze. Over the years she had become accustomed to stares, knew there was no avoiding them. In high school it had been different. Back then if older men raked her body with looks of unrestrained lechery, she resented it. Even went so far as to tell a couple of them to fuck off. No longer. Over the past several years and countless ogles, she had learned to tune them out.

Yet ... there was an unexplainable aspect of the motel clerk's behavior, something more than simple lust. The way he smirked, as if he had secret knowledge about ... well, something she didn't know or understand. The feeling left her unsettled.

The clerk's restless gaze swept over the other young woman in the motel office, the one he heard the older man call Heather. By physical build and size, she could have been Clair's twin, the major differences being her blonde hair, blue eyes and alabaster white skin. A bosom not as large as Clair's but well formed. She was wearing tight shorts and a revealing tee shirt that clearly displayed her large nipples.

Marshall, noticing the clerk's fixed gaze, frowned. "You can call ahead for us, arrange two rooms for tonight. Family of four. Our names are on the register." With that, he wheeled around and said to Helen, Clair and Heather, "Let's go."

The family left the motel office and loaded their suitcases into the trunk of Marshall's 2009 Lincoln Town Car, a car he cherished and refused to trade in for a newer model.

After they climbed into the car, Heather said in her breathless voice with a slight lisp to it, "I thought we were headed to Ft. Lauderdale." She and Clair had been pre-med classmates at Ohio State, and this trip was their graduation gift. Cleveland to Florida, first class all the way.

Except that yesterday the Lincoln's fuel filter clogged in the sticks south of Nashville and they were forced to spend the night at this dumpy motel while a local garage repaired the car.

"We're going to Ft. Lauderdale, honey," Marshall said to Heather. "But we'll need to stop one more night before we get there. And this resort at Wicked Stop is on the way."

Clair's mouth tightened. No matter how many times she asked her dad not to call her friends "Honey," he persisted in doing so. Not maliciously, of course. He was just old school, reared in a former day when men routinely called secretaries and young women names like honey and sweetheart. Clair sighed. Long-standing habits are so hard to break.

Unfortunately, her older brother Justin didn't have the same excuse. Clair once heard him unabashedly tell a friend that "Women are good for the three Cs: cooking, cleaning and kissing." Then roared with laughter at his feeble witticism. That pretty much summed up her brother's attitude toward women. It galled her but, in the interests of family unity, she kept her mouth shut. Still, in a family where his mother was an architect and his sister was preparing to become a surgeon, she wondered how Justin picked up the idea of woman as homebody and servant to man.

Not that she had to think hard or long about the answer. It came down to the same thing. Dad, of course. He had this antiquated attitude about women. What Clair called jungle thinking. Me Tarzan, you Jane. I work, you cook.

Dad had never fully accepted the idea of Mom working outside the home. Clair sensed that he was jealous of Mom's position as a senior manager with Cleveland's most prestigious architectural firm. Mom brought home more money than Dad, which had to add to his resentment. To make matters worse, Mom, a fiercely independent woman, used her maiden name Matsui, and not her married name, at work.

Once, when Clair was a senior in high school, she overheard a conversation between her parents that crushed her. It was early Saturday afternoon. A small fire in the basement of the high school had sent the practicing cheerleaders home, Clair among them. Mom and Dad didn't know she was in the house. From the shadows of the entrance hallway Clair listened to her parents argue about the necessity of Clair going to college.

"She has her heart set on becoming a doctor, Marshall."

"She doesn't need to. All the girl has to do is get a job as a secretary for one of the nice downtown firms. Meet some fine young man and get married. She'll be set for life."

Dad's objections drove a dagger through Clair's heart. Particularly since he hadn't balked about sending her older brother Justin to Notre Dame for his undergraduate degree in accounting. Nor did he quibble about Justin's selection of the expensive Wharton School in Philadelphia for his graduate studies in business.

So, it fell to Clair to fund her own way through pre-med at Ohio State. Which she did with some clandestine help from her mother. Helen paid for Clair's tuition and books. Clair worked in the university cafeteria as well as a local bridal shop to pay for her room and board and incidental expenses. She intended to borrow her way through medical school, this time without help from either her mom or dad.

While Clair simmered in that long-ago memory, her mother, Helen, drew a cell phone from her purse and punched in a number. Marshall looked at her questioningly.

"I'm calling Justin." Her son, delayed in Cleveland by his employer, a professional accounting firm, to conduct an unscheduled audit of a client company. A last minute emergency that postponed his vacation and prevented him from driving to Florida with his family and Heather.

A few moments passed, then, "Justin? This is Mom." After making sure her twenty-eight-year-old son was getting enough to eat and plenty of rest—ever the doting mother—she reconfirmed his intention to fly to Ft. Lauderdale, Florida tomorrow night and meet them at their resort hotel nearby. He'd join the family on vacation and return with them by car to Cleveland.

"No, dear, we're not driving right through," she said into the cell phone in answer to his apparent question. "We're stopping at a resort hotel in a town in south Georgia off I-75 called The Retreat at Wicked Stop."

She listened and smiled as Justin said something in reply. "No, dear, that's not a joke. The town is actually called Wicked Stop. Can you join us there tonight?"

Marshall glanced at Helen as she listened to Justin's answer. She shook her head and mouthed the word "no." A minute or two more of idle chatter between mother and son and Helen clicked off the phone and put it away.

"Exactly as we thought, Justin can't get away until we arrive in Ft. Lauderdale. Tonight's out of the question. Besides, where would he fly into?"

Marshall shrugged. He put the car in gear and drove out of the parking lot and onto the highway, Helen beside him, the two young women in the back seat. Clair glanced behind her through the back window of the car at a rapidly diminishing motel. Once more she thought of the motel clerk and shivered.

TWO

Marshall

Despite the flow of cold air from the car's air conditioner, Marshall was hot. He wiped perspiration from his face and neck with a handkerchief and turned the air conditioner to its highest setting. A blast of cold air swept through the Lincoln, dropping the temperature several degrees.

The outside thermometer registered eighty-nine degrees, hot for ten in the morning. According to the weather channel on television, the temperature for the day promised to top out at a blistering 101 degrees through most of South Georgia. Humid enough, said the weatherman, cracking a clichéd joke, to make a statue weep. A typical summer's day in the Deep South.

Marshall glanced at Helen next to him and at Clair and Heather through the rearview mirror. None of them had broken a sweat. Indeed, Helen was wearing a thin sweater and hovered in it to ward off blasts of cold air. When Marshall was younger and more slender, the heat never bothered him. That was years ago. The extra weight he carried now at age fifty-two made him sensitive to summer temperatures. When pressed, he'd grudgingly admit to an overeating problem, but wouldn't fully accept that at 5'10" and 253 pounds he was grossly out of shape and heading, as Helen constantly reminded him, for a heart attack.

His slender wife had an hourglass figure, stood 5'2" and weighed 102 pounds. At social functions he was painfully aware of the physical contrast between them. A fact that did nothing to alleviate his feelings of inadequacy.

Over the years, as Marshall's number of chins grew from two to three, Justin and Clair joined the chorus of voices raising concern. A black associate, a lawyer, joked that Marshall's jowly appearance made him look like a chocolate Santa Claus. How he *hated* that description. In fact, how he hated being a half-black, half-white non-entity. He felt like Philip Nolan the main character of Edward Everett Hale's short story, *A Man Without A Country*.

Being half-white hadn't brought him acceptance by white folks. Granted, they went out of their way to put on a happy face when he was around, but underneath the veneer of camaraderie, Marshall sensed Whitey straining to oblige him only as long as he was in their presence. Show the world you're treating the nigger equally and with compassion, that kind of liberal bullshit. It made white people's recognition of him a travesty, more of an accommodation than true friendship. Neighbors chatted with him at occasional weekend cookouts, but when it came time to show their true colors (Marshall smiled inwardly at the pun), they didn't want him as a member of their exclusive country clubs.

That's why he named his son Justin. Not Jessie or Tyrone or Lamarr or Roosevelt. Those telltale black names. At first he thought of naming him Chad. That sounded lily-white, until Marshall discovered that Chad was also the name of a country in Africa. Goodbye Chad.

Justin was a solid upper middle class name, a white name connoting Anglo Saxon heritage and prep school advantage. The kind of image he desired his son to portray to the world. He didn't want Justin to suffer as he had, wanted to assure he'd be accepted by Whitey without reservation.

Bitter childhood memories taunted Marshall,

invading his thoughts at odd hours of the day and night, upsetting him, making him consider at times chucking his small accounting business, everything he'd worked so hard to achieve, and get the hell away from it all. Away from all the senseless racist bullshit and the upside-down world where women considered themselves superior to men and whites handed blacks the short end of the stick.

Memories of a white father and black mother who barely tolerated each other, of a cross burning on the front lawn of their home in Jackson, Mississippi, of black kids shunning him at school and white kids mocking him. Memories of his father, an accountant for a local clothing manufacturer losing his job and packing up in the middle of the night and sneaking out of town, leaving his mother and Marshall to fend for themselves. Memories of a mother who suffered a debilitating stroke after her husband deserted her. Memories of kissing the asses of white social workers for food, clothing and shelter. Bitter memories.

Marshall burped into his closed fist and popped a couple of antacid tablets into his mouth.

Black people weren't much better than Whitey. They barred him from their inner circles, weren't comfortable in his presence. You saw the question in their eyes: Is this nigger trying to pass for white? Most blacks considered Marshall more white than black because as a marginally successful businessman and owner of a small accounting firm catering to local retail shops, he did business mainly with white companies. Those who criticized never stopped to think that most businesses were owned by whites, so what choice did he have? At a cocktail lounge one night, an inebriated black associate of Marshall told him something he already was painfully aware of: that black folks inherently didn't trust zebras, those half-black, half-white concoctions like Marshall. Many blacks intentionally, others unintentionally, looked at him with suspicion, often animosity. So Marshall avoided hanging out with blacks, which reinforced their contention that Marshall was sucking up to Whitey.

Marshall took a deep breath and tried to squeeze the negative thoughts from his mind. The bile rising in his throat made him burp again. He covered his mouth with a fat hand and turned away. When he thought Helen and the girls weren't watching, he popped another antacid tablet in his mouth.

"You okay, dear?" Helen asked, examining him, her brow furrowed in concern. The lady, Marshall had to admit, missed nothing. Had eyes in the back of her head.

"Doin' fine," he responded automatically, as he had countless other times to the same question from Helen and his kids.

Marshall stole another look through the rear view mirror at the three other occupants of the car and reflexively compared the color of their skins to his. His was the darkest by far. Clair looked more like a white girl with a tan than a light-skinned black. Helen's skin was white with the faintest tint of pale yellow. Although Marshall was only a light chestnut-color, he felt self-conscious next to the three women, particularly Heather, whose white skin reminded him of marble. Compared to her, he was the color of a turd.

"Where are we now, Dad?" Clair called out from the back seat, raising her voice so it could be heard over the noise of the air conditioner.

Marshall, phlegmatic as always, nodded to Helen and she checked the map. "Just coming into Chattanooga. Another ten miles or so." She ran a finger down the map. "If we don't stop for lunch and hold it to a couple of pit stops, we can make Wicked Stop in about"—she checked her woman's Rolex wristwatch—"say five hours, give or take."

Clair and Heather groaned in unison. Marshall and Helen looked at each other and exchanged grins. The groans awakened memories of earlier trips and the impatience of their kids to arrive at vacation destinations. Riding in cars, Marshall knew, was difficult for young people bursting with surplus energy. Even twenty-one year-old kids such as Clair and Heather.

The hum of tires on the road lured Marshall back to his thoughts. He had never vented his conflicted racial feelings to Helen, the kids or anybody else for that matter. He was a solid family man, but a loner without any real close friends to confide in. Had he close friends, Marshall never would have opened up to them, anyway. He kept his problems and concerns to himself, tucked deep inside him where they steadily ate away at his stomach lining, forcing him to consume a couple of packs of antacid tablets daily.

Helen examined Marshall with the sharp eye of a concerned wife. "Let's make a pit stop, dear. You look tired."

Marshall grumbled something unintelligible.

"Great idea, Mrs. K," Heather said in her sex kitten lisp.

Clair pointed to a sign alongside the road. "There's a Holiday Inn ahead." When its exit approached, Marshall obediently pulled off the highway and stopped in front of the motel's restaurant. They used their respective restrooms and met in the lobby.

"Marshall," Helen said, "did that motel clerk call ahead and make reservations for us at Wicked Stop?"

"He was supposed to."

"Well, let's make sure, dear. Would you call and reconfirm? Tell them we'll arrive late this afternoon. I'd do it, but my cell phone battery's dead."

Marshall had inadvertently left his smart phone at home, so he walked to the desk and asked to use the house phone. He dialed the telephone number the motel clerk had given him.

"The Retreat at Wicked Stop," a cheery woman's voice announced.

Marshall told her who he was and asked her to confirm his reservation.

"One moment, Mr. King."

Ten seconds later another person, this one a man with as jaunty a voice, got on the line. "Mr. King?"

"Speaking."

"We're expecting you sometime before six. Is that correct, sir?"

"About then."

"Okay, let's see if I have this right. There's you, your wife, and two daughters."

"Actually one daughter and her friend."

"Both in their early twenties, I take it?"

Curious question to ask. "Who am I talking with, please?"

"I'm Werner, sir. When you arrive I'll be your personal guide and help you and your family settle in."

"What's the ages of my daughter and friend got to do with it?"

Werner chuckled. "Nothing sinister, sir. Just wanted to know so we can make their stay more pleasant. We have a disco, juice bar, that kind of thing. The sort of activities younger people enjoy. Drug free and alcohol free, of course, and supervised."

That explained Werner's question. Marshall breathed a sigh of relief, chastised himself for being suspicious of everybody and everything.

"You can expect us late this afternoon."

"That's great, Mr. King. Can't tell you how much

we're looking forward to seeing you and your family."

They hung up. Marshall peered at the phone in his hand. Werner's last comment struck him as odd. Why should the people at Wicked Stop be looking forward to welcoming a simple family from Cleveland? What have we got that's so special? Then he laughed to himself once he realized what they were after was ringing up his American Express card.

He shook his head and popped another antacid tablet.

THREE

Helen

Every day Helen found it more painful to act the doting wife and mother. To behave as if nothing was churning her world, upending her existence. To pretend that Roger, a young architect in her office, half her fifty years, wasn't making love to her (making *out* with her, she had to admit, was a better description, no matter how painful that insight may be). To acknowledge that Roger occupied her thoughts every hour of the day and every minute of long, restless nights. To accept that he was *white!* (Why a white man now? Was he the forbidden fruit, the overwhelming need for him a reaction to her half-black husband and her own lemon-tinted skin?)

The affair thrilled her, absolutely thrilled her.

It also devastated her. She wanted—no, desperately needed—to blurt it out, to confess to her devoted husband of thirty years and her loving children and implore their forgiveness. Her upbringing, her personal values, her enduring Christian beliefs, her consuming regard for family first—all of these made confession mandatory.

On a practical level, Helen knew she'd never unburden herself, was deathly afraid of destroying her family. Which made a mockery of her convictions. And eroded her faith to do the right thing, no matter the pain. Her mother and father had reared her to be selfless and honest, regardless of personal cost. The struggle was tearing her apart, making her life an unending hell of torment and self-doubt.

Regardless, she didn't want to let go of Roger,

couldn't if the truth be known. He meant everything, her raison d'être. So she endured the guilt and lived for the few moments she was in Roger's arms.

Helen squirmed in her seat, hoping that Marshall wrote off her restlessness to the long car ride. As usual, her husband was absorbed in his own problems, most of them focused on race, perceived or real. Helen believed most of them were perceived. He was so preoccupied it blinded him to everything else. That's why, Helen knew, he'd never tumble to her affair. If she wanted to she could bring Roger home for dinner and Marshall would never suspect anything unseemly. Not that she ever intended to. Marshall had never met Roger, knew nothing at all of his existence, and she intended to keep it that way.

Her son Justin was as tone deaf to undercurrents among people as his father, so unless she committed an absolutely egregious faux pas, he'd be similarly oblivious to her affair.

Clair was another matter. She was smart and perceptive and attuned to people's feelings. Thank God she was away at school most of the year. Otherwise she'd soon sense that her mother was cheating. And that would crush both of them.

Riding with her thoughts as constant companions made for an exhausting day. Helen distracted herself by studying the south Georgia landscape as it flowed by. There wasn't much to see; an occasional collapsed barn with a faded advertisement for chewing tobacco painted on its side. Sporadically, a combination gas station-diner with a few dusty pickup trucks parked in front and a sign that read something like "Gas Up, Eat Here." Between those sights an endless flow of farms, woods and fields.

Helen felt uneasy and didn't understand why. It wasn't that she disliked countryside locales. On the contrary, she enjoyed the peace and quiet of pastoral settings. Only this time something felt wrong. It frustrated her. Her feelings were as hard to pin down as a drop of mercury under her thumb.

Perhaps it had something to do with the motel clerk who sold Marshall a bill of goods about Wicked Stop. She didn't like the man, felt repulsed by his openly carnal appraisal of Clair and Heather.

Helen glanced at her watch. They had been in the car several hours and were close to their interstate exit when Helen said, "There's nothing down here, other than scrub pine trees and red clay. It's desolate."

"I'll second that," Clair said.

"Amen," Heather chipped in.

Marshall said nothing, instead set his lips in a thin line and searched ahead for the exit off I-75 that would take them on the final leg of their journey to Wicked Stop.

"There it is, Georgia Route 27."

Helen checked the map and sighed. "Take the exit and drive west, dear."

Marshall glanced at her. "Something wrong?"

"I don't know."

He kept driving. They passed through the country town of Americus.

"I agree with Mom," Clair said. "There's nothing around here at all other than peanut and onion farms. What's the resort going to look like?"

Heather had her nose glued to the window. "Jeez, everything around here is kind of woodsy, but maybe that's cause we're so used to big cities."

"What's everybody getting up tight about?" Marshall asked, heated now. "A lot of real nice vacation spots are in the country. Remember Hot Springs in the Virginia mountains? One of the best resorts in the country. Damned place was so isolated you could hardly get to it."

An uneasy silence followed his outburst. Marshall, stiff necked, exited Georgia Route 27 and continued driving west. Twenty minutes later he found what he was looking for. "Here's the turnoff." He pointed to a dirt road cutting through a thicket of scrub pine and poplar trees. Nothing else around other than open meadows and woods.

Marshall stopped the car and read a small metal sign pinned to a tree trunk: TOWN OF WICKED STOP THIS WAY.

"There. See, I told you," Marshall said.

"There's nothing but a narrow dirt road," Clair observed. "And it's full of ruts."

Helen laid a hand on Marshall's arm. "Why don't we turn around and go back to I-75? We can always find a Holiday Inn or some other motel to spend the night."

Marshall's neck grew thick with anger. Helen saw the arteries in his neck swell to the size of cords. "Damn it, we've come this far. Let's not get paranoid. Everybody relax."

When he got like this, Helen eased off. Marshall was sensitive about issues concerning who made the decisions in the family, and on matters as seemingly inconsequential as this, she felt it diplomatic to give way.

Except, this was different ... somehow. "I have an idea, Marshall. Why don't we go back to Americus, find a nice diner, and have a cup of coffee, relax for a while, then we'll come back."

Marshall looked at her with fire in his eyes. He appeared to struggle, then the fight left him and he collapsed like a fighter between rounds. "All right," he grumbled. "But we come back right after coffee."

They were backing up to turn around and return to Americus when a red Ford pickup truck bounced down the dirt road from the direction of Wicked Stop and braked in front of the Lincoln. A young woman of Clair's age jumped out of the truck and walked up to the driver's side of the Lincoln. She wore blue slacks and a short-sleeved white blouse, the latter with a sewn blue crest over her left pocket with the words "The Retreat at Wicked Stop" stitched in gold. Her blonde hair was tied in a ponytail and a pleasant expression warmed her face.

Marshall rolled down the window, and the young woman leaned over. "Hi folks, welcome to Wicked Stop. Looking for our famous Retreat?" Helen noticed that she spoke with a gentle southern accent and had bone white teeth, the kind professional models display in toothpaste commercials.

"How'd you know that, dear?" Helen asked.

The young woman pointed to two large oak trees guarding either side of the driveway. Helen craned her neck and saw tiny cameras mounted high on each tree and pointed at the road.

"One of the TV reception screens is in the truck," the young woman said, "the others at the Retreat. It's a safety measure. In case one of our guests taking a walk needs immediate assistance. Some of them have health problems."

"How far up the road is the resort?" Marshall asked and looked doubtfully at the dirt road. "Does this road lead to a town or to a resort hotel?"

"Both actually, a very small town and the Retreat. Look, why don't you let me ride with you and I'll take you up there? It's real close."

"You work for the resort, I take it?" Marshall asked, reading the emblem on her blouse.

"Yes, sir, I do. And the boss, Mr. Phester, likes to call it a retreat. Actually, 'the' Retreat with a capital 'R'." She chuckled. "Not that it makes any difference.

You can call it a resort if you like. I promise not to tell."
She stuck a slim hand over her heart and flashed a
warm smile at Marshall. That, coupled with the gentle
lilt of her southern accent, obviously charmed him.
Helen shook her head in wonder.

Marshall smiled back and said, "Slide in front."

Helen was about to object but didn't want to
contradict her husband and embarrass him in front of
the stranger.

The girl – Helen thought of her as a girl, not a
woman – bound away, parked the pickup truck
alongside the road and pocketed the keys. Helen stood
outside the car as the girl slipped into the front seat,
sandwiching herself between Helen and Marshall.

"I'm Melissa," she said. Introductions followed.
Clair and Heather chatted easily with Melissa, who
seemed genuinely happy to see the girls. Helen was
more reserved, shaking Melissa's hand without much
enthusiasm.

Melissa seemed to notice. She picked up on how
Heather addressed Helen. "You'll love Wicked Stop,
Mrs. K. We promise to pamper you."

Helen turned and studied Melissa. The girl was
beautiful, Helen had to admit, but the beauty stopped
at her eyes, which were watchful and not at all in
keeping with her cheerful demeanor. "I'm sure I will,
dear," Helen said and patted the back of Melissa's
hand.

Marshall eased the Lincoln onto the dirt road and
followed its twisting path as it bounced over ruts and
climbed a slight but steady rise. Trees and hedges
flanked the road making it impossible to see more than
ten yards on either side. Treetops merged over the
road, forming a canopy and choking out the sun. Helen
imagined she was riding inside a tunnel, a
claustrophobic feeling she couldn't shake. She

wondered what kind of town was accessible through such an ill-kept and scary road. "Are there any other entrances to Wicked Stop?"

Melissa shook her head. "What you see is what you get."

That made no sense. Helen leaned over and glanced at Marshall to see if he shared her feelings. He seemed oblivious to his surroundings, perfectly happy, as evidenced by the slight smile on his lips, perhaps because he was getting his way and going on to Wicked Stop instead of returning to I-75, perhaps because he had an engaging young girl seated next to him, her leg pressed against his in the cramped front seat. Helen turned and faced the backseat. Clair was quiet, possibly sharing her mother's concerns, and Heather, as usual, was bubbling over with small talk.

Helen turned back, smiled inwardly, almost laughed out loud at her silliness. Told herself to get a grip and stop acting like a schoolgirl who's been spooked by a horror film. Finally, she sighed and leaned back in her seat and tried to relax.

FOUR

Clair

The ride though the woods to reach Wicked Stop took fifteen minutes. Heather and Melissa babbled away while Clair remained silent and brooding. She thought it strange that a town had only one road leading into and out of it. Wasn't there some kind of state law mandating more than one exit in case of a forest fire?

At the crest of the hill the woods ended and the town of Wicked Stop came into view. Marshall drove through it with Melissa directing him. From what Clair saw, it consisted of one main drag and two side streets, the entire town girdled by rocky fields and thick forests.

"Welcome to Wicked Stop," Melissa said.

Marshall craned his neck to glance at Melissa. "How'd it get its name?"

Melissa chuckled. "Got it during the Civil War. The Rebels had a prisoner of war camp not far from here, Andersonville. Ever hear of it?"

"Sure," Clair said. "There was a book written about the camp."

Melissa nodded. "More than one. The town of Wicked Stop – it never had a real name until the Civil War – was a pit stop for the guards and soldiers from Andersonville."

"Pit stop?" Heather said.

"Saloons and a whorehouse, excuse my language. The Rebels came to town to get drunk and have a little fun with the girls. Somebody local, nobody knows who, named the town Wicked Stop. The name stuck for over 150 years now."

Marshall laughed and Heather giggled.

Helen said, "I don't see anything remotely resembling a saloon and ... well, you know."

Melissa grinned. "The whorehouse burned down in 1912, if I remember my facts correctly. The name of the town stuck."

"It's small. How many people live here?" Clair asked.

"Last count, about thirty-five."

Marshall glanced around. "That's all?"

"That's all, and just about everybody here either works for Mr. Phester or sells supplies to the Retreat. What you call a company town. But no whorehouse."

Clair thought the place looked like a set from a Clint Eastwood spaghetti western. A desultory air pervaded. The few people visible wore jeans and T-shirts and slouched around as if they had nothing important to do and no place specific to go. The stores and homes were slapped together with unpainted clapboard. The dusty streets held little traffic. An occasional battered pickup truck or delivery van, even a couple of horses tethered to a post in front of a general store. A single paved road ran through the center of town; its two side streets were dirt roads. The isolated nature of the place depressed Clair, made her wonder if its inhabitants felt closeted, out of touch with the world.

They passed a tall, rangy man dressed in wrinkled khaki pants and short-sleeved khaki shirt, dusty cowboy boots and a ten-gallon hat. He lounged in front of an office with a dusty plate-glass window that read WICKED STOP POLICE DEPARTMENT in faded letters.

Helen turned to Melissa. "Isn't this town too small for its own police department, dear?"

Melissa grinned. "That's our only lawman, Billy Ray Poynter. A good ol' boy from Alabama. Mr. Phester keeps him around in case the locals drink a little too much and harass the Retreat's guests. Doesn't happen often. Billy Ray's like the Maytag repairman, just sits around and waits for something to happen. Not that he's unhappy doing nothing. Gives him more time to drink."

Clair's mouth tightened. She didn't like to hear idle gossip, it made her uncomfortable. Her philosophy was tolerant and progressive, live and let live. Like most upper middle-class liberals, she loathed judgmental decisions about working-class people as much as she abhorred violence, felt that looking down on anybody was a step in the direction leading to exclusion and class hatred, eventually brutality. Clair proudly carried an ACLU card and marched for "Black Lives Matter" at every possible opportunity. Had she been a student in the Vietnam era, she would have opened her arms to the North Vietnamese in a gesture of peace. Jane Fonda was clearly one of her liberal heroes, an anti-war, anti-violence woman Clair believed every young girl should emulate.

Billy Ray tipped his hat in recognition as the Lincoln passed, like the sheriff in an old western movie. The hard planes of his face and hollowed cheeks brought to mind the legendary Gary Cooper in the old movie High Noon. Clair's mouth relaxed and she grinned. She almost heard the imaginary words "Howdy, ma'am" forming on his lips.

But the lawman also invoked other, less pleasant, images of oppressive police officers and their criminal counterparts, especially killers and pedophiles. Barbarians terrified Clair. She couldn't fathom man's savage nature and didn't believe she was capable of harming another human being, even to save her own life. She vividly recalled stories from both sets of grandparents. On her dad's side, tales of rape and lynching in the Deep South, and on her mom's side, the brutal death of relatives in Japan from American bombing raids in the forties that killed thousands of civilians.

To complete a class project on World War II in her sophomore year of high school, Clair watched with sick fascination a particularly graphic video showing scenes from the Nazi concentration camp, Auschwitz. Her eyes filled with horror as she viewed a frightening collage: the gaunt faces and haunted eyes of grown men and women weighing under ninety pounds, dead bodies piled on top of one another in drainage ditches like so much garbage, terrified children clinging to their mothers' skirts, being dragged off to gas chambers, crematoriums stuffed with the ashes of human remains. Afterward, sweating and shaking uncontrollably, she collapsed on her bed. Clair suffered from nightmares for the next several years. She shuddered involuntarily at the recollection.

"Where's the Retreat?" Marshall said.

"We're coming up to it." Melissa pointed the way to another dirt road that rose above the town.

A forest of pine trees soon surrounded them, but the drive this time lasted no more than six or seven minutes. The Lincoln pulled up to a gate and braked, and Melissa hopped out of the car.

Clair looked around. As far as she could see, the property was enclosed by an eight-foot high wrought iron fence with menacing razor-sharp spikes at the top that caught and reflected what little sunlight filtered through the trees. It spooked her. Why should a four-star resort hotel need a fence as intimidating as that of a prison camp? Or any fence, for that matter?

Melissa picked up an intercom from a box mounted on the side of the gate and spoke into it. Moments later the gate clicked and swung open.

Melissa waved the Lincoln through and climbed back in the car. The gate closed behind them and Clair caught her breath.

"What's the fence for, dear?" Helen asked, her voice tight.

"Oh, just to keep out vagrants that make their way up from the town. This is an exclusive resort, Mrs. K. We want to make this experience a memorable one for our guests, free from any intruders."

Then why am I so nervous about it? Clair thought and added up the signs that disturbed her: The hideous clerk at the motel this morning, a four-star resort nobody heard of, the rutted one-way dirt road into Wicked Stop that discouraged visitors, now the forbidding fence topped by razor-sharp spikes.

Clair glanced at Mom, saw the stiffness in her back, knew she shared her anxiety.

What to do about it? Clair leaned forward to get a closer look at Dad. He didn't seem at all concerned. If anything he glowed in the presence of the attractive young woman sitting beside him and the all-too-apparent thrill of her thigh touching his. He sweated freely but probably that was because the outside temperature hovered at 101, according to the latest radio weather report for the region, and with five people stuffed into the Lincoln it was bound to warm up.

They rode again for another three minutes before the Lincoln crested another small hill, the tree line parted and the hotel came into view. When he first saw it Marshall gasped with astonishment and Heather squealed. Even Mom relaxed; Clair saw it in the slump of her shoulders.

Until that moment Clair hadn't known what to expect. Now she did. The Retreat at Wicked Stop by all appearances *was* an exclusive hotel. Just as Melissa said. She had to admit that the repulsive motel clerk was right.

The hotel was spectacular and had a cold beauty about it. Made from marble with burnished aluminum window frames, the circular building rose five stories, with a gilded band that orbited the penthouse floor like a royal crown. A large horseshoe driveway swept between the hotel's grand entrance enclosing a majestic water fountain that recurrently propelled jets of water fifty feet into the air, shot through with red, yellow, green and blue lights. Clair figured that touch was right out of a Las Vegas architectural manual. A little too glitzy for her more subdued tastes, but admittedly expensive.

Two long and separate double-floor buildings constructed from the same marble and burnished aluminum window frames flanked the main building like spokes from a hub. The Bermuda lawn alongside the hotel was deep green and freshly cut and edged by flowerbeds with a colorful array of white and yellow day lilies, purple phlox, daisies and red roses, all carefully tended.

In the breezeway separating the main hotel from one of the double-floor buildings, Clair caught glimpses of a large swimming pool with tempting blue water. Sunlight sparkled on its surface.

"Well, what do you think?" Melissa asked, her face reflecting the pride she obviously felt about the Retreat.

"Gorgeous, absolutely gorgeous," Marshall gushed.

"Oh, I love it," Heather said and squeezed her hands together.

Clair leaned forward. "Reminds me of Las Vegas. Hard to believe you'd find something like this in the sti–" Clair felt her face flush.

Melissa turned to look at Clair. "Go ahead and say it. The sticks. It doesn't bother me. You're absolutely right. This is the sticks."

Only Helen was silent. Clair noticed that her back was stiff again, as if something was bothering her.

"Mom, you okay?" Clair asked.

"Fine, dear, I'm doing fine." But Clair could tell she wasn't doing fine, and abruptly her mother's alarm spread to Clair.

About what? She glanced around the property, puzzled. Then it came to her. There wasn't a single person in sight. Not a soul. In every resort hotel she had ever visited, the guests constantly mulled around the property. Not here. Not at the Retreat at Wicked Stop.

Where were they?

Goose flesh crept up her arms and she held herself and shivered.

FIVE

Billy Ray

After the Lincoln Town Car passed by, Billy Ray shook his head in dismay for the people in the car, knowing the fate that awaited them. His dread for the "innocents," as he called them, was exceeded only by the disgust he felt for himself, for tolerating Phester's evil business, no matter what club that blackmailing bastard held over his head.

Since he first arrived at Wicked Stop nine months ago how many times had he seen a carload of "innocents" parade through Main Street on their way to the Retreat? Enough times to get him sick thinking about it, more than enough to question his manhood, his sense of decency. It brought on a shame so deep that at times he entertained thoughts of ... well, doing something desperate.

Lately, Billy Ray's fits of depression were deepening. His personal anesthesia of bourbon, lots and lots of bourbon, no longer warded off the nightmares that invaded his sleep with increasing regularity.

He doubted the people in the Lincoln Town Car had the slightest idea of the true nature of the Retreat, just like all the innocents who had preceded them. Looked like five, probably a family, two of them, the girls in the back seat kind of young and pretty. He felt sorry for them as he did for all young people unfortunate enough to fall victim to the Retreat.

Billy Ray thought he spotted Melissa in the front seat of the Lincoln, squeezed between the fat guy driving the car and the tiny lady on the passenger side.

He sighed, remembering the one time Melissa favored his bed. They both had been dead drunk after a night of boozing and playing pool at Clyde's Bar & Grill, the town's sole restaurant and cocktail lounge. Scared to death that the snoops at the Retreat would find out, knowing that employees living there, like Melissa, were forbidden to touch alcohol, either on or off the job.

They'd staggered out of Clyde's at closing time and somehow made it to Billy Ray's three-room tumbledown shack at the edge of town. After that, events fuzzed over in Billy Ray's mind. Fact is, he was so drunk he didn't recall if they got it on. The last he remembered was stripping down with Melissa, and climbing on top with her legs straddled over his shoulders before his memory blanked out. He recalled nothing after that; couldn't even tell you if Melissa had a good time. Probably not, cause she never gave him another shot. He often wondered what he did, or failed to do that evening, that turned her off. Guessed too much booze kept him from getting it up. Truth was, Billy Ray became impotent after the fifth double bourbon. At which point the boozing became more important to him than sex, or anything else for that matter.

Billy Ray sighed again, pushed himself away from the side of the building in front of his one-room office. He lifted the wide-brimmed hat from his head and wiped his brow with a handkerchief already sopping wet from sweat. His watch read 5:30 p.m. Time for the first double bourbon and water of the evening. He'd been dry since drinking his favorite lunch of boilermakers: two shots of Jack Daniel's Black Label poured ever so gently into a tall draft of ice-cold beer and gently stirred. His mouth watered at the thought as he ambled down the street to Clyde's Bar & Grill.

His cell phone buzzed.

He cursed silently at the interruption. "Billy Ray Poynter here." His slow Alabama drawl unmistakably identified him. Townspeople told him they could shut their eyes and still know it was Billy Ray the second he opened his mouth.

"Hey, redneck, it's Werner."

Billy Ray felt the heat start to creep up his neck and face. "What do you want, skinhead?"

Werner chortled. "Damn, redneck, you're on high today. Must have slipped a few shots of bourbon in between lunch and dinner."

"Get to the point."

"Got a yellow Mustang with a young boy and girl heading your way. Mr. Phester wants you to intercept them, bring them back. And hurry, they just got through the gate."

"How'd they do that?"

"Melissa went to Americus and forgot to lock up."

"Why not let them go?"

"Haven't you been listening?" Werner's voice raised in pitch. "These are escapees. You better grab them, Poynter, or I go right to Mr. Phester and let him know you disobeyed his orders."

Silence from Billy Ray.

"And try not to let anyone in town see you. You been getting careless, lately."

"I don't take orders from you."

Before he disconnected, he heard Werner snort.

Billy Ray cursed to himself, knowing it would be an hour or more before he tasted that first bourbon. He skipped from slow speed into high, trotted around the corner of his office and jumped into the town's sole official vehicle, an old police car the Retreat picked up at an auction, a Ford Crown Victoria with a rotating red light mounted on the roof and an accompanying eighty-five decibel siren. Both of which he kept off after being warned by Werner not to unnecessarily alert townspeople.

He rode down Main Street in the direction of the woods leading out of town to the state highway, the only road to and from Wicked Stop. Aware that the Mustang would have to travel this way to escape.

About halfway into the woods, he turned the large sedan sideways so it blocked the dirt road at its narrowest point, climbed out and stood close to an old white oak tree, one with a trunk wide enough to shield him in case somebody with a gun opened fire.

Billy Ray didn't have long to wait. About one minute later he heard the sound of a car bottoming out on its springs as it hit ruts in the dirt road, the engine racing, its driver no doubt in a panic. The driver saw the Ford sedan blocking the road and slammed on the brakes at the last minute.

Billy Ray stood next to the white oak, his hand resting on the holster of his nine-millimeter automatic. "Get out of the car."

A scared kid in his late teens climbed out of the Mustang with his hands up, eyes wide with fright. The passenger's door opened and a pretty teenage girl emerged, her lips trembling, fear stamped over her face.

Billy Ray *hated* this part of the job. Terrorizing young kids was not something he enjoyed. He did this because he had no choice. It was either obey his lord and master Phester or lose his life. He ground his teeth and his jaw muscles worked furiously.

The kids mistook the lawman's masticating jaw muscles, thought he was angry. Billy Ray saw the alarm in their eyes. Their faces were dripping sweat, and not only from the heat. He smelled the fear in them.

"Nothing to worry about if you do what I tell you to do." He motioned to the girl, then to a small cleared space off the road. "Take the keys from your boyfriend and park the Mustang there."

After she pulled the Mustang off road, Billy Ray patted down both kids, guided them inside the back seat of the Ford and locked the doors. He refused to cuff them like criminals. Besides, his safety was assured by a heavy-gauge wire mesh screen that separated front from the backseat. And he controlled the door locks.

Billy Ray drove through the woods, into the town and on to the front gate guarding the Retreat. He picked up the intercom and called the main desk, asked Werner to come get his prisoners.

Five minutes later Werner arrived in the Retreat's pickup truck with Bobby at his side, a brute of a guy Billy Ray knew slightly. Rumor mill had it Bobby was a stone killer, that tearing people apart was his favorite pastime. Looking at him anyone could believe it. He stood maybe six foot six and weighed in the neighborhood of 300 pounds. All of it muscle. His thick-lens glasses gave him a demented look, like a scientist peering through a magnifying glass at a kitten he was torturing. His hands were particularly noticeable, large enough to crush a coconut, with fingers as thick as pistons. Menacing looking, even to a lawman who's seen untold numbers of criminals.

When Bobby smiled his face lit up in a cruel grin, the kind that makes your testicles shrivel. He was a buddy of Werner, had served time with him in a Wisconsin prison, but unlike Werner, worked at the Retreat voluntarily. Which made him either sadistic or stupid (probably both), because the wages paid by the Retreat were a cut or two above dipping fries at MacDonald's. Billy Ray feared for the safety of the kids from the Mustang.

Werner and Bobby wore the Retreat's standard

uniform for men: blue slacks, white polo shirt, the shirt with a sewn blue crest over the left pocket with the words "The Retreat at Wicked Stop" stitched in gold.

"Anybody see you?" Werner asked. He was a tall, good-looking guy in his early twenties with a thick muscular body, crew-cut blonde hair, and a disarming smile when he wanted to use it. Every time Billy Ray saw Werner, it brought to mind the picture perfect Aryan-type the Germans and Scandinavians produce by the tens of thousands.

Except Werner had a severe case of un-arrested acne that had scarred his face for life, and he was sensitive about it. Billy Ray didn't know much else about him, other than he was smart, a graduate of the University of Wisconsin, an-ex-con, a professed anti-Semite, anti-black, anti-woman, anti-government, anti-everything, and now employed as a working supervisor at the Retreat. He wondered how Werner wound up in this cesspool, suspected that, like himself, he was being blackmailed by Phester.

"Nobody saw me," Billy Ray said.

"Bobby, bring those two up to the Retreat," Werner instructed his accomplice. "You know where." Bobby grunted and herded the horror-stricken kids into the cab of the pickup truck and drove off, leaving a trail of dust behind him.

"You didn't handcuff them," Werner said.

"Didn't have to. They're not dangerous."

"That's not standard procedure for a cop."

"Look, don't tell me how to do my job. You don't know jack shit about being a cop."

"I don't need to know. That's what Mr. Phester's paying you for. Maybe I'll tell him how you screwed up."

"Go ahead. I'm tired of this whole sick operation. Sick of you, too. Don't push me too far."

Werner's mouth tightened and he gave Billy Ray a withering stare. Tiny streams of sweat rolled down both men's faces as they faced off in the late afternoon heat, staring down each other like a pair of gunfighters preparing to sling hot lead.

Werner broke eye contact first, spun around on his heels and strode up the hill to the Retreat. He called over his shoulder, "Bring the Mustang back and leave it in front of the hotel." Got the last word in.

That night Billy Ray shuttered himself in his three-room shack, took the phone off the hook and guzzled bourbon without his customary refined nicety of drinking from a glass. He chugalugged until he finished the fifth, reeled into his tiny bedroom and collapsed on the bed. Opened a second bottle and took a deep slug. But no matter how much bourbon he sloshed down his throat, the look of abject fear on the faces of those two kids haunted him through the long night.

SIX

Helen

The young man with the acned face who approached them as they got out of the car had an engaging smile that disarmed Marshall and Heather. Helen saw it in their faces, wreathed in returning smiles.

Not Clair. Clair's brow was furrowed as if something was puzzling her. Possibly the same thing that disturbed Helen; a noticeable absence of guests on the Retreat's property. Still, Helen didn't want to jump to conclusions. Maybe the guests were inside dressing for dinner. Or simply relaxing in their air-conditioned rooms to escape the brutal heat of late afternoon. Besides, it was cocktail time, a time when hotel guests enjoyed mingling with other guests over drinks. Yes, of course, that was it. They were all inside, sipping their favorite before-dinner cocktails in a dark, icy-cold cocktail lounge. She exchanged glances with Clair and smiled, tried to signal that she was now a little more at ease.

Melissa, the girl who led them to Wicked Stop from the state highway, said to the young man, "I never got to Americus. Found these wonderful folks first. I'll be heading back there in a few minutes. Got to use the bathroom." She turned to the Kings. "See you folks later." She cut across them toward the hotel.

The young man nodded to Melissa as she passed and turned his attention to the others. "Welcome to the Retreat. My name is Werner."

"Verner?" Clair asked.

"It's spelled W-e-r-n-e-r. The 'W' is pronounced like a 'V.'"

"Are you German?" Heather asked in her breathless voice.

Werner paused to examine her. "You have quite an unusual voice. Very kittenish, if you don't mind me saying so."

Heather blushed.

Werner gave her a blazing smile. "Sorry, didn't mean to make you uncomfortable. To answer your question, Miss, I'm third-generation American. My grandparents emigrated from Germany. I've never even been there, don't speak the language, only a few words in my parents' native tongue." His light blue eyes continued to examine Heather with heightened interest. He shifted his gaze to Clair, then Helen and back to Heather. The intensity of his examination made Clair and Heather noticeably uneasy.

Werner smiled politely and turned his attention to Marshall. Werner grabbed his hand and pumped it repeatedly. "It's a pleasure to welcome you to Wicked Stop, Mr. King. I hope your journey was pleasant."

Marshall freed his hand and wiped the perspiration from his face. "It's been a long trip. Glad to be here."

"Please forgive me. I've been impolite. You're all suffering from this abysmal heat wave. If you'll kindly follow me inside."

Werner led the way. Helen noticed his strong back, the wide sweep of shoulders, muscular arms. Exactly the opposite of Roger, her boyfriend, her darling, her paramour. The very thought of Roger sent chills coursing through her body, made her face flush with pleasure. She covertly glanced at Marshall, relieved that he hadn't seen the surge of excitement in her face.

Roger's build was delicate in contrast to Werner's. You could almost call him slender, yet he possessed surprising strength. Once he effortlessly carried her from the sofa in his bachelor apartment to the bedroom. Of course both of them were excited at the time, eager for intercourse, and hadn't she read in one of those men's magazines (which she consumed with avid interest to learn new ways to please Roger sexually) that the anticipation of imminent sexual activity increases muscle strength in men?

They entered the lobby and glanced around. Marshall whistled. "Wow, look at this place."

The lobby, carved from white marble, was small but as opulent as the entrance to a Saudi Prince's palatial residence. The room was circular, its walls adorned with abstract oil paintings in hues of blue and gray and mounted in glided frames. A huge chandelier in the shape of a teardrop hung over a black leather sofa and matching armchairs arranged in a square near the front check-in desk. The chandelier's hundreds of crystals refracted the late afternoon light and scattered it into a thousand sparkling stars that automatically drew the eye.

Yet ... there was something pretentious about the building, both inside and out, as if it were an elaborate movie set, a hoax that would be revealed when Helen stepped through one of the many doors around the circumference of the lobby and found the walls fake, mere props in an elaborate façade, like a movie set.

"Looks like a setting right out of a movie," Heather said, mirroring Helen's thought.

Werner smiled. "Impressive, isn't it? Know where the marble comes from?"

Marshall pursed his lips. "Italy?"

Werner chuckled. "Actually, from right here in Georgia."

"No!" Marshall shook his head in wonderment.

A few employees dressed in the Retreat's standard uniform were busy behind the front desk or moving across the lobby. Except for an occasional sideways glance at the new arrivals, they went about their business, ignoring Marshall and his party. Not a single guest was in sight.

"Where is everybody?" Helen asked.

Werner shrugged his shoulders, averted her eyes. "Most are probably in one of the cocktail lounges or in the restaurant upstairs, maybe a few around the pool, some in their rooms resting before dinner, I suppose. This is the hottest time of the day. Too hot to be milling about."

Clair pointed across the lobby. "There're some guests." A white-haired man and woman in their sixties were being led by a Retreat attendant from the elevator bank to a side door. They shuffled along like zombies, as if they were sick and on pain medication. Before they exited, the man turned around and glanced at Marshall with dulled eyes. Helen picked up on what she thought was a look of warning. She tensed, glanced at Marshall, but he apparently hadn't noticed. Or was so impressed by the luxurious surroundings that his natural instincts were dulled. Or, more probably what she thought she saw, she didn't, the result of her hyperactive imagination. Yet...

"Tell you what, folks," Werner said. "Let me make you comfortable in our reception room and we'll register you there."

He led them across the quiet lobby and ushered them into a room behind the front desk. It contained an eclectic collection of furniture in a South Sea motif: an upholstered bamboo sofa and matching armchairs and end tables, a bamboo bar along one wall flanked by two potted palm trees. Against the other wall, soft-leather longing chairs with teak trim setting in front of a matching teak credenza in the shape of a schooner. Behind a nearby teak desk, the only business-like furniture in the room, a sideboard holding a computer and flat screen monitor. Despite the comfortable looking furniture, the room imparted an impersonal feeling of coldness and sterility, like a doctor's examination office. Helen noticed the room's absence of windows.

"Sit down and relax," Werner said. "I'll get the registration cards and return in a moment." He stopped at the door and swiveled around, smiled. "Oh, by the way, if you have any cell phones, we charge them for free. Part of our service."

"You people are Johnny-on-the-spot," Marshall said, beaming. "We do have one that needs charging." Helen wished Marshall wasn't so accommodating. She reluctantly handed her cell phone to Werner.

"Any others?"

"One's enough," Marshall said, grinning. "Women and cell phones equal gab, gab, gab. You know how that goes."

Werner chuckled and left the room. Helen choked off a reply to the sexist remark. Clair's face turned red.

Marshall, oblivious to the women's reaction, plopped onto a sofa and sighed, wiped sweat from his brow and neck. Helen sat beside him and the girls arranged themselves in chairs around the sofa.

After Werner left, a woman attendant in the Retreat's standard uniform walked into the room and smiled. "What can I get you nice people to drink?"

"Where's Melissa?" Marshall asked.

"She's gone to town. Back in a jiffy."

Everybody ordered soft drinks other than Marshall who asked for a Budweiser. The attendant delivered the drinks from the room's bar and said, "If you need a refill, help yourselves. Please feel like you're in your own home." She left the reception area and closed the door behind her. Helen heard it snick shut.

Marshall, with a smug look, turned to Helen. "Feel better now?"

"No."

"No? You got to be kidding. Look at this place. It's five star."

"There's something wrong."

"I'll second that," Clair said.

Heather looked wide-eyed at Clair. "I don't understand."

"I do," Marshall said, his voice taut. "Every time I get a good idea, Clair and her mother get a better one. If we'd listened to them, we'd be stuck right now at some seedy motel on I-75."

Helen leaned forward and touched Marshall's arm. "It's more than that, Marshall. Listen to me, there's something about this place I don't like."

Clair nodded. "That older couple the attendant led out of the lobby. The man was trying to signal something."

"You saw it, too?" Helen asked.

"It was scary."

Marshall's brow furrowed in puzzlement. "What in hell you talking about? All I saw was a couple, probably on their way out to dinner or something."

Helen said, "I think we should get out of here ... now."

Heather's eyes widened. "What's going on?"

Marshall's back stiffened. "Nothing, absolutely nothing. About the worst that's going to happen to us is we get a great meal, maybe a swim and a good night's rest. Then on to Florida tomorrow morning."

Clair, restless, stood and moved around the room, inspecting everything in sight. The desk was locked, the computer shut down. She moved to the door leading to the lobby and rattled the doorknob.

Helen followed her with her eyes. "Dear, what's

wrong?"

"The doors won't open. We're locked in here."

Marshall rose ponderously. "Can't be. Damned thing's probably stuck." He walked over and rotated the doorknob to the lobby, lost patience when the door wouldn't open and shook the handle. Nothing happened.

"There's another door," Heather said and pointed to the opposite side of the room. Clair walked over and turned the knob. "This one's locked, too."

Helen rose and walked to the desk, picked up the telephone and dialed the hotel operator.

"Yes?"

"This is Mrs. King in the reception room. We'd like to get out but the door is stuck. Would you please send somebody over to fix it?"

"No."

Helen gasped. "No?"

"That's what I said, Mrs. King. No. There's nothing wrong with the door. It's just locked. Werner will explain later." She hung up.

Helen clutched the phone as if she could squeeze it to life, and jiggled the hook. The line was dead. When she turned to face Marshall, Clair and Heather her face was pale.

"They won't let us out. We're prisoners."

SEVEN

Werner

Werner knew that his boss, Mr. Phester, would be happy with this catch, at least with the females. The husband, Mr. King, was too old and too fat to bring a decent price at market. Besides he was black. Or looked black. While a buyer might make an exception a for light-skinned black woman with a straight nose, no buyer would be willing to fork over hard cash for a fat old black man. Which meant Mr. King was destined for the hunt. A fate that made even Werner cower.

The two pretty girls and the one older lady, Mrs. King looked to be in good shape. The girls should bring top dollar. Of that Werner was certain. The older one might well become a domestic provided she didn't fight it. If she did, well ... that would be her misfortune.

Werner shook his head in astonishment. By his estimate, ninety-five percent of the women who passed through the Retreat at Wicked Stop accepted their fates docilely, often willingly, as if their lives weren't worth much anyway and any change, no matter how repulsive, was preferable.

For many of them it was. Particularly the women they once rounded up from the inner cities of Atlanta, Birmingham, Memphis and New Orleans. The ghettoes were chock full of sexually precocious light-skinned Latino and black girls living in squalor, for whom slavery or prostitution was a step up. At one time, Mr. Phester sold those girls in wholesale lots to foreign corporations in markets such as the Balkans or the Middle East. The more attractive girls among them often wound up whoring for corporate employers, high roller businessmen, madams or street pimps. It was a matter of economics. Which option, prostitution or slave labor, brought a higher rate of return on the owner's investment? Werner listened with rapt attention once as a human trafficker listed the costs and selling prices of slave labor: initial purchase price (from a dealer like Mr. Phester), transportation to a new location, pay-off of immigration officials in host countries, food, clothing, housing and sundry supplies during transfer. Sales prices for slaves varied from country to country, depending on going rates, and remained mostly steady, with an anticipated inflation rate of five to eight percent per year. An expensive business with a medium to high initial investment for the businessman, but one with potentially lofty profits. The demand for slaves and whores simply never seemed to abate.

According to this same trafficker, the business had flip-flopped over the past few years. Foreign competition intensified, making the low end of the business less profitable. The supply of cheap labor from the Philippines, Vietnam, Cambodia, Bangledesh and other third-world countries exploded, forcing Mr. Phester to concentrate on the high end of the business, selling young women between the ages of fifteen and thirty as high priced whores. Which meant attracting more upscale white girls who brought in the big dollars.

The upscale girls, most of them with white skin, came from middle and upper class homes, and unlike their counterparts from the ghettoes, Mr. Phester handled them individually rather than in groups. He lured the older ones to the Retreat via referrals from travel websites that earned a handsome commission for their efforts. He also had procurers find runaways at bus stops of large cities and lure them to the Retreat. These girls, unlike their lower class counterparts, resisted at first, put up a fight, but usually gave in once they understood the futility of opposition.

All of Mr. Phester's girls received special attention in an effort to assure their suitability as slaves or prostitutes, including physical examinations to determine their health and the absence of sexually transmitted diseases, and psychological profiling to determine their fitness to serve. Girls unable to meet the stringent standards of the Retreat were sold off at bargain rates or ... otherwise disposed of.

Werner thought about the girl called Heather, the one with the sex kitten voice. He smiled to himself. As a member of the Retreat's senior staff he was entitled – with Mr. Phester's permission, of course – to "sample" his guests every now and then. And, indeed, Heather was one he very much wanted to sample. The thought aroused him and he grew hard.

He hoped she wasn't a virgin, because absolutely *nobody* was allowed to touch virgins, much less fondle those rarest of creatures. They brought the highest bidders in the world to the table, oil-rich sheiks and foreign billionaires from Eastern European countries, who'd pay astronomical prices in American dollars for the privilege of breaking in young Anglo-Saxon beauties. But only if they were sexually uncontaminated. That's why Mr. Phester paid hefty fees to have likely virgins examined and certified by a reputable gynecologist. His customers were never disappointed. Virginal certification by the Retreat was recognized in the white slavery community as the gold standard. It meant that customers could rest assured they were purchasing genuine virgins, not pretenders. A fact that Mr. Phester took great pride in.

Werner recalled a conversation with Mr. Phester: "Werner, it's not simply the virginity of our girls that appeals to our buyers. It's the fact that they're white.

The whiter the better. That's why Anglo-Saxon girls command higher prices than their Asian or Hispanic counterparts. And, of course, in that regard, dark-skinned black girls are out of the running altogether. Buyers can get them by the dozen from most African countries. It's white that commands a premium."

"Even black girls who are virgins?"

"Yes, even them. The girls in this business who bring in the biggest bang for the buck, if you'll excuse the expression" – Mr. Phester paused and grinned at his pun – "are pure white skinned Anglo-Saxon girls, the kind one finds in Great Britain and seldom elsewhere. The skin of those beauties is often the color of alabaster. They are the rarest of jewels and are in great demand. Unfortunately, we seldom run across such girls in the USA. But in the continuum of desirability, blonde virgins come in second, redheads third, brunettes fourth. And that's our market as it stands today. All with light skin, of course."

Mr. Phester often claimed that if he sold but one virgin a month he could keep the business profitable. Regrettably, not that many virgins found their way to the Retreat. Or elsewhere. In this day and age such creatures were uncommon. You had to catch them young, eleven or twelve. While those tender ages appealed to perverts with a pedophiliac bent, most of the Retreat's white slave buyers preferred girls with more fully developed bodies. Which meant teenagers or post-teenagers.

Werner fondly recalled a thirteen-year-old girl named Ivy from his home state of Wisconsin, the daughter of a cheese company executive. When the Retreat captured her, Warner was terribly excited by her fresh beauty, robust health, the provocative contrast of her innocent looks with her lush, over-ripe body. He was shocked when he got her in the sack and she mounted his pony and rode it so long and so hard, blood mixed with his semen. Wonder of wonders. One of the best pieces of ass he ever had and from a thirteen-year-old girl at that. Last he heard, Ivy was turning tricks in Belgrade for her owner, a Serb politician, making a ton of money for him and loving every minute of it.

Werner understood the sordid nature of the world. His old man had kicked him out of his Kenosha, Wisconsin trailer after finding Werner, age fifteen, playing house with his eleven-year-old sister, thereby hogging the old man's action. To survive, Werner became a male prostitute in Milwaukee, turned tricks for both men and women he picked up freelance in the streets. Until the day a white pimp, whose territory Werner was violating, beat the living hell out of him. From that moment on Werner worked for the pimp, eventually became his lover and protégé.

The law repeatedly hassled Werner as it did most whores, male or female. He became an habitué of Milwaukee police station holding cells and jails. His pimp's lawyer sprung him usually within hours of his arrest. Except for the one time Werner got careless and greedy. He beat up one of his tricks and robbed him. The trick turned out to be a prominent neurosurgeon, and Werner served six months in the county lockup.

In spite of the fact that he was pulling in big bucks, Werner, bright and ambitious, wanted to do better for himself. Two years into the whoring, and with the blessing of his pimp, he took and passed his general equivalency high school exams and entered college. He attended classes during the day and whored at night, proudly graduated with honors five years later with a degree in history, a subject that utterly fascinated him.

Werner read the great philosophers. His favorite was the German Nietzsche, whose reasoned doctrine

Werner believed in: a breed of supermen whose dominant will assured their triumph over inferior human beings. The same credo Hitler followed when he cleansed impure Jewish and Gypsy blood from the German race.

Werner chuckled at his recollection of the Jewish matron he was servicing weekly. The lady was married and a pillar of Milwaukee society. The relationship lasted until the day she found Werner rifling her purse. When she told him to get lost, Werner, half in the bag from too much of the lady's scotch, called her a dirty Jew bastard and spit in her face. Without flinching, she wiped the spit from her face and calmly told Werner "You can take the blood out of a German, but you can't take the Nazi out of his blood. Now get out of my house, you cocksucker." Werner replied using a quote from his precious Nietzsche, greatly admiring his own clever repartee: "Whatever does not kill me makes me stronger."

Werner's pimp was also a skinhead, an American Nazi and a fellow Nietzsche traveler. He indoctrinated Werner into the movement, taught him to hate Jews (he didn't need much urging), feminists, blacks, foreigners, the American government, cops, judges, liberals from the country's Northeast, rich bastards and damned near everybody else who didn't like Strohs, wienerwurst, Harley-Davidson hogs, skinhead emblems and trailer park haute monde.

Werner immersed himself in the skinhead movement, became the local group's brain trust, planned its capers until the day the group pushed beyond its capabilities of petty burglaries and muggings and slit the throats of two prominent Jewish brothers, owners of a famous Milwaukee department store. From that moment on, Werner was on the run with the entire state of Wisconsin hunting him down.

Mr. Phester rescued him, brought Werner to the Retreat and made him a senior staff member, kept him buried in the Retreat, out of the public eye and away from the law. True, Werner didn't serve at the Retreat voluntarily. Mr. Phester held him as a captive of sorts. Their relationship was strictly employer-employee or, as Werner put it in darker moments, blackmailer-victim.

Blackmail. Such an ugly word when it's used against you. And, as he came to realize, the way Mr. Phester held sway over every Retreat employee.

Werner didn't intend to remain a victim forever. Give it another year at the most. Once Milwaukee forgot the two dead Jews he'd be home free. Well, maybe he couldn't return to his hometown, but at least he could get the hell out of the Retreat and make some serious money elsewhere in a metropolitan area, this time pimping instead of whoring. Run a few girls and a couple of hung studs. The market was wide open and the competition fragmented in the smaller Midwestern cities, and not controlled by the Mob. He could make his mark someplace like Toledo and eventually control the whole territory.

Not that escaping Mr. Phester's clutches would be easy. Werner was wary of him, reasoned that someday Mr. Phester would dispose of him because he knew too much about the Retreat's business. He intended to blow the scene long before that, and he thought he knew Mr. Phester well enough to predict when that time would come.

For now, Werner couldn't get Heather out of his mind. He was due to register his new guests, the Kings and Heather, and knew it would be a day or two before he'd be able to get the girl alone. A day or two was much too long. If he didn't get some immediate relief, he'd burst. He dialed the public announcement system.

53

"Melissa, please report to Werner's office." He repeated the message, hung up the phone, eased back in the vinyl swivel chair behind his desk and rubbed his crotch in anticipation.

Three minutes later Melissa knocked on the door and walked into his tiny office.

"Get what you needed in Americus?"

"What's on your mind?"

"Lock the door behind you."

She did and Werner stood and dropped his pants.

"What if somebody hears us?" Melissa asked, staring at Werner's erect penis.

"This won't take five minutes."

"That's the trouble. It never does."

Werner's neck muscles tensed. "Shut up." He reached for Melissa and loosened her belt. She slipped out of her dress pants and stood before him, grabbed his penis. Werner's breath came fast as he placed his thumbs in her panties and slid them down her bare legs. He lifted Melissa and placed her on her back lengthwise on top of his cleared desk, her legs over his shoulders. Werner dropped to his knees, buried his face between her legs and closed his eyes. From that moment on he was muff diving Heather, not Melissa.

EIGHT

Clair

Marshall paced the locked reception room. Despite the air conditioner running at full blast he was drenched with sweat. Clair, Helen and Heather sat huddled in their chairs warding off the blasts of cold air.

Heather's eyes revealed how frightened she was. "Why are we being locked in?"

Although Helen was scared, she gave her a comforting smile. "No need to be worried, dear. There's just some sort of misunderstanding. We'll work it out."

Marshall snorted. It came out in shaky waves, displaying his anger and fear.

"Please take a seat, Marshall," Helen said, in a calm soothing voice, "and calm down."

Marshall sank into a chair. "Jesus Lord, what's going to happen to us?"

Helen reached over and patted his arm. "The answer is nothing is going to happen to us. As soon as Werner returns, we'll ask to leave Wicked Stop immediately and he'll escort us to our car. Don't worry, dear, it's going to be all right."

Like hell it is, Clair thought, they were in real trouble. She felt a warning bell deep inside her sounding the alarm. She wasn't sure what Werner wanted, but it wasn't going to be enjoyable and it wasn't going to result in them leaving the Retreat. Not without a fight or the payment of an exorbitant ransom. Were they being held for money? Maybe. And maybe it was something far more sinister. The uncertainty made her shiver.

Clair guessed that Werner wasn't calling the shots in the Retreat. He was too young and too much a lightweight to be in charge. Bright, yes, but not experienced or mature enough to run an enterprise the size of the Retreat. Not in her opinion.

Which meant there was a Mr. Big behind the scenes. Somebody else who would determine their fate. Somebody she might be able to appeal to if Werner got out of hand. She was anxious to meet this Mr. Big, discover what his intentions were and, if necessary, probe for his weaknesses and fashion an escape plan. Escape from the Retreat, she was beginning to realize, might be a necessity. Hopefully before her father and Heather went to pieces.

"I got us into this mess," Marshall said and his voice cracked. "I'm so sorry."

Helen sat next to Marshall and put her arms around him and held him tight. "It's not your fault, Marshall. We all agreed." Clair was surprised at how guilty her mom looked. Why? Coming to the Retreat wasn't her fault; if anything it was because of Dad's stubborn insistence.

Her attention was diverted when a key scraped in the lock and the door from the lobby swung open. Werner marched in, clutching a folder in his hand. A huge man the size of a nightmare followed Werner into the room and locked the door behind him. The tranquil blue and white uniform he wore was in sharp contrast to his blunt features. His hands alone were monstrous and crude looking, as if they had a life of their own, a life steeped in mayhem. He stood at attention, his back to the door, arms folded, cold, indifferent eyes behind coke-bottle glasses raking Clair and the others before coming to rest on Werner.

"Everybody please stay seated," Werner said and gave everybody another one of his throwaway smiles.

Marshall shot up from his chair. The sudden movement shook his jowls and made him appear ridiculous, like a clown entertaining children at a circus matinee. "I don't–"

Werner grinned at the ridiculous sight and held up his hand like a traffic cop to stop Marshall. "I'll explain everything, Mr. King. Please sit down and listen." Marshall hesitated. The man at the door scowled and took a step forward.

Marshall took one look at the large man with the mean eyes and collapsed onto a chair, his legs visibly shaking. "It's okay, Bobby," Werner said. Bobby stepped back to the door.

"Sorry, Mr. King," Werner said. "I didn't mean to intimidate you. It's just that Bobby gets impatient. He's a man of action, not words." The phony smile returned to his face and he pulled up a chair to face the Kings and Heather. He opened the folder in his lap.

"Okay, I've got a few questions for each of you, starting with ... Let's begin with the man of the house, Mr. King."

Helen stood and faced Werner defiantly. "We want to leave this hotel immediately. No, let me change that. We *demand* to leave this hotel immediately. Take us to our car."

Werner sighed and waved Helen back to her seat. "I don't believe you fully understand what's happening, Mrs. K. You're not in a position to demand anything. That should be clear by now. Please sit down."

"I'm *not* sitting down. I'm going to get the police." With that she paraded to the door. Bobby effortlessly scooped her up with his intimidating hands and brought her back and dropped her onto her seat. The air rushed out of Helen's lungs, leaving her speechless, humiliated.

"What do you want from us?" Clair asked in a

tremulous voice.

"In time, Clair, in time," Werner said and paused. Then, as if struck by a good idea, his face beamed. "Tell you what, let's get through these formalities as quickly as possible, and I'll escort all of you to our four star dining room for a sumptuous dinner." He rubbed his hands together in anticipation. "How does that sound?"

Helen mustered her courage for another assault. "You can't hold us against our will."

Werner frowned. "Please, Mrs. K, let's get off on the right foot. I ask the questions and you and the others respond. Please do not add any unnecessary comments. It'll only slow down your processing and make this a late evening for everybody." He glanced impatiently at his watch.

The edges of Helen's mouth tightened and turned white. Marshall's head trembled as if his neck was no longer able to support it. Tears gathered like storm clouds in Heather's eyes. She sat still, pale hands clasped tightly together as if in prayer.

Clair stood and said in a quiet but firm voice, "Let me speak to the person in charge."

Werner glared at her. "I *am* the person in charge."

"You don't run this place. Somebody else does."

Werner's face turned fiery red, accentuating the pockmarks of his acne. "Sit down and shut up."

Clair planted her feet wide apart. "I won't." Her jaw muscles rippled. "I want to speak to your supervisor."

Werner turned toward the door. "Bobby."

Bobby moved with a speed that took Clair by surprise. She inhaled sharply as he seized her by the upper arms, lifted her a foot off the floor and shook her. Bobby dropped Clair and she crumpled like a limp doll onto a chair. Her heart thudded so violently against her rib cage she was afraid it would explode. She squeezed the arms of her chair, holding on for dear life.

Helen's lips trembled. "How dare—"

Bobby's frigid eyes drilled into Helen's, numbing her, stopping her mid-sentence. She shivered as if a chilled wind from the grave had swept over her.

Werner rose and faced the group. His voice was icy. "This is getting out of hand. Any more trouble and ... well, it won't be agreeable. That I promise."

A dead silence greeted his comments. Bobby returned to his guard position at the door.

Werner sat and reopened the folder. "Let's get back to the business at hand." He faced Marshall and his face was serious, intent. "Question number one, Mr. King? Are you Negro or do you have Negro blood in you?"

NINE

Marshall

Marshall thought he might faint. He had not heard that horrible racist word applied to him in many years. At least not to his face. His head swam and he gulped air to keep from passing out.

"Marshall, are you all right?" Helen asked, alarmed.

Clair bounded up. "I'm going to the bar to get a washcloth." Bobby, standing guard, tensed.

Werner nodded his approval. Bobby relaxed and Clair trotted to the bar, searched and found a bar towel, soaked it in cold water and brought it back to her father. Helen took it and patted Marshall's forehead.

"I'm okay," Marshall said between deep breaths. He was pale with shock, his face an ashen-brown color. He recited the Lord's Prayer over and over to himself.

He had learned long ago to keep a low profile when the heat was on, to tune down the angry rhetoric, bottle up the anger, blend in with his background. Not to stand out in any way and become a target of racial hatred. That's how he had survived so long in Whitey's world.

Years before, a member of the NAACP issued a stinging rebuke when Marshall refused to march in a demonstration. Called him a coward, a lackey for white folks. Marshall knew better. His accuser was wrong. Marshall wasn't a coward, he was a survivor.

Werner sighed. "Can we please return to the questioning?"

Helen and Clair sat down on either side of Marshall, each holding one of his hands.

"You didn't answer the question, Mr. King."

Helen snapped, "I'll answer it for him. Yes, he's half black."

"And half-white, I presume?"

"What else?" Helen asked sarcastically.

"And you, Mrs. K. You're...?"

"Japanese American."

"Full blooded Japanese, correct? Mother and father from Japan?"

"Yes," she said between clenched teeth.

Marshall couldn't believe he and Helen were being subjected to a racial interrogation. This wasn't Nazi Germany in the forties, for God's sake, or Birmingham, Alabama in the sixties. This was politically correct America at the start of the twenty-first century. He swallowed two antacid tablets.

Helen, mirroring Marshall's thoughts, said, "It's against the law to ask those questions."

Werner guffawed and turned to Bobby, who returned his smirk with a malicious grin. Ceiling lights reflected off his glasses, accentuating the cruelty in his eyes.

"And your daughter, Mrs. K. If I get this right, she's part Jap, part Negro and part white. A mixed breed if I ever saw one."

Helen sputtered something unintelligible.

Marshall saw his daughter's face turn red.

Bobby broke his silence and spoke. "What the KKK calls a mutt."

"A mutt," Werner agreed, a wicked grin twisting his features. "Very good, Bobby. That's what you are Clair, a mutt. Although I must admit, a very nice looking mutt."

Clair bottled up an answer, her face blotchy, eyes blazing.

"Why are you asking these questions?" Helen

asked.

Werner raised an eyebrow. "Not that it's any of your concern, but I suppose it won't make any difference if I tell you. ... The answer is, it may affect the sales price."

Helen blanched. "What sales price?"

Werner grinned. "No more questions." He turned toward Heather. She cowered in her seat. Clair moved her chair and sat next to Heather to bolster her.

"By the color of your skin," Werner said, his eyes roaming her body with obvious lecherous intent, "you're unmistakably white."

Heather bobbed her head. She huddled against Clair.

"Are you white all over?" Werner's stupid grin appeared again, Marshall thought.

Heather blushed.

"Here, let me see." Werner leaned forward and lifted Heather's tight shorts an inch. Heather squealed and pulled away. Clair's lips curled down and she started to say something until Werner froze her with a withering look.

"I thought so. Such a beautiful white. I take it you're of British extraction?"

Heather opened her mouth to reply, but only a few muddled squeaks emerged.

"Damn it," Clair said. "Can't you see you're scaring her to death?"

Werner's neck stiffened. "You're starting to annoy me."

Clair crossed her arms and rubbed them where Bobby had grabbed and bruised her. The memory made her shudder. "Why don't you leave Heather alone?"

"Do you want Bobby to caress you again, you stupid girl?"

Clair sat in stony silence.

Werner turned back to Heather. "Your parents or grandparents were from England, correct?"

Heather bobbed her head.

"Speak to me, Heather."

Heather said "yes" in that kittenish voice that so stirred men, made them do foolish things. Werner and Bobby exchanged leers.

Werner went on for another thirty minutes gathering information from Marshall, his family and Heather: ages, occupations, background, schooling, jobs held, religious affiliations, living family members. He had them fill out short multiple choice tests aimed at revealing their characters and personalities. Part of their psychological profiles.

Marshall sat through the "processing" as Werner referred to it, with a growing sense of fear. He grappled with the meaning of the interview but couldn't come up with anything that made sense. The questions and written test seemed pointless to him, as if Werner were categorizing them for a collection of sorts. But what sort of collection? A feeling of dread enveloped Marshall, perhaps as it had his ancestral Virginia slaves, certainly as it had his parents and grandparents who had felt the heel of racism grind them into the dirt.

Werner's cell phone buzzed. He snapped it open. "Werner here."

He listened for a few moments and said, "Yes sir. We're ready. I'll have the room prepared." He closed his cell phone, rose and whispered something to Bobby, who nodded and left the room.

Bobby returned moments later with four straight back collapsible wooden chairs, carrying two in each one of his ham-like hands as easy as if he were lifting toothpicks. He arranged a straight line of chairs in the center of the room. He pointed to Marshall, Helen,

Clair and Heather. "You four, sit here."

They obediently moved to the chairs and sat down. Bobby arranged three comfortable leather wing back chairs in a row facing the four of them, the two lines of chairs about twenty feet apart.

Werner glanced at his watch and signaled Bobby to return to the door. Moments later somebody tapped and Bobby unlocked the door and let the new party in.

The first to enter was a small dapper man carrying a Chihuahua. The man, probably in his mid forties, stood about 5'4" and weighed maybe 110 pounds, no more. He was dressed impeccably in a well-tailored midnight blue suit, muted striped tie, off-white French-cuff dress shirt with gold cufflinks, and glossy black dress shoes. His freshly trimmed shiny black hair, graying at the temples, was swept back behind his ears. He wore a small well-trimmed black mustache that complemented his dark good looks. The Chihuahua he held and petted had the spoiled look of lap dogs coddled by their owners.

There was something effeminate about the man. Nothing you could define specifically from his businesslike appearance, yet Marshall felt it immediately. His features were gender neutral, but tiny and delicate, as if they belonged to a doll's face. The expression the man wore was as disinterested and indeterminate as his features. No smiles, no scowls, the eyes unfathomable. He sat down in the center leather chair provided by Bobby, eased the dog to a position on the chair beside him, crossed his legs and coolly examined the four people facing him. Werner handed him the folder containing the group's personal information. The man opened it, flipped through the pages and examined them with casual interest.

The woman who had followed him into the room was perhaps in her late sixties with a well-preserved body. She wore cosmetics from the Lady Gaga school of make-up: a lavish slap of wet red lipstick, thick pancake powder, a wide swath of eye shadow the color of ravens' wings and nail polish as bright as arterial blood. Her short dark-blue evening dress and high-heeled shoes accentuated damn fine legs for a woman her age, well shaped, with no visible sign of cellulite or varicose veins, although Marshall couldn't be sure since her legs were masked by mesh stockings.

The woman's eyes were as sharp and glacial as an eagle's. They speared Marshall, Helen, Clair and Heather in turn with a look so predatory and calculating that it scared the living bejesus out of Marshall. She sat down next to the small dapper man and folded her hands in her lap.

Melissa was the last in and stood behind Marshall. Bobby remained at the door. The small dapper man fingered the sharp crease in his trousers and frowned as if lost in thought. He patted the seat on the other side of the lapdog, signaling Werner to sit down.

"Sure thing, Mr. Phester." Werner obediently took his seat.

"My name," the small dapper man said in a quiet, modulated tone, "is Gilbert Phester. I am the sole owner of the Retreat and much of the town of Wicked Stop." He said this not with a sense of pride, but with the evident intention of stating a simple fact. "To the right is my mother, Mrs. Mildred Phester, and to my left is Werner, whom you already know." He used the antique grammatical word "whom," not "who," the more colloquial form.

"And, less I forget and hurt her feelings," – he pointed to the dog lying quietly beside him – "this adorable little creature is Pootie, my award-winning Chihuahua. I'm proud to say she won Best in Show honors at the Memphis Dog Festival last year."

He paused to smile and pet the dog. Pootie responded by closing her eyes contentedly.

"On behalf of myself, my mother and the staff at the Retreat, I welcome you to our community." He bowed his head in a solemn, courtly gesture.

"As for all of you," he said, sweeping an arm to include the four people sitting apprehensively in front of him, "whether or not you are aware of it, you are now my property to do with as I please."

The dog barked for the first time.

TEN

Clair

Clair watched in wide-eyed astonishment as Gilbert steepled his fingers. "If you think that statement false or ill-advised, think again. Your lives and your futures are solely in my hands. Acceptance of that unalterable fact will make everything that follows so much easier." He stressed the word "unalterable."

Helen bolted up from her chair. "I demand that my family and I be allowed to leave this horrible place." The Chihuahua, bug-eyed, sat up and growled at her.

Gilbert examined Helen with mild interest. He paused for a moment while she stood defiantly before him, hands on hips. Then lowered his voice and spoke directly to her:

"Madam, may I suggest you take your place among the others and be absolutely quiet until asked a question, at which time you will be given the opportunity to reply. But only then. Your conduct—"

Helen tensed and stepped forward threateningly. Werner leaped up and slapped her face. She shrieked and fell back to her chair. Clair froze, desperate to help her mother but unable to conquer her fear of the in-your-face confrontation and the accompanying violence it invariably spawns. Yet, for the first time in her life she felt the compulsion to physically hurt another human being, that awful Werner, to make him pay in kind for slapping her mother.

She couldn't do it. Instead, tight-lipped, her whole body shaking with repressed rage, she glanced around shedding tears of frustration. Helen was quietly sobbing but otherwise all right. Marshall and Heather were glued to their seats, bodies heaving with fright.

"You d-didn't have to do that to my wife," Marshall said. He seemed startled by the daring of his outburst and shrank back into his chair.

"The fun's not over until the fat man sings," Mrs. Phester said and giggled at her own play on words. She had the soft, dulcet tones of a younger woman, the opposite of the cackling speech Clair expected from the mother of this evil man sitting so nonchalantly beside her.

Gilbert nodded to the chair beside him, a signal for Werner to sit down. Werner obediently slid back into his seat, fire in his eyes, his gaze bouncing back and forth between Helen and Clair, the twin objects of his rancor.

Gilbert, who had sat quietly during the entire melee, shook his head in dismay. "This is such a waste of my valuable time." He turned to Mrs. Phester. "What shall we do with these horrid people, Mother?"

A sadistic, lecherous smile lit Mildred's face, exposing lipstick stuck to the edges of her teeth. "We could tie the young ladies up and let Bobby have his way with them while we watch."

Gilbert semi-seriously mulled the idea around. "I'm sure Bobby would enjoy that. Wouldn't you, Bobby?"

Bobby's lips trembled in anticipation. "Oh, yeah."

Clair took a closer look at Bobby. His brutal demeanor hid an animal cunning hinted at by the raw intelligence behind his eyes. Somebody else to watch out for, Clair decided, an extremely dangerous man. Probably the most dangerous of the bunch.

"Let me tell you something about Bobby," Gilbert said, "if you haven't already guessed by his behavior. Bobby was brutalized as a child, beaten and raped so savagely by a succession of barbaric pedophiles that compassion and guilt were brutally stripped from his emotional persona. Those are feelings he no longer possesses or understands. The only stimuli he responds to are lust and greed."

Bobby stared straight ahead. Not a flicker of emotion crossed his face.

"We save Bobby's singular ... talents for recalcitrant guests. Guests like you, madam." He nodded to Helen who cowered in her seat. "His success rate at converting rebellious candidates to willing, agreeable participants in our venture is one-hundred percent."

"One way or another," Mildred said.

"What Mother means is that guests either learn to obey our orders or Bobby disposes of them in a manner unique to him, an event I assure you that you want to avoid at all costs."

Clair shivered. She glanced at Heather. A cloak of abject fear covered Heather's face.

"Now, how about you young ladies?" Gilbert faced Clair and Heather. "Would you enjoy a romp in the hay with Bobby? Rumor has it he's big enough in the right places to give you a good time." He paused to assess the effect of his words on the young women.

The very suggestion of impending rape and its associated pain, followed by a manner of death too horrible to imagine, shoved Heather over the line into a frenzy of dread. She bawled hysterically and clung to Clair.

Gilbert frowned. "May I please have quiet? I do not tolerate noise well."

Clair held and shushed Heather, cooed to her until her cries gradually subsided.

"That's much better. Thank you, young lady." Gilbert inclined his head to Clair. "In consideration, we'll hold the séance with Bobby in abeyance." He stopped and beamed as if he had just done the girls a big favor.

"Regarding the young lady in hysterics, it's entirely possible we may have a virgin on our hands. What say you, Mother?"

The sharp-eyed old lady leaned forward. Her intense gaze seemed to penetrate both girls in turn. "Maybe the blond, not the other one."

"Which begs the question." Gilbert picked up Pootie and placed her on his lap. "Are either of you two unspoiled, if I may put it delicately?"

"None of your damn business," Clair spat out.

Gilbert chuckled. "But, you see, young lady, it's *exactly* my business."

Clair assessed Gilbert. From the little he had revealed so far, he was bright, focused and tougher than he looks. The lap dog called Pootie, the man's sissified gestures, a soft-spoken voice were signs that seemingly pointed to his sexual orientation. She wondered if he was gay, not taking it for granted, knowing that some effeminate men were strictly heterosexual, others bisexual and a few didn't bother with sex at all. Which category did Gilbert Phester fall under and could she use that information to hatch an exit plan?

Of one matter she was certain. The man was what her dad called cocksure, full of himself. That he had built a business the size of the Retreat and set it in a captive town out of reach of the law was enough to swell anyone's head, to satisfy his feelings of invincibility.

That cockiness was his greatest vulnerability and one she intended to exploit. When he let his guard down, she intended to make a run for it, then return accompanied by police to rescue her parents.

She recalled seeing a few cars and trucks parked around the front of the Retreat. If she stole one and drove it to Wicked Stop, she'd find the town's lone police officer, get him to call the county sheriff or state police.

Gilbert punctured her daydreams. "Believe me, we'll find out if you and your friend are virgins. But enough of that for now. All of you, please take off your clothes."

"What?" Helen said. Clair and Heather gasped. Another blow that sent Marshall reeling. He had an absent look in his eyes, a look that revealed he was slipping away from reality. A look that alarmed Clair.

Gilbert signaled Werner who, along with Bobby and Melissa, stepped in front of Marshall and the women in an intimidating manner.

"Take off your clothes," Werner commanded, staring at Heather.

"It'll be okay," Clair cooed to Heather. "They're not going to hurt you. I'll help you get undressed."

Clair lifted a trembling Heather to her feet and undressed her. She kicked off her clothing at the same time so both young women became nude together. Heather clung to Clair, burrowed her face in Clair's neck.

"Ladies, please part," Gilbert said. A sob tore through Heather's throat when Clair gently nudged her aside.

Werner sucked in his breath, his gaze leaping from Clair's to Heather's bodies and settling on Clair's. "Jesus, look at the tits on the brunette!"

"You're so eloquent at times like this, Werner," Gilbert said.

Melissa stared at the naked women in admiration of their bodies. Bobby, whose eyes, peering through the magnified lenses of his glasses, seemed as big as two fried eggs, drooled. A bulging hard-on, which he did nothing to hide, revealed his all-consuming interest.

His mouth hung open and his breath came in short rasping spurts. His look said it all: I stand ready to devour, to *hurt* these two soft insignificant creatures the moment the boss man gives me the okay.

A dreamy look softened Mrs. Phester's flinty eyes as her gaze roamed the bodies of the two young women. "I used to look like that once. Of course, I'm still not that bad, am I boys, particularly in stockings and high heels?"

Clair steeled herself to pay attention to the conversation, to explore for weaknesses and escape opportunities, despite her nudity. Relieved that Mrs. Phester's comment took some attention away from her. She watched with fascination as Werner blushed. His eyes darted back and forth between Gilbert and his mother. "I wouldn't know, Mrs. Phester."

Mildred chuckled and batted her eyelids.

Clair was amazed at this self-evident confession, pondered how Gilbert Phester tolerated the thought of his mother having sexual relations with these ... these animals.

Gilbert, either seemingly oblivious to the not-too-subtle nuances, or, more probably, ignoring them altogether, said, "Please, Mother." He turned his attention to Helen. "Now for you, madam. Undress now."

Helen sucked in air and shucked her clothes with a look of defiance. Although there were tears in her eyes, she held her head high and met Gilbert's neutral gaze.

Werner nodded his appreciation. "Not bad for an older lady," he said. Bobby tore his gaze away from Clair and Heather, sneaked a look at the older woman, grinned and licked his lips appreciatively.

"I can match the mother," Mrs. Phester said. "Easily. I'm bigger in the bust and have better legs. This lady's too skinny if you ask me, Sonny."

Gilbert ignored his mother's comment, instead turned to Marshall. "Now for you, sir."

"No, goddamn it," Helen snarled. "Leave him alone."

Gilbert raised his eyebrows. "Madam, I must admit that I do admire your spunk. You are resilient, if nothing else. Tell me why we shouldn't insist that this disgustingly fat old man remove his clothes."

"Because he's got nothing to offer. You've got three naked women in front of you. What more could you want?"

Gilbert seemed to ponder her question. After a few moments he chuckled and nodded to Helen. "I'll accept that rationalization. You're absolutely correct. We have no further use for your husband ... Melissa, pictures, please."

Helen breathed a sigh of relief. Clair thought Phester's remark ominous and worried about her father.

Melissa picked up a camera from a drawer of the desk. She waved Clair away from Heather. But Heather wouldn't step away.

"Is this necessary?" Helen snapped.

Gilbert sighed. "Please, madam, let's not cause any more strife. You know all I have to do is wiggle a finger at Bobby and you're, what's the popular expression? Ah, yes, toast."

"It's okay, Heather," Clair said. "I'll be right over here."

Heather let go and Clair stepped away. Melissa took several pictures, both frontal and rear views, including close-ups of Heather's breasts, rear, legs and vagina. Two or three of her face. Finally, a full-body view. Heather bordered on hysteria. She took constant propping up and reassurances from Clair. As soon as Melissa finished with her she collapsed onto a chair and covered her body with her clothes.

Melissa took pictures of Clair and Helen. Marshall, dripping sweat, kept his eyes pinned to the floor, an anguished expression knurling his brow. Clair's heart went out to him. Her throat swelled and she wanted to cry, but refused to give Phester and his gang the satisfaction.

"Melissa, measurements, please," Gilbert said.

Melissa set the camera aside and from her pocket removed a cloth measuring tape, the kind tailors use.

A flash insight came to Clair. "You're going to sell us, aren't you? As slaves. White slaves."

Every eye in the room found Clair. It suddenly became very quiet.

"Young lady," Gilbert said, "to paraphrase that famous quote from *The Charge of the Light Brigade*, 'Yours not to reason why, yours but to do or die.'" He turned back to Melissa, his nose in the air. "Continue the measurements."

Melissa checked all three women's essential measurements: chest, waist, hips, height, leg length. She called out the numbers and Werner, between peeks at Clair and Heather, recorded the measurements in his folder.

It was the opportunity Clair had been waiting for. Melissa and Werner were busy. Bobby was so fascinated by the parade of flesh he was drooling.

Clair bolted to the door. It took everybody by surprise. By the time Bobby and Werner reacted she was past the door of the reception room and racing through the lobby.

The few people in the lobby stared dumfounded at her, mouths agape, as she sped by naked. In front of the hotel a blast of hot, humid night air smacked her in the face and made her catch her breath. Her eyes darted in every direction, searching, until she found and ran up to the same red Ford pickup truck Melissa drove when they first met her. She prayed the keys were in the ignition, counted on the arrogance of the people working at the Retreat not to take simple precautionary measures.

Sure enough, the keys were still in the ignition. Clair would have sighed with relief but there was no time. She jumped inside the truck and cranked the ignition as Werner and Bobby came flying through the front entrance. Spinning the tires, she wheeled the truck around and slid down the road leading down to the town of Wicked Stop. Bobby, running flat out and with remarkable speed, caught up to the truck and grabbed the tailgate with one hand as she sped away. Clair jammed on the brakes and the top of Bobby's head smacked into the back of the truck. He dropped to the ground like a sack of cement. She heard him curse as she pulled away and raced down the narrow road. Sweat poured off her in rivulets, her bare rear uncomfortably stuck to the vinyl seat of the truck.

Then remembered the gate. She had to get through the gate. But how?

At the foot of the drive she slammed on the brakes, leaped out of the truck and picked up the intercom mounted to the closed gate. She inhaled deeply and often to calm herself. Over the thudding of the pulse in her ears, she listened to the night. The unmistakable sound of a car engine alternately racing on straight sections of the dirt road and braking for curves came from the direction of the Retreat. No time left! Quick now!

She flicked on the intercom, took a deep breath. "Werner says to open the gate," she said in a hurried voice.

"Who is–"

"Damn it. Open the gate quick or Werner will fry

your ass."

It worked. The gate clicked open. Clair climbed into the truck, clashed the gears and jerked forward. She drove down the dirt road and onto Wicked Stop's main street, past the building marked "Wicked Stop Police Department." Not a sign of town's lone police officer. No time now to stop and hunt for him. Not with Werner in hot pursuit. Instead she raced ahead into the woods leading to the state highway. She flicked her eyes toward the rearview mirror. Found no signs of a car following her.

That puzzled her. But only for a moment. She came around a bend at a narrow point and almost slammed into a police cruiser blocking the road, its roof lights flashing. She jumped out of the truck and guardedly approached the police car. When she was almost upon it, a man stepped out of the woods and stood in the headlights from the truck. Clair froze and sucked in her breath. "It was the police officer from the town of Wicked Stop, the one she had heard Melissa call Billy Ray."

Billy Ray said, "No need to be afraid. I'm a policeman, the law." He pointed out the badge pinned to his shirtfront.

"Officer, thank God I found you." She walked up to him.

"Jesus, you're naked," Billy Ray said, an incredulous note infecting his voice. "They didn't tell me that."

"Tell you–" Clair stopped and gaped at Billy Ray.

The lawman grabbed Clair and held her by the wrists. Careful not to stare at her body.

"I don't mean to hurt you, Miss. Just don't give me any trouble."

Clair struggled against his grip. "You're part of it. You're part of that awful gang," she said, her voice shaking with fear and resentment.

The lawman released Clair to grab a blanket from the trunk of the police car. Clair staggered away, running blindly into the woods. Once out of reach of the truck's headlights she became disoriented and dropped behind a large bush, hoping the lawman wouldn't find her.

It took him about fifteen seconds with a flashlight. He guided Clair to her feet and wrapped her in the blanket.

He was gentle but persistent. "Time to go back, Miss."

Clair broke down and sobbed.

ELEVEN

Billy Ray

When Billy Ray first saw the girl running toward him, back lighted by the headlights from her truck, he didn't realize she was naked. Once she moved closer he was amazed to find that not only was she naked, she was also barefoot.

Werner had warned him, called and told him about the girl escaping from the Retreat. Out of breath and agitated, he hadn't mentioned anything about her state of dress. Or undress in this case.

Billy Ray drove into town with the girl locked in the back seat. She was quiet now, huddled and shivering in her blanket despite the hot night air. In deference to her needs, he shut off the car's air conditioner. Even with the vents set wide open in the front and the fan on high, the sweat oozed from every pore of his body and soaked his uniform. He glanced at the car's outside thermometer. The temperature of the night air washing over him was 81 degrees with humidity so high it felt he was immersed in a hot bath.

His cell phone buzzed.

"Billy Ray Poynter here."

"No shit. Who else would pick up your cell phone, redneck?" Werner calling.

"Get to the point, skinhead."

"You got the girl?"

Billy Ray hesitated.

"Goddamn it, you got the girl?"

"Werner, how come all these people are escaping? Security at the hotel's your responsibility, isn't it? Suppose I tell Phester you suck at what you do?"

Billy Ray heard choking sounds, visualized Werner bristling with resentment. "I'm wise to your tactics, redneck. Just answer the question. You got the girl?"

"I got her."

"Bring her up to the gate. I'll meet you there."

"Maybe I will, and maybe I won't."

"Know something, Poynter, you're stupid. You better bring the girl to the gate and right now or I'm going to have Bobby shove a pinecone up your ass sideways. Then I'm going to tell Mr. Phester how the sorry piece of shit he hired as a town cop never cooperates with me."

"Don't get excited, Werner. It makes those ugly scars on your face turn red."

"Listen to me, you redneck jerk," Werner replied in a low sibilant voice. "Bring the girl up and bring her up now." Werner slammed the phone down hard enough to make Billy Ray jerk the cell phone away from his ear.

As it was, Billy Ray was disgusted with himself for acting like Pavlov's dog every time some poor bastard had the common sense and gumption to escape from the Retreat, and his masters sent him like a trained retriever to fetch them. He hated returning captives to the Retreat, knowing what Phester had in store for them. Wished Werner and the rest of them would leave him the hell alone, but knew that was a fantasy, never to be realized.

This one girl in particular bothered him. He didn't understand why. There was something different about her. Maybe it was because she appeared more intelligent and vulnerable, maybe because she was a looker with raven black hair that reminded him of his former wife ... Oh, hell, he wasn't sure what it was, couldn't reach down far enough inside himself to pull it out.

Disturbed by his lack of insight, blaming it on a

booze-soaked brain, he stepped on the accelerator and drove through Main Street on the way to the Retreat.

Then abruptly braked at the edge of town when a flash insight gripped him. One that took roots as he sat there and tossed it around. It came down to this: the boozing was his way to forget the ugly scene at the Retreat, to blank out the human sorrow he was part of.

Except drowning himself in booze wasn't working anymore. His nights were a torture. He increasingly hated himself with an intensity that he realized would eventually destroy him. So he either acted now and got the hell out or waited until the booze killed him. Because sure as hell it would.

There was only one way out of the Retreat. It was full of risks and had a nasty downside, but with mounting excitement he knew he was going to chance it. He smiled wryly as he recalled a saying that had stuck with him like Krazy Glue over the years, a saying that probably more than any other described his career, such as it was. "To hell with the consequences, full speed ahead." A war cry, one that repeatedly landed him in hot water. The redneck version of Dirty Harry.

Billy Ray scorned what others called playing politics and what he called by its real name, plain old ass kissing. He wasn't about to cut slack for bad guys simply because they had high political connections. Never had, never will. In any case, Billy Ray suffered because of it. At first a rising star in the Florence, Alabama police department, making chief of detectives at age thirty based on an outstanding arrest record, Billy Ray flushed it down the drain one frosty January evening when he nailed the rapist of a seventeen-year-old girl. Unfortunately, the perpetrator wasn't just anybody, he happened to be the mayor's teenage son. So, when holier-than-thou Billy Ray turned down the mayor's request to drop the arrest because, as the mayor put it, "the slut and my boy were having consensual sex," his career was finished. He started sliding downhill, one demotion following another. Billy Ray became the cop to avoid in the Florence Police Department. And remained that way until the murder.

He knew what he was about to do now would more than likely result in prison time. Not a pleasant thought for a lawman who in prison would become the natural prey of every deranged convict hell bent on revenge against cops. More likely, he'd wind up in protective custody, what cons called PC, a section of the prison set aside for lawmen gone bad, child molesters, cons on suicide watch, psychos and faggots. Pretty terrible way to live. Still, he had to do it.

He spun the police cruiser around and drove to his small home, shut off the car lights and climbed outside. The night air remained blistering hot. Billy Ray removed his hat and wiped the sweatband. Inside his house he picked up a fifth of Jack Daniel's, then a dress and some sandals left at his place by his bedmate of last Saturday night, the plump waitress who worked night shift at Clyde's Bar & Grill. He returned to the car, arms laden.

"Are you taking me back to the Retreat?" the girl asked in a frightened voice.

He unlocked and opened the back door and handed the dress and sandals to her. "Put these on."

She looked up, surprised, then slipped into the dress and strapped up the sandals. "The outfit's too big. So are the sandals. They look awful on me."

Billy Ray grinned. Even at a time like this, the girl was concerned about her appearance.

He threw the bottle into the front passenger seat and climbed back into the car, cranked up the engine. Glanced at the girl through the rearview mirror. "We're not going back to the Retreat."

Billy Ray heard her sharp intake of breath. She leaned forward and gripped the mesh screen separating them. "Where are you taking me?"

"To the state cops."

She was silent for a moment, then, "If you mean it, let me sit up front with you."

Billy Ray considered her request. "How do I know you won't try to run away?"

"I won't, not if we're going to the state police."

That sounded reasonable. "All right, why not?" He popped the door locks. The girl climbed out of the back and slid into the front. She noticed the fifth of Jack Daniel's on the bench seat between them.

"I remember you now. You're the police officer Melissa pointed out when we drove through Wicked Stop on the way to the Retreat."

"Were you in that Lincoln with Melissa?"

"Yes, along with my mom and dad and a close friend."

Billy Ray said nothing, as if the subject of her family was somehow painful.

Clair turned to him with an anxious look. "How are we going to free my parents and my friend Heather?"

They were driving down the access road from Wicked Stop to the state highway. "That would be a bad move. If only the two of us bust into the Retreat we're going up against some pretty rough people. I'm sure you've met some of them, like Bobby and Werner. Better we get the state troopers to do it for us."

"Why are you helping me? If you knew about my escape from the Retreat, then you're connected to them." To punctuate her concern, the girl moved closer to the door, away from Billy Ray.

"I'm not part of that bunch. Not anymore. I've had my fill."

"Can I count on that?"

"Do you have any choice?" he sounded annoyed.

Clair decided not to press the point. She looked at the bottle. "Melissa said you drink a lot. You're not going to drink now, are you?"

Billy Ray swore at Melissa under his breath. "No, Miss, you don't have to worry. I'm not going to assault you or rape you or hurt you in any way. Not tonight."

The girl tensed. Billy Ray mentally kicked himself for a stupid lapse of sensitivity. Blamed it on the booze again. "That was a joke, Miss, a feeble one. ... Say, what's your name, anyway?"

"Clair King," she said in a voice betraying her fear.

"Look, don't be afraid. You got to understand I'm on your side."

"And you're..."

"Billy Ray Poynter." He extended his hand. She hesitated at first, then shook hands. Hers was ice cold and dry despite the night's heat and humidity.

"May I ask you something?" Clair said.

"Sure, why not?"

"The people at the Retreat kidnapped my family and me and God knows how many others. You seem like a decent man. Otherwise you wouldn't let me get away. How in the world did you get involved?"

Billy Ray winced, retreated within himself. How in the world, indeed? Because Phester was blackmailing him, that's how. He vividly recalled the horrible events that turned his life upside down. That warm Spring night in Florence when he stopped at a convenience store after work to buy a six pack and interrupted a robbery in progress. The robber, wearing a stocking over his head, pointed a shotgun in Billy Ray's direction and Billy Ray, blessed with quick reaction time, instinctively drew his automatic and shot and killed the robber before he squeezed the trigger of the shotgun. Unfortunately for Billy Ray, the robber was a fourteen-year-old black kid. Now a dead fourteen-year-old black kid.

That was all she wrote. Killing a black today, particularly a black youth, was enough to get any cop in trouble. Regardless of the circumstances. Add to that the seething animosity of the mayor of Florence, and Billy Ray had dipped his toe in a cauldron of boiling water. His wife of three years, a social climber, knowing what was in store for Billy Ray, wasted no time walking out on him. Worse, the chief of police, thirsting for Billy Ray's blood, issued a warrant for his arrest. Billy Ray panicked and ran. Looking back, he knew that had he stayed and faced the trumped-up murder charge, it never would have held up in court. The district attorney might not even have pressed charges.

But that isn't what happened. Billy Ray scooted out of Florence as fast as his long legs would carry him. He compounded his problems by stealing a car, later ditching it in Birmingham. He bussed to New Orleans and hid out until Phester found him and gave him a home. Such as it was.

"That older man at the Retreat," Clair said. "The one who's in charge—"

"Gilbert Phester."

"That's him. He scares me." She huddled in her blanket.

"He scares me, too."

"Any person who starts a white slavery business in a town called Wicked Stop is either crazy or arrogant or a little bit of both."

"You got to admit," Billy Ray said, "it takes gumption. And a lot of smarts."

Clair turned to face Billy Ray. "He's got something on you, doesn't he?"

Billy Ray kept his eyes on the road and his voice level. "Know something, you're a smart young lady."

"I'm not that much younger than you. About ten years."

"Like I said, a smart young lady. Maybe too smart."

Clair ignored the barb. "What in your past was so bad that Mr. Phester got his hooks into you?"

Billy Ray sighed. "You're persistent, I'll give you that. But what's past is past. Right now we're going to the law. Not this fake law." He flicked a finger at the tin badge on his chest.

"This Mr. Phester, he's running a white slavery ring, isn't he?"

Billy Ray looked startled, kept his eyes forward, hoping the girl didn't notice his reaction.

Clair picked right up on it. "Then it's true. God, how awful. How does he get away with it?"

"Look, I don't want to talk about anything right now, okay?"

She said nothing, instead focused on the road highlighted by the car's headlamps.

Billy Ray pointed ahead. "The state highway's coming up." He pulled the cruiser aside at the entrance to the state road, out of range of the Retreat's cameras mounted on the two oak trees flanking the entry road. Then sat back and closed his eyes for a moment, rubbed them with the back of his hands. "You okay, Clair?"

He saw her nod in the light reflected from the dash.

He flipped open his cell phone and dialed a number. "Police Chief Billy Ray Poynter here. I need a state trooper at the entrance of the road leading to Wicked Stop."

He listened for a moment. "No, it's not an emergency, but it is urgent. There's two of us. We'll be waiting right here."

He closed the cell phone and reached for the bottle of bourbon.

Clair's eyes widened. "You're not going to start

drinking now, are you?"

"Not unless I can get the bottle to my mouth." He upended the bottle and guzzled a mouthful of bourbon.

"You shouldn't be drinking. The state police are on their way."

"Look, Miss, don't tell me what to do. I've had enough of that crap to last me a lifetime."

"Sorry." She paused momentarily. "Look, one thing I don't understand."

Billy Ray sighed. "Go ahead, ask me. You will anyway."

"How long has the Retreat been in business?"

Billy Ray thought about it. "Now that you ask, I don't rightly know. But it's been a bunch of years."

"How do they get away with selling girls into slavery? I don't get it?"

Billy Ray sighed.

Clair pivoted around in her seat and examined him. The reflected light from the instrument panel tinged his face a ghostly green.

"If they've been selling women into slavery all these years, you think by now somebody would have run away—"

"Like you?" Billy Ray snorted.

"I guess I wasn't too smart. Surely somebody before me must have run to the state police or the sheriff."

"Believe it or not, not that many run away. And all those who do are caught. Out of the hundreds of girls the Retreat's sold into slavery, maybe a dozen or two made the attempt. They give up as soon as they run into me or Bobby or Werner. But they're the exception. Most girls accept their fate, like contented cows." He shook his head in disgust.

"That doesn't make any sense."

"Look, I don't know much about history, but what

I learned stuck with me. Remember reading about World War II? How five million European Jews were promised by the Nazis they were being moved to resettlement camps. Absolute lies, but the Jews bought it because they didn't want to accept the truth. It was too horrible to believe. And the truth was those god-awful concentration camps where Jews were gassed by the millions."

"I know," she said in a low voice.

"Well, the same principle holds true here. The girls the Retreat captures don't want to believe the worst. They tell themselves they're going on vacation to exotic lands, things like that."

"Like the Jews thought in Nazi Germany."

"Exactly. I'm not the smartest guy in the world, but this I know: people would rather stick their heads in the sand than accept the truth."

"It's awful."

"We're all too damned civilized. If a few of the girls at the Retreat had picked up knives and stabbed a few attendants, maybe they'd have gotten away and the Retreat wouldn't be in business today."

Clair shivered. "I could never hurt anybody like that."

"Maybe someday you'll have to."

Clair sat in stony silence while Billy Ray repeatedly tipped the bottle.

"Are you married?" Clair asked, breaking the silence.

"She left me."

"Was she–"

"Look, I'd rather not talk about it."

Silence again. The only sound the gurgling of the bottle as Billy Ray drank from it.

By the time the state patrol car arrived, roof lights flashing, the bottle was a third empty.

The trooper climbed out of his patrol car, adjusted his hat. With one hand resting on the holster flap of his handgun, he cautiously approached Billy Ray and Clair, the headlights from his car behind him illuminating Billy Ray's police cruiser and blinding its two occupants.

Billy Ray and Clair climbed out of the car to greet him.

"You're officer Cody, right? Remember me? I'm Billy Ray Poynter, police chief of Wicked Stop. This young lady was a prisoner of the Retreat."

"I know who you are." The trooper had a Southern accent thicker than Billy Ray's. He motioned Clair to join Billy Ray on the other side of the car. When she did, Billy Ray said to the state trooper, "I'll fill you in on the way to the Retreat."

The state cop unholstered his handgun and pointed it at Billy Ray. "Hands on your head."

"Hey, I'm a cop."

"Do it now!" The snarl in his voice left no room for argument.

Billy Ray laced his hands behind his head and the cop patted him down and removed his sidearm. He handcuffed Billy Ray and Clair.

"What in hell's going on here?" Billy Ray asked, his accent growing thicker, the words coming faster in tune with his rising alarm.

The state cop ignored him, instead snatched Billy Ray's cell phone and punched in a number. Billy Ray gaped at him.

"Werner, this is Jack Cody, state police. I've got a couple of escapees at the entrance to Wicked Stop. I'm bringing 'em in now."

The cop snickered in response to something Werner said. "Don't worry, Werner, I promise not to shoot them. ... Unless the assholes are stupid enough to make a break for it."

TWELVE

Gilbert

"**W**ell, well, well," Gilbert clucked as he stroked the Chihuahua on his lap. "The two most stalwart employees of the Retreat, brought together by circumstances neither one of them could have foreseen."

The acne on Werner's face turned fiery red. He felt shamed by the presence of others in the room: Gilbert's mother, Marshall, Helen, Clair, Heather, and Billy Ray. "Don't put me in the same category with Billy Ray, Mr. Phester." Werner stole a glance at the Kings and Heather.

"Pay no attention to them, Werner," Gilbert said. "Our guests have been sedated enough to obliterate any memory they may have of this conversation."

"Not that bastard Billy Ray or the girl." Werner pointed to Clair, hands and feet bound, mouth gagged. Her teary eyes bulged with a mixture of resentment, defiance and fear. She sat next to a subdued Billy Ray. The side of his face was swollen from the blow Werner had delivered the moment the state cop brought him to the Retreat.

Gilbert chuckled. He guided Werner to the far side of the room where they sat down and talked in hushed whispers. "She won't be with us long enough to make any difference, Werner. The buyers are just now starting to arrive. We'll have our show and auction tomorrow afternoon as scheduled. Bobby and Melissa are setting up the auditorium to handle a group of about twenty-seven, if memory serves me. Assuming everything goes well, and I have no reason to believe differently, Clair King may find herself a new home before the weekend is over."

"I'll be happy when she's out of here. Girl's been a headache."

"Agreed. Now on to some business. We may have a record quarter."

"Mostly men buyers coming?"

It was a good question. Male buyers tended to spend more than female buyers, so Gilbert encouraged the men to attend his auctions as much as possible, although he still invited their female counterparts if scheduled turnout appeared low.

It was equally important to have enough girls on hand so each buyer could leave the Retreat with one or more white slaves in tow. These traffickers came from distant locations around the globe, and to have one leave empty-handed was tantamount to seeing that particular buyer and his cash never again.

"For this auction," Gilbert answered Werner's question, "we'll have twenty-three men and two women."

Werner nodded. "Better than last auction. There were fifteen men and six women as I recall."

"A decided improvement." Gilbert dusted off his hands to signal the end of that subject.

"Got enough hunters coming, Mr. Phester?"

"Yes, and the hunt's still scheduled for the day after tomorrow, provided our hunters arrive on time. I believe two or three of them will also attend the auction. One of them is Harry Phieu, a regular buyer. His second time around."

"I've got the game preserve ready for their arrival, the blinds positioned, the traps set."

"How about the perimeter?"

"It'll be secure. I'll have attendants positioned

around the perimeter to chase away any outside hunter who accidentally stumbles onto the property. And to keep our game inside the property."

"I can always count on you, Werner. This hunt's important. Remember, it's only our second. The first one wasn't overly successful. If you recall, we had three hunters, but only Harry Phieu bagged game. A teenage boy, if I remember correctly. The other two hunters didn't get a thing and we were forced to refund their money."

"Yeah, and it took damned near everybody working the Retreat to round up the other three teenage boys they were hunting before they bagged them."

Gilbert raised an eyebrow. "That was too close, much too close. This year we must do a better job by keeping the game close enough so the hunters can bag them. I'm relying on you."

"Will do, Mr. Phester."

"As far as the hunt's concerned, we need at least two hunters to have a hunt, but three to breakeven. Anything above that is pure profit. In fact, I won't conduct a hunt without a minimum of three. And, needless to say, based on our last experience, every hunter must score a kill."

"You got three for this hunt, right?"

"We have four scheduled and no cancellations so far."

"Are we going to use the fat guy, Mr. King, as game?"

"The problem with that is the hunters may be disappointed. They prefer their game to be in better condition, give them more of a fight. There's no challenge in bagging a fat, tired old man."

Werner nodded in the direction of Billy Ray. "How about the cop? He's strong enough, looks like he's in good condition."

"Our friend, Billy Ray? I believe he'd be an outstanding adversary for the hunters, if we can keep him sober long enough. I just don't know how far gone his alcoholism is. The drinking may have sapped his strength as well as his will. Actually, I'm not quite sure what I want to do with him. I'll mull it over tonight."

"Anyway" Werner said, "we have those two teenagers Billy Ray brought back to us, the ones who tried to escape yesterday."

"The boy, anyway. I don't know how the hunters will react to hunting a girl. In any case, it makes more business sense to sell her at auction. Nevertheless, I believe your concern is justified. We may be forced to add both Mr. King and Billy Ray to the hunt."

"We also have that old guy with the white hair, the one I got locked up, along with the teenage boy."

"Yes, we'll definitely include both of them in the hunt. The older man seems to be in pretty decent physical shape and the teenager definitely is. Enough to give the hunters a run for their money."

He stopped petting his dog for a moment and considered the problem of Billy Ray. Pootie whined, the dog's signal to continue stroking her. She had been at Gilbert's side for twelve years, and he loved Pootie with unreserved devotion. Next to his mother, there was no one he more dearly cherished. He unashamedly kissed the dog's forehead, and the dog returned the kiss by licking Gilbert's face.

Gilbert rose and led his mother and Werner back to where they held Billy Ray.

"Needless to say," Gilbert continued addressing Werner, this time in earshot of Billy Ray, "I'm quite upset about Billy Ray's disloyalty. If it weren't for me, he'd be rotting away in an Alabama prison this very moment. And, as we all know, police officers do not fare well in prison. Particularly police officers who kill young blacks. The prisons are overflowing with black men who hunger to rape and kill such racists."

He wagged a finger at Billy Ray. "What particularly disturbs me about you Billy Ray, is that you underestimated me. Never once did you consider the possibility I was smart enough to have another police officer in reserve. Your disloyalty is bad enough, but your lack of respect for my intelligence is unforgivable."

"Billy Ray's been a naughty boy, hasn't he, Sonny?" Mrs. Phester said.

"He certainly has, Mother. What shall we do with him?"

She examined Billy Ray, from head to toe, with a look as sharp as a hawk's talon. "We might try to sell him to a foreign corporation as factory or farm labor, but it'll cost too much to ship him overseas."

"Agreed," Gilbert said. "There's an excess of competition from Africa and Asian countries for good cheap male labor as it is. We wouldn't recoup our costs. You can buy a male slave in his late teens from the Sudan for a thousand dollars."

"They're not white, Sonny."

"True, Mother, but for factory or farm labor their color or nationality makes no difference as long as they can work sixteen hours a day."

"I suppose we could turn Billy Ray over to Werner or Bobby as a bonus."

"I'd like that very much, Mrs. Phester," Werner said. His eyes gleamed with pleasure at the thought.

Billy Ray, hands tied behind his back, head hanging on his chest, stared at his boots and said nothing.

Werner threw a withering glance in Clair's direction. "Bobby's lucky he didn't break his glasses when the King girl knocked his head with the truck she was driving. Banged him up real good, though. He's got a real hard-on for her, and for Billy Ray for running to the cops. He'd love to tear both of them to shreds."

"He'll do no such thing," Gilbert said. "Clair and Billy Ray represent income to the Retreat, sales dollars." Gilbert hesitated. With disgust, he recalled the money he paid out to politicians, police and other governmental parties to protect the anonymity and security of the Retreat. Although he was careful to disguise the trail of white slaves he lured to Wicked Stop, there had been instances when outsiders traced the last known location of their relatives and friends to the Retreat. Hence the considerable payoffs to politicians and police for protection. Gilbert sighed to himself.

"Before we go any further, I think it best that we bring these two errant souls, Billy Ray and Clair, in line with the rest of our guests." He nodded in the direction of Marshall, Helen and Heather. All three sat side by side on a sofa as if glued together, subdued, hands in their laps, faces expressionless, a blurry, distant look in their eyes. They brought to mind three rag dolls that a child, playing house, arranged on a doll sofa.

"Werner, if you will," Gilbert said.

Werner stepped forward with a syringe and a small vial with some fluid in it. He upended the vial and inserted the needle, filled the syringe.

"The girl first," Gilbert instructed.

Clair struggled to free herself. Werner grabbed Clair's arm and wrapped a rubber tourniquet above her elbow, found a vein and injected her.

"Now Billy Ray," Gilbert said.

Werner injected Billy Ray, who put up no resistance.

"Young lady," Gilbert said to Clair, "from your dossier I gather that you recently completed your pre-med studies at Ohio State. So you might have some clinical interest in knowing that the solution Werner injected you with is Temazempan, a sedative that will help make you less restive."

"She certainly needs it," Mrs. Phester said. "She's been hyperactive from the moment we met her."

Clair struggled to speak.

"Remove her gag, please," Gilbert said to Werner.

Werner jerked the gag from Clair's face and she gulped in air. Her chest heaved with the effort.

"You might be further interested to know, that from now on your stay at the Retreat will be a happy, even a euphoric one, thanks to the addition of a narcotic called Dilaudid in your food – four star meals, I might add. We're quite proud of our cuisine at the Retreat – and you'll remain drowsy but quite content. I tell you this so you'll understand there's no sense in resisting. We can easily adjust the dosage should you become, shall we say, antagonistic. It all depends on you."

"Mom and Dad, Heather ... are they going to be okay?"

"They are perfectly fine, quiet and content. You'll be joining them in moments, just one great big happy family."

Clair's eyelids fluttered and her head gradually floated back, then flopped onto her chest. And came back up again, but this time with a faraway look in her eyes.

Gilbert nodded at Werner. "Take them to their rooms and lock them up for the night."

"How about Billy Ray?"

"Him, too. Lock him with the other men in the basement." We'll decide what to do with the scoundrel in the morning. I want to think about it overnight." He idly scratched the dog behind its ears. Pootie cocked her head sideways to receive the full benefit.

Werner stood. "One question, Mr. Phester."

Gilbert arched an eyebrow. "Yes?"

"The girl, Heather? When are we going to find out if she's a virgin?"

Gilbert allowed a tiny smile to caress his lips. "You're unrepentant, aren't you Werner? But to answer your question, tomorrow. The physical exams will be performed first thing in the morning. The doctor will contact you."

"Sure thing, Mr. Phester."

Mrs. Phester's nostrils flared. She stared openly at Werner's crotch until he became uncomfortable under her scrutiny and walked away. He lifted the phone and called the front desk, told them to send two attendants to the reception room. Moments later the uniformed attendants arrived and escorted the Kings and Heather away. Werner seized Billy Ray by his collar and dragged him from the room.

"Mother," Gilbert said, "why don't you have a beverage in the lounge upstairs? I'll join you later."

Mrs. Phester knew when her son wanted to be alone. She bent over and kissed him on the forehead. "I'll be waiting for you, Sonny."

After she left, Gilbert mixed himself a martini from the bar and eased himself into the executive chair behind the teak desk. He leaned back, lifted his feet onto the edge of the desk and closed his eyes. His thoughts drifted to Mother. Bawdy old woman, he thought and smiled to himself, a real bitch in heat. Utterly amazing for a woman her age.

Mother's sexual appetite was voracious. Indeed, were he interested in such matters, he could count a dozen or more Retreat attendants, both male and female, whom she had seduced over the past year or two. Including Werner and Melissa. But not Bobby.

Mother seemed to know intuitively whom to avoid. Bobby simply was too unpredictable, too dangerous.

Only a few weeks ago, Gilbert had entered their suite at an obviously inopportune time, and found her entertaining two of the Retreat's younger male attendants. Gilbert murmured his apologies and departed hastily, not in disgust, but in self-reproach for having intruded on her private life.

Afterward, the two male attendants hastened to beg Gilbert's forgiveness. He had sat behind his oversize desk that made him look Lilliputian, his fingers steepled, and pretended to be unhappy. The two attendants, sweat pimpling their brows, scared not only for their jobs but for their lives, pledged to do anything Gilbert asked if he would only forgive them. Precisely the state Gilbert wanted his employees in. The implicit threat of loss of life motivated employees to work with renewed vigor. He gave them scathing looks while admonishing the two young men for their purportedly offensive behavior, dismissed them and chuckled after they left. And made a mental note to keep an eye on those two in case they decided to bolt.

Gilbert's thoughts drifted further back. Mother had named her only child after the Latino movie star Gilbert Roland because of her attraction to swarthy, earthy types. An earthy type herself, she and her husband, Gilbert's father, frequently participated in threesomes, with the third occupant of their bed frequently a young sailor or airman from nearby military bases. When Gilbert's father traveled his mother picked-up young men and women and brought them back to her home in the hills for afternoon dalliances. Some of which lasted for days on end.

As fate would have it, Gilbert's sex life was diametrically opposite that of his mother's. He rarely indulged his sexual fantasies (seldom had any), preferring occasional masturbation to the complications of a relationship. On those few times when he felt an urgent need for female flesh, he'd arrange to have a trollop brought from Americus directly to his quarters at the Retreat where, for the princely sum of fifty dollars, he would take his pleasure copulating, but only in the missionary position and *never* with any of that messy business such as kissing, caressing, licking and sucking that habitually accompany the vulgar act of sex. Activities that made Gilbert gag. As the male pundits would express it, Gilbert's fornication was confined to "Wham, bam, thank you, ma'am." With his eyes closed. That single encounter would hold Gilbert for several months, until the abominable need surfaced again.

Gilbert was a proponent of that crude but true maxim, never shit where you eat. Accordingly, when his need for copulation reached its peak, he abstained from helping himself to any of the female attendants working at the Retreat, although most of them would have jumped at the chance to ingratiate themselves with the boss. He held himself aloof, kept an arm's length in his business relationships.

Gilbert knew the Retreat's employees made unkind remarks about him behind his back. The rumor mill had it that he and his mother were ... fornicating. A grossly offensive notion that sent shivers of revulsion pulsing through him.

That contemptible assertion was as far from the truth as possible. Their relationship was strictly wholesome and ... Christian, for want of a better word. Gilbert dearly loved his mother, owed his life to her in more ways than the traditional one of giving birth to him. She had been the buffer between Gilbert and his burly, mean-spirited father. Her interventions saved his life.

Gilbert sighed and his thoughts drifted further back in time to his childhood in San Diego. His father ran twin businesses, an illegal animal importing business and a money laundering operation for associates in the drug trade. For the latter business he owned and operated a bank in Chula Vista, a California border town south of San Diego.

The money poured in. Gilbert grew up in fashionable La Jolla and lived in a million dollar home. His father drove a Mercedes, his mother a BMW. But there was trouble in paradise, notably, Gilbert's frequent and recurring health problems. At age five, Gilbert developed pneumonia, which brought on rheumatic fever and a scarred heart. He was confined to a wheelchair for a year.

After that, concerned about the fragility of her boy's health, his mother over-protected him from the vicissitudes of growing up: boyhood sports, roughhouse games, all the physical activities that normal boys enjoy, but for a boy with a delicate condition ... well, who knows if his heart would have handled the strain.

Gilbert turned inward and became a loner, withdrawn and bookish. Long after the disease faded from memory, he steered away from close associations with classmates and neighborhood kids and abstained from physical activity of any nature. He was frequently ill, suffering periodic bouts of flu, common colds and all manner of aches and pains. His dear mother, of course, always managed to nurse him back to health. The two became inseparable.

Because of his various illnesses, he never fully developed physically, had skinny arms and legs. And, since both his parents were on the shorter side, he topped out at 5'4". A tiny scarecrow of a boy and later a man.

His father, a lover of sports, drinking and screwing, a real American he-man in every sense of the word, never forgave Gilbert his disability, simply couldn't fathom siring a "defective product" as he called Gilbert. He spurned the boy, whipped him whenever convenient, until the boy, at age ten, was bordering on psychotic withdrawal. In simpler terms, becoming a basket case.

Without the interference of his mother, Gilbert was certain his father would have killed him with the same glee he once displayed when drowning a litter of kittens birthed by Gilbert's cat, Sammie. An act that sent Gilbert screaming into the night until the police returned him to his home the following morning.

The memory of his father's cruelty sent chills bucketing through Gilbert's body and made him reach for a throw blanket on a nearby sofa to warm his body. He took deep breaths to calm himself and then slowly, ever so slowly, a smile took hold on his face and within seconds he was beaming, a rare sight, one that few employees of the Retreat ever witnessed.

Because seared in Gilbert's memory was his twelfth birthday. Mother, panic-stricken when her drunken husband attacked her precious son yet again, and sick to death in general of the contemptuous way the bastard treated him, hefted a twelve-gauge shotgun and emptied both barrels into her husband, blasting his midsection into a thousand pieces over the birthday cake as Gilbert stood by and watched.

THIRTEEN

Helen

Helen floated through an erotic dream with her young lover, Roger. Unconsciously, she slipped a finger between her legs and with a gasp of pleasure found her clitoris and massaged it. As soon as Roger's face came into focus above her, she wrapped her legs tightly around his slender body and squeezed, nuzzled his head to her breast and licked his ear. He lifted his head to gaze into her eyes. His features blurred and dissolved and reformed again, this time into an alternately grinning and snarling Werner. Helen shrank back, pushed against his chest. But Werner was too strong. As he pinned her down and groped her breasts, Mrs. Phester drifted ghost-like to a position beside Werner and slowly disrobed in a grotesque caricature of a stripper. She shed her clothes to reveal a hideously wrinkled and deformed body. Her lips, like those of a clown, were smeared with lipstick that covered her entire lower face. The lewd old woman reached out to Helen with gnarled fingers.

Helen opened her mouth to scream and bolted to an upright position. Her heart threatened to leap through her chest, her head throbbed, her mouth was as dry as dust. Dear Jesus, it was a dream, merely a dream. Thank the good Lord.

But where was she? She pivoted her head to each side, disoriented, searching for someplace familiar to anchor her position and not finding it. The sudden motion made her nauseous. Calm down, she told herself, calm down. She closed her eyes and took deep breaths until her heartbeat gradually subsided, then opened her eyes and glanced around.

She was in a long narrow room with cots lined up in two orderly rows, one row on either wall. The room resembled an army barracks. Early morning light filtered through window blinds, illuminating the sleepers around her with dappled light. Most of the beds were filled with women, some mumbling through nightmares or dreams, others snoring. One women perched upright in her bed, shaking off the mantle of sleep and looking around with a dazed expression.

The events of the past day came flooding back. Helen along with Marshall and Heather had been drugged. Where were they? And what happened to Clair? She dimly recalled seeing Clair after her escape. But where? Her recollection was fuzzy.

Head splitting, Helen staggered to her feet and stumbled from bed to bed searching for her daughter and Heather. Thankfully, she found them sleeping in adjacent beds at the far end of the room. By her count, the beds held thirty women, all of them in their teens or twenties with the exception of herself and one other woman about her age.

She prodded Clair and Heather until they awakened, shushed them. The girls groped through clouds of sleep to reach full consciousness. As far as Helen could tell, all the women in the room, including her, were dressed in gray institutional nightgowns and nothing more, other than ankle bracelets.

Ankle bracelets? She lifted her gown and glanced at her ankle. Sure enough a bracelet adorned her ankle. It looked like nothing more than a strap made from some sturdy metal. She bent over and tried to remove it and couldn't, no matter how much she pulled and tugged.

Helen shrugged her shoulders and searched for street clothes and shoes, found nothing. The room was devoid of closets or lockers.

She whispered to Clair, told her to keep Heather quiet. Helen tiptoed to the end of the room and tried opening its only door. Locked. Next she examined one of the windows. It was built into the frame without any way to open it, like a hotel room window. She tapped it, found it was constructed from unbreakable glass which she guessed wouldn't fracture even if hit with a sledgehammer.

Helen returned to Clair and Heather. "Do you know where Marshall is?" she whispered.

Both girls shook their heads.

"What's happening to us?" Heather asked. "How do we get out of here, Mrs. K?"

Helen squeezed Heather's hand. "There's got to be a way, dear. Don't worry, we'll find it." But her voice lacked conviction.

Clair clasped her head with both hands. "The drugs wore off. My head's a war zone."

"So's mine," Heather said. "What do we do now?"

As if to answer her question, the entranceway door flew open. Werner strode inside like a drill sergeant ready to inspect the troops. Melissa and three other female attendants tagged behind him, all neatly attired in their blue and white uniforms with the gold insignia of the Retreat.

"Up and at 'em, girls," Werner intoned in a drill sergeant's commanding voice. He clapped his hands. "It's six a.m. Everybody out of bed. Let's go. We have a busy schedule."

His no-nonsense greeting was met with a series of groans as the women slowly emerged from their cocoons of drug-induced sleep.

Werner had them form a double line of fifteen women each and marched them abreast from the room. The female attendants herded the women back into line when any drifted away. Many of the women, girls really, were openly sobbing. Clair kept Heather from falling apart by whispering encouragement to her as the girls tramped along, out the building (which Helen recognized as one of the hotel's flanking double-floor structures) through a breezeway and into a stairwell, where they climbed to the second floor of the main building. Werner led them into a dining room where the delicious breakfast smell of coffee filled the room. It was cheerily decorated with solid-looking maple tables set for breakfast, six hardback chairs at each table, brightly-colored floral pattern wallpaper and a large bay window overlooking the swimming pool behind the hotel. Helen gazed out the window and saw a bored male attendant lazily sweeping the pool bottom with a long vacuum attachment.

Werner stood near the tables, hands on hips. "Okay, girls, everybody sit down."

They did so with a murmur of dissent.

Werner clapped his hands; the slap sounded like a rifle shot. "Enough of that or I'll turn Bobby loose on you."

Some of the girls moaned, somebody mumbled a curse and finally a silence enveloped the room. Evidently, Helen thought, every girl here had met or knew of Bobby. She shivered at the memory of Bobby's ice-cold eyes magnified by the thick lenses of his glasses, as he salaciously examined her body. The very thought of his knockwurst-sized fingers running up and down her body was gruesome and sickening enough to make her stomach churn.

The girls obediently sat down in clusters of six. At each table a female attendant hovered nearby, grim and watchful.

In minutes, two male attendants, emerged from the kitchen, carrying steaming breakfast plates to each girl loaded with scrambled eggs, bacon and buttered toast. They scooted back to the kitchen and returned with carafes of coffee and milk and orange juice for each table.

A few girls, voraciously hungry, dug in. Most didn't. "Eat, goddamn it," Werner roared and the other girls quickly picked up their forks and hesitantly ate what they knew or guessed was food laced with tranquilizers. The attendants walked among the tables, making sure that the thirty girls consumed their breakfasts.

Helen, Clair and Heather were seated together.

"Mom, I've got an–"

"No talking," the female attendant for their table barked. Her stern demeanor left no room for doubt that she meant it.

Helen and Clair exchanged glances. Helen realized that Clair wanted to tell her something important.

Werner glanced at his watch and tapped a foot. "Eat fast now, girls. You're going for your physical examinations and we're leaving in fifteen minutes."

From the expressions on some of the faces around her and at adjacent tables, Helen knew they were thinking the same thing: This might be a chance to escape.

It must have been apparent to Werner, too. "Just so you don't get the wrong idea, the physicals will be held here, in the Retreat."

A few groans greeted this announcement, followed by the attendants snarling at the girls to shut up.

After breakfast, Werner commanded the girls to stand up and form two lines. The attendants took their places policing the lines.

"Okay, now for an interesting demonstration," Werner said as he paraded up and down the standing girls. "A few of you noticed that thing on your ankles.

Go ahead, all of you look down."

The girls obediently lifted their gowns and examined their ankle bracelets.

Werner grinned. "Try to rip them off. C'mon, go ahead, give it a try."

Most of the girls bent over and jerked the edges of their bracelets.

"They don't come off, do they?" Werner asked. "Don't even bother trying. They're made from space-age metals. Know why you're wearing them?" The attendants snickered.

"Okay, let me show you." He turned to the girl nearest the door. "You, go ahead and get out of here. Go ahead, leave." He pushed his hand in the air telling her to scat. She stared back at him wide-eyed.

"D-d-do you mean it?" she asked in a husky voice, obviously suspicious.

"Damn right. Go on now, get out of here."

The girl examined Werner for a few moments then bolted for the door. Werner pressed the button of a device he held in his hand and the girl's body convulsed as if shot through with a thunderbolt. She shrieked and collapsed in the doorway.

"Revive her," Werner told an attendant who scurried to the girl's side. Werner stared at the rest of the girls who looked on with eyes filled with dread.

"That's what happens if you try to run away. The ankle bracelet you're wearing contains electronic circuits. You'll get as far as that girl did. Every window and every door leading out of this building has built-in electronics that will trip the circuits in your bracelet if you attempt to escape. Circuits that will zzzzzap you." He grinned maliciously and pointed at the girl convulsing at the doorway. Everybody watched the spectacle of attendants reviving the girl and helping her to her feet. She groaned, appeared dazed and disoriented.

"Okay, let's move out," Werner said after the spectacle was over.

The girls obediently trudged forward.

Clair raised her hand. "I got to pee."

Melissa ran up to Clair. "What the hell are you trying to pull now?"

"I got to pee bad."

"Get moving," Werner bellowed.

"Look," Clair said and pointed at her leg. A rivulet of urine snaked down her leg and her gown was stained in the front. "I mean it. I got to go."

"You filthy pig," Melissa shouted, furious. She slapped Clair's face. Clair cried out and cringed.

"Melissa," Werner said with evident disgust, "take the bitch to the john, then catch-up with us. We're falling behind schedule."

He herded the girls out of the dining room.

Melissa grabbed Clair's arm and twisted. "I'm going to kick your ass, troublemaker."

Clair howled with pain.

FOURTEEN

Clair

Once inside the restroom, Melissa kicked Clair in the ass. "Get in the stall. Now!"

Clair scampered into the stall. She shut and locked the door behind her.

"I'm standing outside, bitch, waiting for you. Make it fast."

"I'll be just a minute," Clair said, her voice choked.

She felt the drugs from the breakfast starting to take hold. Quickly now, she told herself. She peeked between the partitions to make sure Melissa wasn't watching and lifted the toilet seat. She vomited into the toilet, concealing the noise by flushing. She stuck her fingers down her throat again and vomited some more, the flushing toilet covering the sounds.

"Get the rag out," Melissa shouted.

"I'm coming," Clair replied, her throat raw. She unwound a long strand of toilet paper and wiped her eyes, nose and mouth. Spit into the toilet and prayed that Melissa wouldn't smell the bitter odor of vomit. She offered a hasty prayer, unlocked the door and stepped out of the stall.

Melissa pinched Clair's arm and forced her ahead. "Keep on moving."

Clair winced and obediently marched forward. Her head began to clear and she thanked God she threw up in time before the drugs took hold. At the breakfast table, she had wanted to advise her mother to try the same gambit, but an alert attendant stopped her. Her mother was now drugged, but at least Clair could face whatever lay ahead with a clear head. She dragged along as if in a drugged state to fool Melissa.

Melissa hustled Clair into a room in one of the double-floor wings, where she joined the other girls. The thirty of them lined up single-file against the wall facing a closed door to yet another room. Clair covertly searched for and found her mother and Heather. Their eyes didn't return Clair's signal. Rather they glanced into the distance with dreamy smiles. Clair noticed the same listless appearance and vacuous gaze on the other girls. She slumped against a wall, imitating the others, a neutral expression on her face, her mouth hanging open, as she stared off into space, pretending to be drugged.

"Any trouble?" Werner asked Melissa while nodding in Clair's direction.

"A pain in the ass, as usual, but look at her, she's quiet now, zonked out of her mind like the rest of them."

A woman in a dirty white smock stuck her head out from behind the door in front of the line of girls. Her brunette hair was disheveled and a lit cigarette dangled from a corner of her mouth. The smoke drifted up and made her squint. She brushed the smoke away with hands wearing surgical gloves. "This one's no virgin, but physically an excellent specimen." She pushed the somnolent girl through the door and an attendant led her away. Clair tried to see where they were going but didn't want to turn around and disclose her alert state.

Werner smirked. "Only the best for you girls. A doctor who smokes. A gynecologist, no less."

"And a warden," the doctor shot back with a snort, "who quotes Nietzsche and hates Jews. Hope none of these lovely ladies are Jewish."

"You know what Nietzsche said about women, don't you doctor?"

The doctor snorted. "I'm afraid to ask."

"I quote, 'God created women. And boredom did indeed cease from that moment ... but many other things ceased as well!'"

"How droll."

Werner and the doctor hurled barbs at each other. Despite any number of insults he threw her way, the doctor remained unflappable, kept her cool. Which seemed to goad Werner on, making him reach for more challenging taunts. In a friendly way but with a bite.

"I could give you a taste of Nietzsche you'll never forget."

The doctor took a puff on her cigarette. From behind a cloud of smoke she said, "You'll never get the chance."

"You don't know what you're missing."

The bantering continued. Despite the doctor's scruffy appearance and the smelly cigarettes she chain-smoked, underneath her smock Clair saw a large bust with dominant nipples protruding through both her dress and smock, and a well rounded rear (which seemed to appeal inordinately to Werner since his eyes kept on returning to that section of her anatomy).

"Shut up, Werner," the doctor replied to his latest dig, "and send in the next girl." She coughed as one of the attendants ushered the next girl on line into the examination room, a stunningly attractive Latina teenager with glossy black hair.

Five minutes later the door swung open and the doctor said, "Werner, this one may be real pretty but she's got a rash around her groin and the lower portion of her stomach. I'm not sure what it is, but it doesn't look good. I won't know until the blood work returns from the lab."

Werner cursed. "I'll take it from here." He turned to an attendant. "Put surgical gloves on and take the girl to the reception room and lock her in there. Tie her to a chair so she can't move around the room. I'll tell Mr. Phester about this."

The attendant led the Latina away.

"Doctor," Werner said, "why didn't the rest of us see this rash when we had the girl strip?"

"How long ago was that?"

Werner struggled with his memory. "Maybe two, three days."

"Enough time for a rash to develop," the doctor concluded. "Don't blame yourself." Then her eyes lit up with a sudden thought. She smirked. "Not to worry. If Gilbert Phester says anything, I'll explain. He won't blame you."

Werner smiled and gave the doctor a thumbs-up gesture along with a winning smile. "Thanks, I owe you one." He signaled the attendant near the front of the line. "Send in this one next." He pointed to Heather. Clair tensed. Afraid she'd be noticed, she consciously relaxed and slouched against the wall. An attendant led a compliant Heather into the doctor's examination room.

Clair was glad Heather was drugged. Otherwise, her friend might have been in hysterics by now. Notwithstanding that Heather dated infrequently, her provocative appearance and kittenish voice often lead men to believe she was a hot conquest. How wrong they were. Heather was a virgin. Or so she had confided in her best friend Clair. And Clair had no reason to doubt her. They had been best friends through high school and college. Each kept nothing substantive from the other. Including their sex lives.

The influence of Heather's virtuous parents, her father a Baptist preacher, and mother a Sunday school teacher, both of them true believers, (and both now dead), combined with her pious Baptist upbringing, instilled in Heather an unswerving moral compass she persisted in following. She intended to remain a virgin until exchanging marriage vows, and had yet to meet the man of her future.

Clair, in contrast, surrendered her virginity one Sunday afternoon during her sophomore year in high school to the young, handsome and fast-talking manager of a shoe store on top of the desk in his tiny, cluttered office. She looked back on that event as a mistake. Wrote it off to a deadly combination of childlike gullibility and raging teenage hormones. Since that seminal event she had admitted only one lover, an anesthesiologist professor in college. Clair and the professor, both close-mouthed, managed to keep the affair hidden. Other than Heather, nobody else knew.

Clair and the professor, a bachelor, weren't in love. Their liaison was a convenient arrangement serving the physical needs of both. Once Clair graduated college, the affair was over without regret, at least on Clair's side, although she often felt the professor had feelings for her that went beyond sex.

Clair turned her attention to Werner. He called Gilbert Phester and told him about the girl with the suspicious rash. Clair strained to overhear Werner's side of the conversation, but Werner turned his back on her and the other girls and spoke in undertones. All Clair heard was a murmur.

Ten minutes later, the doctor's head popped out from behind the door. "This one's okay," she said. And then slyly, "Actually better than okay."

Werner's head shot up. "Is she a virgin?"

The doctor beamed. "Never been used. Gilbert's going to be elated."

"Oh, how bloody wonderful," Werner said in a despondent voice.

The doctor shook her finger at Werner and

chuckled. "Had your mind set on this one, did you? Well, too bad."

"You'll do as a poor substitute."

The doctor grinned. "Not in this life. Or any other." She ushered the next girl into the examination room. When it came Clair's turn she docilely followed the attendant. A nurse mounted her onto a table fitted with stirrups. Her heart started to accelerate, she felt a pounding in her head, it was difficult to lie still. She consciously breathed deep and slow to keep the doctor from noticing that she wasn't drugged. When the doctor probed between her legs Clair emitted a tiny cry. The gynecologist stopped what she was doing and examined Clair's eyes. Clair kept a dreamy expression on her face and the doctor resumed her work.

She next examined Clair's lungs, heart, checked her pulse and took blood for a work-up. Then it was over. The doctor helped Clair off the table and eased her out of the room.

"Werner," she said after lighting a cigarette, "this one's not drugged enough. Time to make her go sleepy bye."

FIFTEEN

Mildred

At 9:30 a.m. Mildred cracked open Gilbert's bedroom door in the penthouse suite to see if her son, a late riser, was still asleep. Her eyes took in the large king-sized bed that dwarfed Gilbert, the pink sheets with lacy frills, the sky-blue wallpaper, the sparkling stars embedded in the ceiling, the adjacent fireplace with dainty porcelain figurines displayed on the mantle.

She often wished that Gilbert had been more masculine. Yet, she understood that his immersion in feminine surroundings was attributable to Gilbert's unease around anybody or anything masculine. A direct result of the punishment he took at the hands of that cruel fuck of a father. May the bastard roast in everlasting hell.

Contrary to the hot gossip racing through the Retreat's grapevine, she knew Gilbert wasn't gay, that he didn't indulge in incest and that his sexual appetite, while infrequent, was pedestrian. Certainly no different than many of the Baptist prudes Mildred had met during her infrequent shopping tours in Savannah and Brunswick.

When she heard Gilbert's gentle snores, she tiptoed out and walked down the hall to her bedroom. She stood in front of a full-length mirror, stripped off her shorty nightgown and examined her body.

For a woman approaching sixty-eight, Mildred had to admit what her bedmates said was true; she looked twenty years younger. Hell, knock off another ten years in a dark room. Her breasts were full and well formed. Sure they sagged a little, but for Christ sake, what the hell did anyone expect from a broad her age?

She turned sideways and glanced at her profile. Her belly swelled out to a pleasing roundness that men found sexually alluring. Her legs were long and slender, like a Vegas showgirl's (she hid her mottled skin and varicose veins in dark hose). Her favorite costume when entertaining was black mesh stockings hooked up to a red garter belt, sheer black panties with a rear cutout that played peek-a-boo with the cheeks of her ass, and red high heels. Nothing else. It drove men wild. Exactly where she wanted them, panting and begging for it. She loved being in control. That's why her favorite position was on top, riding the pony and looking down (in more ways than one) on her partner of the moment.

She inspected her face and let out a whoosh of air in relief when she didn't find any new wrinkles. Then examined the rest of her body for new pockets of cellulite, varicose veins, sagging flesh and mottled skin. Nothing new. All in all, she awarded her body a passing grade for the day. Well, make it a B+. Infinitely better than other women her age who were wrinkled, stooped-over, worn-out old crones. Not Mildred. For whatever reason, she had escaped the ravages of time. Call it part DNA (her mother looked forty when she died in a car accident at age sixty-three), part science (collagen to smooth out the wrinkles).

Satisfied with the results of her survey, a ritual she managed every day of her adult life, she applied the usual thick layer of lipstick, rouge and eyeliner. Then splashed on perfume as if it were cologne. Some criticized her for wearing too much makeup and dipping into a bath full of perfume, enough to smell like a Paris whorehouse on Saturday night. But that's the way she liked it, and nobody was about to criticize her less they raise the ire of her son and protector, Gilbert.

Ah, Gilbert. Her precious son. Mildred truly loved her only child, had devoted her entire life to nurturing him and guiding his career. She was the perfect helpmate, standing shoulder to shoulder with her son through the good years and bad.

She had reared Gilbert as a single mother after blowing away that cruel son of a bitch, Gilbert's father. The man never believed Gilbert was his son (truth was, even Mildred wasn't sure who the real biological father was) and took it out on poor Gilbert through verbal and physical abuse.

Disposing of her husband's body had been no trick for Mildred. She was thirty-three at the time and a woman of stunning beauty. She exuded an aura of sex that was almost tactile, sufficient to entice any man who could still get aroused. At the time, one of the men she was fornicating with regularly was her husband's business partner, a thug who knew his way around the criminal underworld and had mobster connections. Within sixty minutes of her call to him, two hulking men she had never seen before arrived with cleaning equipment and solvents. They wasted no time mopping up the mess of bone and flesh and blood and shit spattered over the dining room. Then whisked away her husband's body, and that was the last she heard of either the two men or her husband. The body, or what remained of it, was never discovered. Just like Jimmy Hoffa. One minute he was here, the next minute he was gone. An eye-opening evening teaching a contemplative Mildred that anything beyond the law was possible if only you knew the right people.

The only aspect of the bastard's death she regretted was that Gilbert stood there open-mouthed as she blew his son of a bitching father away. To keep the poor child from being traumatized she kept him close to her side for the next several years, indeed would rarely let him out of her sight. Took him to school and picked him up afterward. Right through his sophomore year in high school. Until Gilbert, sick of his over-nurturing mother, swore he'd run away from home if she didn't back off. Only then did she pull back. Always restless when Gilbert was out of sight, she snooped on him, but discreetly, from a distance. As much as possible, she stayed his companion and closest friend and adviser throughout both Gilbert's high school and college years.

Yes, she had wrapped Gilbert in a protective cocoon that both comforted and at times admittedly stifled him, but what else was she to do? Yet, that close bond yielded a partnership that had stood the test of time. Thirty-five years after his birth, Mildred and her son were as inseparable as ever.

Most folks who met Mildred left with the impression of an old broad who refused to age gracefully (true), a woman with a ravenous sexual appetite who could take on two young men simultaneously and tire them out (true), a useless old fool who leeched off her son and contributed nothing to his career (definitely untrue).

She deliberately cultivated an image of a self-indulgent old fool. People underestimated her intelligence and creativity, wrote her off as a non-entity. Which prompted them to relax in her presence as if she wasn't there. Hence their vulnerability. Mildred kept her mouth shut, listened and watched and spied on everybody. Every evening in their penthouse suite atop the Retreat, she reported her findings to Gilbert. On many an occasion, Gilbert used that information to punish disobedient employees, a few of them severely.

Evenings were usually reserved for the two of them and nobody else. Mother and son discussed the

Retreat's problems and opportunities over small glasses of sherry while a Brahms lullaby played softly in the background.

People who knew Mildred would have been shocked to discover that she was the impetus behind the Retreat. Indeed, it was Mildred who first identified the white slavery business as one with great potential. It was Mildred who discovered the town of Wicked Stop, Georgia and immediately appreciated its remote location and the hermit mentality of its inhabitants. (What delicious irony, locating a white slavery business in a town named because of its long-ago immersion in prostitution.) And it was Mildred who, over many evenings of talk, convinced Gilbert of the idea's viability. Her drive and imagination fueled the development and turned concept into reality.

Standing before the full-length mirror and admiring her body, Mildred slid into her standard costume of seduction: panties, stockings, garter belt, high heels. She shrugged a mink coat over her shoulders, left the suite and climbed down one flight of stairs to the fourth floor.

In the stairwell, she eased open the fire door and walked silently down the carpeted hall before tapping on the door to room 412. Harry Phieu's suite, the Asian white salve trafficker from Singapore. The forty-something, 6'4", muscular 265-pound stud, hung like an elephant. The biggest tool Mildred had seen in her long life, and she had seen enough to fill an exhibit hall.

This was Harry's second trip to the Retreat to buy slaves, and the last time Mildred and he had cohabited as some would call it, or in Mildred's more direct terms, fucked their brains out. After his visit, she was so drained and sore the very thought of sex was repulsive, an abstention that wore itself out in a matter of days and was never repeated.

Upon her knock, Harry immediately opened the door. "Mildred, my sweet, please do me the honor of coming in. I've been waiting with great anticipation." He bowed and swept his arm in a welcoming flourish. Mildred strolled in and turned to face him, fluttered her eyelids in a coquettish manner.

He stood in front of her in a pair of briefs. Her sharp eyes swept over his body and took in his shaved head, slanted eyes, manicured goatee, barrel chest, strong arms, muscular legs. Her eyes found his crotch and lingered there.

"I've got good news, my sweet."

"What's that?" she said, her gaze cemented to Harry's briefs which, as she watched, seemed to be writhing with internal movement like a caged snake. Or perhaps it was her over-stimulated libido reacting to his masculine presence.

"A virgin. The Retreat has a white virgin for me. A blonde, no less with marble-colored skin." He clapped his hands in delight.

Mildred's gaze shot up and drilled Harry. "How do you know?"

"Werner called moments ago. The doctor certified her."

Mildred nodded. "The blonde with the sexy voice that came in yesterday. I'd bet on it."

"Pardon me, my sweet?"

"Nothing." She waved the thought away. "The virgin's not necessarily for you, Harry. She goes on auction tonight. If you got the bucks, your customer gets the fucks." She giggled at her comical rhyme.

"My best customer, an Arab prince, will pay generously for his heart's desire, an Anglo-Saxon virgin. But, alas, I must first win the bid. Perhaps you can help."

"That may be difficult," Mildred said coyly. "You

know how hard virgins over twelve years old are to find nowadays."

Harry fingered his crotch. Mildred's eyes followed its every movement like a hawk eyeing its prey before swooping down to snatch it up. "I'm counting on you, my sweet, to help persuade Gilbert to look upon my bid favorably."

"It's a matter of the highest bidder," she said and shucked off her coat. "You're up against twenty-five other buyers, all hungry for a white-skinned virgin."

Harry sucked in his breath as he took in her body. "I must admit, my sweet, you haven't aged one bit since we first met. You obviously grow more sexually appetizing every year."

"Flattery will get you everywhere, Harry ... So will this." She fondled his genitals and felt his growing interest.

"How about it, my sweet? Will you talk to Gilbert?"

A silence pervaded the room for a few moments as Mildred reached inside his briefs and gasped with pleasure. "Well, maybe I could do something."

"I knew I could count on you." Harry stepped out of his briefs and Mildred dropped to her knees in front of him. She closed her eyes and got busy.

SIXTEEN

Werner

"You gonna let me help?" Bobby asked Werner. His eyes, big as clam shells as seen through his thick glasses, pleaded with Werner.

"Sure thing. We wouldn't exclude you, Bobby. Not for the show and auction. Mr. Phester wants you to guard the entrance door to the dining room and theatre." What Werner didn't dare tell him was that neither he nor Mr. Phester trusted Bobby to contain his savage impulses around the girls. Bobby was volatile, virtually uncontrollable when sexually aroused.

Last quarter, Bobby, then a newcomer to the Retreat, was assigned guard duty over two girls who failed the physical while Mr. Phester decided their fate. The decision was taken out of Mr. Phester's hands when one of the girls thought she could outsmart Bobby and escape. Her plan was to disrobe and entice Bobby while the other girl hit the menacing giant over the head with a hammer.

The girl managed to remove her blouse before Bobby, aflame by the sight of a fine set of swinging boobs, savagely attacked her. He ripped off the remainder of her clothes and slung the hapless girl to the floor. The standing girl was foolish enough to come up behind Bobby with the hammer in her hands while he had the first girl pinned down and was pumping away. Bobby grabbed the attacking girl by the throat and crushed her windpipe without missing a stroke on the girl wrestling for her life underneath him. The hammer clattered to the floor, Bobby climaxed, strangled both girls and flung their corpses in a corner.

After that incident Mr. Phester issued a standing order that under no circumstances was Bobby to be left alone with any of the girls for sale or for that matter any of the Retreat's female attendants.

Werner and Bobby and the women to be auctioned were standing in the back of the Retreat's theatre where the auction was scheduled to take place. "Shit, I can help back here, you know, give you a hand," Bobby said. His eyes roamed over the young girls with the intensity of a hungry shark sniffing blood in the water. Until his gaze came to rest on Clair. Then his eyes flooded with hate.

"Tell you what, Bobby," Werner said, noticing Bobby's agitation and patting his arm to placate him. "The boss wants you to take Pootie for a walk." He threw Bobby the key to Mr. Phester's suite. "After the dog shits, bring it back to the suite and come on back here. Then stand guard outside the main door to the dining room. When the show's over, I'll let you help me bring the girls to their dorm." That was taking a chance and Werner knew it, but he had to do something to keep Bobby from throwing a fit.

Bobby grumbled his agreement and shuffled away, clearly disappointed. Werner kicked himself for bringing Bobby to the Retreat in the first place. Sure, he was strong and useful and scared the living hell out of the girls, kept them in line, but Werner wasn't sure he, or anybody else at the Retreat for that matter, could bring Bobby to heel when his emotions got out of control. And Bobby's tantrums reflected poorly on Werner who had recommended the lumbering giant to Mr. Phester in the first place.

Werner checked the girls to assure their readiness for the upcoming show and auction. All twenty-nine, including the two older women among them, roosted on benches in a holding area at the back of the theatre, like birds perched on a swing, all of them zonked out sufficiently on drugs to thwart escape attempts but awake enough to walk and move around on command. A delicate balance needed to keep the show and auction moving along smoothly and the girls serene and compliant. The last problem buyers wanted were slaves they purchased ready to bolt at the first opportunity.

Buyers, of course, were not naïve. They understood that the girls were being held against their wishes, but ordinarily, once having arrived at their final destinations, in the homes and businesses of their ultimate owners, most girls docilely accepted their fates. True, on occasion, a mustang slipped through the screening process, a fighter who would never surrender her freedom under any circumstance. Every buyer dreaded purchasing such a rebellious slave. It was equivalent to burning money, because not a single ultimate owner in his or her right mind would buy such a servant or prostitute. Reputable buyers would rather swallow the money spent on a mustang than defraud a client. That meant certain death for the buyer's business, perhaps even his life in countries such as Saudi Arabia where reneging on a contract was dealt with harshly.

The woman doctor hired by the Retreat was responsible for regulating drug dosages, so the girls, while conscious, hovered in a state of disorientation. The doctor circled her thumb and forefinger in a universal sign to indicate that the girls were ready for the show, flashed it to Werner who nodded his approval and appreciation.

Werner needed a good show. Mr. Phester was clearly unhappy when the blood work came back on the Latino girl with the rash showing that she had genital herpes. An unhappy circumstance that exempted her from the show and auction. She was now locked up in a separate room until Mr. Phester decided what to do with her.

Not that Werner was responsible for the girl's condition. It's just that Mr. Phester would be impossible to live with if sales dollars fell below budget and Mr. Phester was forced to dip into company reserves to keep the Retreat afloat.

Werner walked farther backstage and knocked on the door of the dressing room reserved for Heather, the Retreat's star catch this auction.

"Yes?" asked a cautious voice on the other side of the door.

"It's Werner."

The lock snicked open and Werner stepped into the dressing room. Heather rested in a Barcolounger recliner, eyes shut, a peaceful expression on her face. The female attendant who let Werner in stood guard at the door, a 650,000-volt stun gun in one hand to defend against intruders, cell phone in the other to call for help if need be.

"How is she?" Werner asked and bit his fingernails.

"Doing fine. Don't worry."

"I do worry," Werner said. "A lot is riding on how sales go tonight. And how sales go tonight may rest upon this lovely young hunk." He paused and stared at Heather. He was itching to run his hand up and down her legs, lick her belly, do all sorts of delightfully nasty things to her.

The attendant sniggered. "Looks like you'd like to eat that cake before it's served."

Werner snapped out of his reverie. "Keep her quiet until I come back."

"Will do, mein fuehrer."

Werner grabbed the cheeks of the attendant's ass and said, "Playful, eh? Well, do your job right and I've got a special reward for you later tonight."

The attendant's voice turned frosty. "Since you seem to prefer Melissa, I'll be waiting ... with this." She pushed Werner away and pointed the stun gun at his genitals.

Werner smirked and left the room. The attendant, muttering to herself, slammed and locked the door behind him, making Werner ever mindful of Nietzsche's words, "In revenge and in love woman is more barbarous than man."

He glanced at his watch, 7:45 p.m., fifteen minutes before the curtain was scheduled to rise. He stood center stage and peered about to make sure everything was in order. The dock where the girls would stand while being auctioned, the spotlights that exposed every inch of the their bodies, the cameras surrounding the dock and connected electronically to three 80" split screen monitors, one in the back of the dining room and the other two on the sides in the front so buyers could get a close look at what they were bidding on. A nice trick that kept every view of the girls front and center. Some buyers were especially attracted to facial looks, others to legs, some to hips and asses, others to breasts.

That morning, Werner had tested the computer system connected to each dinner table that recorded bids. All a buyer needed to do was click a mouse at his dinner table to signify placing a bid. A giant screen behind the dock flashed each bid along with the name of the buyer making it.

Mr. Phester prided himself in keeping up with the latest technology, claimed it made his operation both cost effective and more interesting to buyers. Product differentiation, he called it. A necessity in a market choked with slaves for sale.

A pleasant buzz of dinner conversation ebbed from the dining room on the other side of the curtain.

Earlier, Melissa had supervised setting up the tables for dinner. She reported to Werner that a total of twenty-five people, including places for Mr. Phester and his mother, were arranged in tables of five. An intimate setting, one carefully planned by Mrs. Phester, designed to relax the buyers and put them in the mood for spending money freely on the girls. The wine and booze budget for the evening alone was more than Werner made in a year when he hustled the streets of Milwaukee.

Werner's stomach churned as it always did before showtime, fearful that Mr. Phester would punish him for any slip up. His job was to corral the girls, shuffle them through their physicals, receive the blood work results back from the lab, obtain a release for each girl from the gynecologist and get the girls dressed and on the stage in their respective places ready for the show and auction. Once the curtain rolled up, Mr. Phester took over and Werner's role was confined to making sure the girls appeared on stage at their scheduled times for both the gown and nude exhibitions and the bidding that followed. Often a scheduling nightmare.

"Bring the girls to their spots," Werner instructed the attendants backstage. They scurried away to the holding area and guided twenty-six girls, minus the two older women and Heather, to marked spots on the stage, a choreographed setting arrayed in a dazzling display of colors and lights. The girls wore ankle length white gowns (the color of purity), high heels, tiaras of false diamonds and gold. The ankle bracelets were removed for the evening. No makeup. Mr. Phester claimed that girls without makeup looked more wholesome, au natural as he expressed it, and thus more attractive to buyers.

The girls' hairdos were fashioned to match their individual features under the careful supervision of

Mildred Phester who had an eye for such things. Some of the girls sported upswept hairdos, others natural falls. One girl wore a ponytail.

Werner's cell phone rang.

"All set?" Gilbert asked. His voice betrayed opening night jitters.

"All ready to go, Mr. Phester." Werner wiped the sweat from his brow. His handkerchief was sopping.

"We begin in five minutes." He hung up.

"Clear the stage," Werner called out. The attendants scurried away, leaving the girls standing in their marked spots.

Werner rushed into the backstage restroom and vomited.

SEVENTEEN

Gilbert

Minutes before the curtain rose, Gilbert and his mother excused themselves to their guests in the dining room and hurried backstage.

"The estimate, Mother, let me look at it one more time."

"You're going to wear holes in it, Gilbert."

Gilbert sighed. "I'm doing my very best to remain calm, Mother, but there's a lot riding on how well sales go the next few hours."

Mildred handed Gilbert the sales estimate. It looked like this:

Sales Category	No. Girls	Probable Unit Price	Total Sales Dollars
Virgin	1	$500,000	$500,000
Highly Desirable (Not shopworn, unsophisticated)	9	100,000	900,000
Desirable (Still malleable)	17	70,000	1,190,000
Older women (House servants or prostitutes for those who prefer older women)	2	30,000	60,000
TOTAL:	29	NA	2,650,000

Gilbert handed the sheet back to his mother. "We need that two point six million to have a good auction. At least $900,000 to break even."

Mildred patted Gilbert's hand. "Don't worry, Sonny. I have a feeling we're going over the top tonight."

"So I fervently hope, Mother."

"Besides, we have income from the hunt."

Gilbert nodded. "After expenses that should net us

an additional $100,000. We do that four times a year and we gain an extra $400,000 that goes right to the bottom line."

"Another sweet avenue of high-profit income."

"How true, Mother, how true."

"Are we all set with Harry Phieu's bids, Gilbert?"

Gilbert sighed. "We are, although I must confess, I'm not comfortable with the arrangement."

"It's to our advantage. Harry can open the door to big dollar buyers."

Gilbert studied his mother and smirked. Yes, I agree, he thought. And from what I've also gathered, he's quite well endowed. Dear, dear Mother, what am I going to do with you? "If any of the other buyers get even the faintest whiff of this side deal, we'll lose them, and probably the business."

Mildred chuckled. "Not to worry."

"I do, but it's much too late for that. I've already agreed to the arrangement. Harry will take the virgin with a bid of $500,000. If somebody bids over that amount, Harry will bid up to win, but we'll sell the virgin to him for no more than $500,000."

"That way we all come out ahead."

"In addition, Harry committed to buy two other girls at not under $100,000 if they're not bought by other bidders. That's not on our sales estimate sheet, but it's what he agreed to."

"Correct, Sonny. As a backstop, in case we have any girls left over."

The sound of a rustling curtain behind him made Gilbert catch his breath. He pushed the curtain aside and caught a fleeting glimpse of somebody's back before that person rushed through the outside door leading to the pool in the back of the Retreat.

"My God, who was that?"

Mildred ran behind the curtain and searched the

area. "I don't see anybody."

"The outside door. He went through the outside door."

Mildred opened the back door and peered around. A wall of hot, humid air greeted her. All she saw were nightlights bouncing off the water's surface of the pool in iridescent fragments. "Nobody here."

"There was somebody there, I know it."

Mildred touched her son's shoulder. "Maybe it's a case of nerves. You're strung out, waiting for the show and auction to begin."

Gilbert wiped his brow with an initialed handkerchief. "You may be right, Mother. A simple case of nerves." He looked hopeful.

"Of course, Sonny, that's all it is. The best way to lose the jitters is to start the show."

"You're right, Mother. As usual."

"You'll be okay once you get center stage. Like an actor. And a fine one you are. You'll have them eating out of your hand."

"A comforting thought. Well, as the Bard said, 'Let's get the show on the road.'"

"I don't believe he said that, Gilbert."

Gilbert chuckled. "Neither do I, Mother. Neither do I."

Mildred left the stage and returned to her seat in the dining room. Gilbert remained backstage.

The curtain rose. As the girls came into view, appreciative whistles and polite applause emerged from the guests at the dinner tables. Then a hush fell over the crowd. Gilbert knew this was a critical moment, when buyers examined the flesh before them for the first time and made initial decisions about which girls they thought would please their customers. First impressions were so important.

The room was thick with smoke and redolent with

the bouquet of fine brandy as buyers puffed on Cuban cigars and sipped Remy Martin or Hennessy XO from snifters.

Gilbert, a non-smoker, discreetly waved the cigar smoke from his face and stood before his audience, a smile creasing his tiny features.

"Ladies and gentlemen, my dear friends and valued associates of long standing, it's an honor and pleasure to welcome you to the Retreat and our quarterly show and auction. Behind me stand some exceptionally alluring young women, carefully selected in a stringent process of quality control that makes the Retreat stand head and shoulders above its competition." He was interrupted by scattered applause.

"We have for your consideration tonight twenty-seven exceptional girls, those standing before you. And in the wings two mature but highly attractive women. Best of all, one young lady in the dressing room who I'm proud to say is a twenty-one-year-old virgin."

The crowd stood and roared its approval. A few, unaware until now that a virgin was up for auction, wolf-whistled with delight. Harry Phieu winked at Mildred and she battered her eyelashes at him.

Gilbert watched the buyers closely as he made this announcement, saw in their eyes a look of calculation, each wondering how much he or she could afford to bid and who among their clients would pay the hefty price for that rarest among females, a virgin in her early twenties. Gilbert had a moment of panic when he realized that the virgin might bring a price considerably higher than the agreed-upon $500,000, extra money lost because of his side deal with Harry Phieu.

"As you know, we distributed nude pictures of these young beauties to your rooms earlier today so you can appreciate what we have in store for you tonight.

Did you get them?"

More whistles and applause. One buyer called out, "I almost didn't leave my room tonight, the pics were so good. If you know what I mean."

"Yes, I think we do," Gilbert said dryly.

Another round of hearty laughter.

"Enough talk. Are you ready to begin the show?"

"Yes," the buyers howled in unison and clapped their hands.

The curtain dropped. A buzz of heady anticipation rippled through the crowd. Werner and his attendants herded the girls back to the holding area, less one, a stunningly beautiful raven-haired teenager with pale skin. Gilbert believed in starting the program with a bang, to auction one of his most attractive girls and condition buyers to place high bids.

Attendants moved the girl to center stage and positioned her in a dock that stood about one foot higher than the stage, girdled by a waist-high circular safety rail to prevent the girl from falling. The dining room and stage lights dimmed and Werner shone a single spotlight on the girl in the pitch black of the stage. She stood there zombie-like, a beatific smile plastered across her face, eyes dull from the drugs.

The curtain rose and a perceptible murmur of appreciation escaped the lips of buyers.

Melissa emerged from the kitchen in the back of the now darkened dining room and stood before a dais. A small light clipped to the dais shone on papers held in front of her. She tapped a microphone to make sure it was live, found it was and cleared her throat.

Gilbert, now standing to the side of the stage, said, "Ladies and gentlemen, one of our attendants will now read the specifications of the exquisite beauty standing before you." He nodded to Melissa.

Melissa slipped on a pair of frameless reading

glasses. "The name of the first lovely girl on our program is Dawn. She is seventeen years old, 5'5", 120 pounds, with measurements of thirty-two, twenty-three, thirty-eight, well-proportioned as you can see—"

"Better believe it," one of the male buyers shouted. The others cheered and clapped.

"Please notice her marble white skin, a sign of true Anglo-Saxon heritage. While Dawn is third-generation American, her grandparents emigrated from New Zealand and settled in the American South. She hails from Montgomery, Alabama. According to the results of her physical examination, Dawn is in perfect physical health."

More whistles of approval, sprinkled with a few titters.

"Some of you first time foreign buyers may not be aware of it," Gilbert said, "but girls from the Southern part of the United States are vastly different than girls from other sections of America. As a rule, Southern girls are well-mannered, gracious, keep themselves physically fit and have been reared to attend to a man's needs."

Polite applause.

"As an aside," Gilbert said, "I would never recommend that any of you buy a girl from America's Northeast without a careful personality screening. Most of that region's girls are feisty proponents of equal rights for women. What's more they've been conditioned from childhood to believe they are on an equal footing with men. Apologies to the women in our audience, of course."

A chorus of boos erupted, including from women buyers who understood the basics of their business, namely that their customers, almost all of them men, lived in cultures where a woman's place was on her knees, either scrubbing the kitchen floor or attending to a man's sensual needs. Some customers even resided in countries where men legally held the power of life or death over women.

"Continue, Melissa," Gilbert said.

"From our in-depth scrutiny of Dawn's background, combined with a thorough physical exam and our pinpoint psychological profile, the Retreat concludes that Dawn's sexual experience has been limited to intercourse with one boy, a classmate in her high school, and to a few petting sessions with another boy before that. She lost her virginity only three months ago and contact with her sexual partner since then has been infrequent."

"In other words," Gilbert added, "she is relatively uncontaminated, certainly not yet inducted into the more sophisticated aspects of sexual union."

"A near virgin," somebody yelled from the dinner crowd.

"Is that like being near-pregnant?" another buyer retorted, and that brought the house down.

After the laughter subsided, Gilbert held up his hands and pointed at Dawn. "Because of her relative lack of experience, whoever purchases this budding young blossom in the height of her sexual bloom will be able to mold her in his or her fashion. In the opinion of the Retreat, this young woman is a prime property."

Enthusiastic cheers.

"While Dawn looks elegant dressed in formal wear, believe me when I tell you she is absolutely delectable au natural." Gilbert rolled his eyes and the audience laughed appreciatively.

"Tell me, my friends," Gilbert said, and his voice rose with every word, "are you ready to see her in the nude?"

Wild cheers erupted from the crowd.

Two female attendants held a large beach towel in

front of Dawn, shielding her from the crowd while another attendant undressed her. The towel was in the Retreat's colors of blue and white with the name of the Retreat monogrammed in large gilded letters. Buyers stood as if in unison and their hungry eyes attempted to pierce the towel.

Gilbert stepped in front of Dawn and whisked the towel away in a dramatic flourish, like a magician waving his cape. The crowd was left speechless. Had their eyes been drills, nothing would have been left of Dawn's body.

"Mother of God," an American buyer said, "Look at that perfect body."

"Magnifico," a Spanish buyer added.

"Molto bene," from an Italian.

Harry Phieu jabbed Mildred in the ribs. "This one's for me."

Gilbert guided the girl stage front so buyers could get a closer view, both front and rear, then brought her back to the dock. Wolf-whistles and cheers accompanied her every step of the way. The three 80" electronic monitors exposed every square inch of Dawn's perfect body.

"Are you ready to start the bidding?" Gilbert yelled over the noise of the crowd.

"Yes, yes, yes," the crowd chanted, every man and woman on his or her feet, stamping the floor enthusiastically.

From past shows, Gilbert knew this was a key moment. "We have a base of $100,000 for this outstanding specimen with increments of bidding starting at $10,000 or more. Who will open the bidding?"

Gilbert glanced up at the giant screen over the dock. It immediately flashed "$100,000, Dahesh Rantoon, India." Gilbert glanced at the Indian and bowed his head in acknowledgment and appreciation for getting the ball rolling.

All the buyers' names, of course, were phony. As they had to be in this highly dangerous criminal undertaking. The laws of the United States, as well as most countries of the world, deal severely with human traffickers.

Immediately the screen flashed a second bid, "145,000, Achmed Habi-Ban, Saudi Arabia."

Then a third and a forth. Gilbert raised the microphone to his lips. "Our high bid is $170,000. Surely, this endearing young lady, a picture of physical beauty men would kill for, deserves far more appreciation."

The screen flashed again. "$200,000, Harry Phieu, Singapore."

A whoop of astonishment burst forth from the crowd. Gilbert bowed in Harry's direction. Harry's shaved head glistened in the reflected light from the stage.

"Mr. Phieu," Gilbert said, "recognizes the value of this enchanting young lady. Does anybody else?"

The screen flashed. "$250,000, Dahesh Rantoon, India."

Gilbert nodded again at the Indian and said, "Any other bids?" His eyes scoured the audience. Harry Phieu glowered.

There was dead silence for twenty seconds.

Gilbert smiled. He was relieved; the auction was off to a grand start. "Very well. Sold to Mr. Rantoon for $250,000."

The buyers applauded politely. Except for Harry Phieu and one or two frustrated others who wanted to buy Dawn but had budget limitations that kept them from offering higher bids.

Rantoon jumped to his feet and raised his thin

arms and tiny hands in a gesture of victory. "This girl is a jewel. A thousand thanks, Mr. Phester." He turned to face Mildred. "And to his hospitable and gracious mother." He blew kisses to the crowd and sat down, face flushed, a happy man.

The bidding continued as girl after girl went on the auction block. Gilbert and Mildred kept track to assure that each buyer had an opportunity to walk away from the evening's festivities with at least one purchase.

"And now, ladies and gentleman," Gilbert proudly announced, "a bonus for you, our friends of the Retreat. Not only do we have a virgin waiting in the wings, we are also offering our special for the evening, a mother-daughter combination. Buy the daughter and get the mother thrown in free. Our gift to you." With that he bowed deeply and with a flourish swept his hand to the side. The curtain rose and Clair and her mother Helen stood in the dock.

EIGHTEEN

Helen

By the time Werner led Helen to the dock to stand side by side with Clair in front of eager buyers, the drugs were starting to wear off. Helen vacillated between moments of clarity and fuzziness, with each succeeding minute returning her to a state of mental alertness. She had always been resistant to drugs, a condition that surfaced years ago when she underwent minor surgery for a lacerated finger.

"Hey, look at this," somebody yelled from the audience, "a whore tag team." The buyers howled with glee and stamped their feet in approval of the joke.

After the audience hushed, Melissa read off Clair's particulars, then Helen's: sexual history, results of their physical examinations, psychological evaluations. What she left out, Gilbert filled in:

"The Retreat has a well-deserved reputation for honesty and for delivering the goods as advertised. This is why, my friends, I must inform you that what you see before you, the physical specimens of mother and daughter, do not tell the entire story. The daughter is half-black. She's also feisty and has made two attempts at escape—"

"Gee, why would anyone wanna do that?" somebody called out from the crowd, and the buyers guffawed in response.

Gilbert smiled. "As you can see, neither attempt was successful. For those among you with clients who enjoy taming a wild mare, this young lady, Clair, presents a challenge."

"How about the mother?" Harry Phieu asked as he

reflectively stroked his goatee.

"She, too, is quite spirited, although not to the same degree as the daughter."

"Let's cut the talk and see what they got," somebody yelled from the audience.

Gilbert grinned. "A man who drives right to the heart of the matter. I like that. Very well, let's not waste any time." He signaled to Werner who scurried center stage and disrobed the two women as two attendants held up the Retreat's large beach towel. Helen held her breath and played along as if she were still drugged. It was all she could do to keep from screaming. Easy, she repeatedly told herself, easy, or they'll find you out.

As before, Gilbert whisked away the towel. Buyers appreciatively clapped and whistled their approval.

"Jesus, the girl's got it all," one lady said from the audience.

"And none of it's bad," somebody else rejoined. Which cracked everybody up, of course. Buyers slapped their thighs and cackled.

"Hell," another said, "the old lady's not that shabby, herself. She's still got a few miles left on the odometer."

Gilbert nodded. "I agree. All in all, from a physical beauty standpoint, a perfect mother-daughter combination." Gilbert opened the bidding.

"I have exactly the client for both of them," Phieu said. He sat next to Mildred and felt her hand underneath the table copping a feel of his slumbering snake. "A Malaysian businessman, an animal of a man in the drug trade, who enjoys domesticating wild beasts like these two. I'll open the bidding at $150,000."

Helen's arms pimpled with goose flesh. She prayed that if people noticed, they'd attribute it to her standing naked in a drafty place.

Gilbert looked aghast. "Surely, these two, a perfect

matched set if I ever saw one, are worth more than a mere $150,000?" He searched the faces in the dining room, a question mark on his face. "Don't any of you other wonderful people have clients who appreciate the sport of taming a mother-daughter combination?"

"My customer, the Malaysian, is such a man," Phieu said. "He's tamed many wild animals in his day, most of them women."

Several members of the audience tittered nervously, the women among them. Helen, feeling the undercurrents of lust and greed sweep through the crowd, felt nauseous.

Two other buyers threw in bids, driving the price up to $175,000.

"Look," Harry said to Gilbert, "I'll make you a proposition. Let me tryout both women tonight and if all goes well, as I'm sure it will, I'll offer a flat $200,000 for the two. A more than fair price."

Gilbert hesitated. "We've never done this before, offer tryouts."

"Take it or leave it."

Gilbert turned to the other buyers. "I can do this only if you agree it's a one-time occurrence and if you, my valued customers, grant your approval."

"I don't like it," Dahesh Rantoon, the buyer from India, said. Normally quiet and invariably polite, he appeared upset enough by the suggestion to speak his mind. "It smacks of a private deal." A grumble of agreement greeted his words.

"Very well, then," Gilbert continued, sensitive to the needs of his buyers, "If some of you do not approve, we can go no further with the proposition ... Is that a problem, Mr. Phieu?"

Phieu stood and placed his large hands on his hips and frowned. "I'm not happy about it. But I want these two and I'll bid $185,000 for both right now." With that he slapped the dining table in front of him and the silverware and plates jumped an inch and clattered. Mildred and the other buyers at the table jerked back. Phieu's histrionics allowed Helen an opportunity to sneak a look at her daughter. Clair was totally doped up, a walking android.

"Are there any further bids?" Gilbert glanced around the room. Dahesh Rantoon raised his hand, then apparently changed his mind and lowered it. When Gilbert looked his way, Rantoon shook his head.

"No further bids? Then the mother-daughter combination is officially the property of Mr. Phieu for $185,000."

At a signal from Gilbert, the curtain dropped. An attendant moved Clair and Helen backstage. From her new vantage point, Helen was able to observe everything around her. She kept her eyes half-closed to appear drowsy.

Werner next ushered Heather to the dock. Her dulled eyes told Helen that Heather was still drugged beyond comprehension.

From behind the curtain, Helen heard Gilbert address the group:

"This is the moment, we've all been waiting for. The sale of the Retreat's most exquisite of all creatures, a virgin. One of the finest properties we've had in quite some time. And allow me to indulge myself, ladies and gentlemen, by informing you that the young lady you're about to see is not merely an ordinary virgin. She's an Anglo-Saxon beauty with stunning looks and a voluptuous body, a tender grape bursting with the juices of youth, ready for plucking. A twenty-one year-old knockout who has yet to be despoiled. Certainly, as I'm sure you'll agree, that's a rarity in this day and age.

"This young beauty's been certified a virgin by our resident gynecologist so you can rest assured you're getting the real goods, not some heroin-addicted phony of thirty with a little alum smeared on her private parts to fool buyers. A crude tactic one of our competitors actually used to foist off a sullied woman on an unsuspecting buyer. In stark contrast, the Retreat has principles. It holds itself about such nonsense, as I'm sure you know. Our reputation for delivering the goods as advertised remains the highest in our industry.

"In any case, without further adieu, here is our lovely young flower."

The curtain rose and the audience collectively drew a breath, then rose to its feet as one and voted its approval with thunderous applause.

Heather, even in a drugged state, was breathtaking in her evening gown of white, particularly with the aura of virginity enveloping her.

"Isn't she a stunning creature?" Gilbert asked the crowd.

More thunderous applause answered the question.

Gilbert walked to the dock, led Heather from it and paraded her around the stage to the accompaniment of wolf whistles and cries of enthusiastic approval. She followed his lead quietly, a small smile playing across her luscious lips.

"Beauty is not strictly for the eye, " Gilbert said. "It's also for the ear. Listen to this lovely young plum speak, and tell me if you've ever heard a voice as sensual." He quieted the audience and whispered something in Heather's ear. Heather, drugged but responsive, said, "What may I do for you, thir?" in her typical lisping sex kitten way, the kind that drives men to do dangerous things.

The crowd drew a collective breath and then exploded in a frenzy of endorsement. One buyer yelled out, "I can't take it anymore. I'm going to the john and lock the door." A chorus of ribald laughter followed.

Gilbert held up one hand to silence the crowd. A hush fell over the buyers as he led Heather back to the dock. He nodded and two female attendants lifted the beach towel to hide her from the audience as another attendant stripped her.

Watching this, Helen felt sick to death. She squeezed her eyes shut and took deep breaths to keep from throwing up. Her eyelids snapped open and she furtively glanced around to see if anybody saw her. But every eye in the room, on the stage, behind it and in the audience was fixed on Heather.

When Gilbert yanked the towel aside a stunned silence swept the room until one buyer broke the silence with "My God, I don't believe it." His reaction was the valve that opened the floodgates. Gilbert felt the building shake as buyers pounded the dinner tables and bellowed their support in the wildest demonstration of the evening.

After a full minute of this exuberant display, Gilbert waved his arms in a downward motion, signaling the crowd to silence.

When it did, a murmur of excitement rolled through the room like surf racing toward a beach.

Gilbert opened the bidding. "For this exceptional young lady, we will bid in increments of $50,000. Who will open the bidding at $500,000?"

A woman buyer signaled her acceptance. The board flashed "$500,000, Janet Smyth-Rawlson, U.K."

Another buyer, a portly man from Spain, held up a plump hand. The board identified him, "$550,000 Jose Portaberro, Spain."

"The current bid is $550,000. Who else among you will enter the fray for this luscious young example of virginal girlhood in her prime, one of the most treasured prizes ever to grace the halls of the Retreat?"

Three other buyers threw in bids, raising the price to $700,000.

Gilbert was sweating freely. Carefully, he wiped his brow with a monogrammed handkerchief. "This unexcelled beauty, one of the loveliest the Retreat has ever auctioned, will deliver great pleasure to whoever owns her. She's the—"

The board flashed again. "$800,000, Harry Phieu, Singapore."

Gilbert bowed to Phieu. "The bid is $800,000. Are there any further bids?" Helen noticed that Gilbert's voice was shaky. Because of the side deal with Harry, he was losing $300,000.

Three buyers signaled their intentions simultaneously. The board displayed in rapid order:

"850,000, Janet Smyth-Rawlson, U.K."

"900,000, Simon Jiminez, Columbia."

"950,000, Achmed Habi-Ban, Saudi Arabia."

Complete silence now as potential buyers held their breaths and others watched on in wonder.

Gilbert's chest was heaving as he gulped in air to calm down. He cleared his throat. "The bid is $950,000. Are there any other bids?"

Silence. Gilbert glanced at Harry Phieu who sat in his seat expressionless.

"Then going, going—"

Harry Phieu jumped to his feet. "Goddamn it, $1,000,000 and not a penny more." He glared at the other buyers as if to defy any of them to up the bid.

Nobody did.

"The gentleman from Singapore wins the virgin for a total of $1.000,000."

Harry Phieu bounded to his feet, almost knocking over the dinner table in the process. He rushed onstage and shook Gilbert's hand and examined the three women he had purchased. When he came to Helen and Clair he winked at Gilbert. "Send these two to my room for the evening. Might as well break them in right."

NINETEEN

Justin

"This isn't like Mom and Dad," Justin said as he paced the motel room. "I'm worried." He stopped and glanced at himself in the mirror over the dresser, tightened his stomach muscles so his fat, sagging middle wouldn't show through his T-shirt. He stood 6'1", three inches taller than his father, Marshall King, and at 230 pounds was almost as large. His skin was the same cocoa butter color as his sister Clair, the composite result of his father's half-white, half-black parents and his lemon-tinted Japanese-American mother.

Unlike his dad, Justin considered his color an advantage. In America today, a dark skin provided special opportunities if one knew how to play the game. And Justin knew how to play the game. He had pressured his employer into two promotions and hefty annual raises based on his minority status. The company was afraid to challenge him regardless of how terrible his work was. Not unless it wanted to see its offices picketed by militant groups and its reputation besmirched by an overarching liberal media. And Justin's work was terrible. His shoddy performance was exceeded only by his surly attitude.

"Maybe they had car trouble," April said. "It could be as simple as that."

Justin sighed with impatience and shook his head, asked himself why he even had asked April to come. She was, as Justin described her to business associates, "short, dumpy and mousy looking with frizzled brunette hair that won't stay combed. She even wears granny glasses, a real throwback to the sixties."

"They should have been here hours ago. I haven't heard a word from them." Justin glanced at his watch. 10:19 p.m. He was really worried now. *Where in hell were they?*

"Did you try their cell phone?"

"Do I look stupid?" he snapped at her. When her eyes registered the shock of his unexpected churlishness, he pulled back. "Sorry, I guess this is getting to me. I tried calling a dozen times, but there was no answer." He stopped at the motel window and scowled at the evening sky over Ft. Lauderdale as if it held the answer to his parents' whereabouts and had better fess up or else.

"I didn't know you tried calling," April said in a tight voice. "I just got here."

April and Justin worked as auditors for the same national accounting firm, Justin in its corporate Cleveland office, April in its Ft. Lauderdale branch. They were part-time lovers, getting together only when their paths crossed during occasional business trips, and for Justin, only when he was both drunk or stoned and had nobody else to turn to. Their liaisons lacked anything beyond the immediate satisfaction of lust. Afterward both would fall into gloomy silences, ended by his quick departure.

In the silence that ensued she tried reasoning with him again. "Maybe they're still at the hotel where they spent last night. Somebody could have gotten sick."

Justin snapped his fingers. "Of course. Why didn't I think of that? That has to be it." He smiled at her and her face brightened.

"Actually, I remember the name of the place well. It's called the Retreat at Wicked Stop. Apparently some resort hotel in the sticks of Southern Georgia."

What a funny name. What does it mean?

"Damned if I know. ... Let's see, where's the phone number?" He rummaged around in his suitcase and over-stuffed work notebook and found nothing. "I guess I didn't ask Mom for the telephone number. Never thought I'd need it."

"Call the operator at area code 912, the one for Southern Georgia. One of my clients is in Valdosta. There's not much around there as I recall. Should be one area code only."

"Hey, good idea." He dialed information and asked for the Retreat at Wicked Stop. The automatic dialer put him right through.

"The Retreat at Wicked Stop. May I help you?"

"I'm trying to reach my parents, Mr. and Mrs. Marshall King."

"One moment, sir."

Ten seconds later a man came on the line. "Yes sir?"

"Put me through to Mr. or Mrs. Marshall King, please."

Silence.

"Did you hear me?" Impatient now.

"Yes, sir, I heard you distinctly. But I'm afraid there are no guests staying her by the name of King."

"Then they left. Look on your register for last night."

Silence again. "I'm afraid there was no party by that name staying with us last night."

"That's impossible."

"Sir, I'll check again, but I'm a supervisor here and I know the names of all our current guests, and the names Marshall and Helen King are not among them."

"What's your name?"

"Werner, sir. And who am I addressing?"

"I'm Justin King, Marshall King's son."

"I wish I could be more helpful, sir."

"Is there a Clair King there or a Heather Cahill, her friend? They were traveling with my mom and dad."

"Those names do not ring a bell, but as we speak I'm checking our computerized guest list and, one moment now ... Ah yes, none of those names appear." He sounded satisfied with himself.

Which infuriated Justin. "Goddamn it, there's some screw-up in your computer. I know my parents stayed the night. They called and told me."

"There's no reason to be abusive, Mr. King."

"Shit," Justin sputtered and slammed the phone down so hard the base cracked.

"Jeez, Justin, take it easy," April said.

"Son of a bitch was lying."

"How do you know?"

Justin threw a smoldering look in her direction. April backed up and opened her purse. She pulled out a stick of marijuana. "Hey, chill out, okay? You're frightening me." She lit the joint with trembling fingers.

"Fuck this," Justin said to himself and sunk onto the bed. He placed his hands behind his head and stared at the ceiling.

April took a few drags on the joint and handed it to Justin. "Here, this will help," she said in a choked voice, showing the effects of the marijuana.

Justin grabbed the joint and inhaled deeply several times. He handed the joint back to April, lay back on the mattress and closed his eyes.

April smoked quietly for a few minutes, then dropped the butt in an ashtray and lay down next to Justin. She put her arms around him and he reached for her shorts and unzipped them.

"Wearing anything underneath?" he asked, his eyes closed, voice calm now.

"No." She shrugged out of her shorts and unzipped

Justin's pants, pulled out his penis, already growing hard in the embracing clutch of her warm hand. Without further undressing, they went at it, quietly, like two aging seniors, more out of habit than out of passion. An impersonal, stress-relieving coupling, devoid of love or affection. A few isolated animal grunts and groans. Simply the nature-compulsive mating of two animals.

Afterward, while Justin was washing up, he said to April, "Bastard I was talking to on the phone, that Werner guy, at the Retreat."

"Yes?"

"He was lying about my parents."

"How do you know?"

"Because when I mentioned my parents I asked for Mr. and Mrs. Marshall King."

"So?"

"So he later said they had no Marshall and Helen King registered."

"I don't get it."

"I never mentioned my mother's name, Helen."

April's jaw dropped. "Jeez, that means—"

"It means that this guy Werner saw my mom and dad, but for whatever reason, he doesn't want to acknowledge they were at the Retreat." A light faded in Justin's eyes as he pondered the fate of his parents

.

TWENTY

Clair

Melissa poked Clair in the ribs with her elbow. "C'mon, bitch, move."

The blow was cushioned by Clair's drugged state, but it still sent a sharp pain rippling through her body. She moaned and trudged forward. The blow had the side effect of reducing her drug-induced lassitude, already starting to wear off fast.

"You, too, mama bitch," Melissa said and cuffed Helen on the side of her head.

Helen snarled and Melissa dropped back, surprised by Helen's reaction.

"Time for some more sleepy bye drugs for both of you. As soon as I lock you in Harry Phieu's room. Get moving." Melissa prodded both women forward. Mother and daughter were dressed in their gowns and high heels and had difficulty maneuvering the hotel corridor. Helen held the side of her head and moaned.

"Ladies, you remember, Harry, from the party? He's got a present for you two." Melissa held her arms about a foot apart, then circled her fingers to the diameter of a beer can, and tittered with sadistic glee. "When he gets through plowing your holes, you'll be able to reach in there with a shovel."

Who is Harry Phieu? Clair wondered as she fought through the cloud fogging her mind. Her recollection of the past few hours was dim. All she recalled was the presence of many people in a smoky and crowded room, a lot of cheers and catcalls, and the naked bodies of other girls floating past her. Naked? Was that possible?

Melissa stopped in front of room 412. Clair's head was clearing fast. She became aware of her surroundings and the fact of her imprisonment, realized with a start that Mom and her were alone with Melissa. The time to act was now. Nobody else was in the hotel corridor.

But what could she do?

Her mother answered the question for her. As soon as Melissa keyed open the door to Phieu's room, Helen shoved her inside and jumped on her back. She circled Melissa's neck with her thin but strong arms and squeezed.

Melissa's arms flailed wildly and she lurched across the room like a bucking bronco trying to dislodge its rider. Clair had the presence of mind to enter the room and close the door behind her.

Melissa reached behind her and grabbed Helen's hair and yanked. Helen cried out but kept on squeezing. Harder and harder. Melissa's face changed from a beet red to a light purple. Her eyes bulged. Clair circled the two, looking for a place to grab Melissa, to help her mom somehow. Still in the residual grip of the drugs, all she could do was pry one of Melissa's fingers away from her mother's hair and bend it backwards. Melissa screeched and jerked Helen and herself away from Clair. Which shocked Clair. This was the first time she had ever physically hurt somebody.

Helen and Melissa, locked in a deadly struggle, staggered and fell across the bed. Choking sounds emerged from Melissa's lips. Her eyelids fluttered as Helen refused to relinquish her death grip. Moments later, Melissa passed out and she slumped to the floor. Helen, gasping for air, collapsed on the bed next to Melissa, exhausted from the combat. The strain showed on her tense sweaty face.

"Give me a minute," she said between gasps of air.

Clair struggled to her feet and stumbled into the bathroom, rinsed a washcloth in cold water, washed her face, rinsed it again and returned to the bedroom.

Never before had Clair even remotely considered that her mother was capable of harming another human being. Until that moment when she choked Melissa she had always acted so ... civilized. It shattered the belief Helen had preached to Clair over the years: violence only begets violence.

Helen sat up and wiped her face with the washcloth. She glanced at Clair, then, brow wrinkling, searched her eyes. "Are you okay?"

Clair nodded.

"I had to do it, dear. I had no choice."

Clair bent over and examined Melissa. "She's still breathing. Thank God."

"No time for that now." Helen struggled to her feet. "Let's tie her up and go. This Harry Phieu, I saw him downstairs. He's dangerous, like Bobby. We've got to get out before he arrives."

Clair caught the note of desperation in her mother's voice. It propelled her to action. They tore bed sheets into strips and bound and gagged Melissa, pulled her body into the bathroom and shut the door. Both women removed their high heels, which left them barefoot.

Helen searched the room.

"What are you looking for, Mom?"

"Anything to protect us." She rummaged through Harry Phieu's luggage, found nothing, opened the dresser drawers. "Here's something interesting." She extracted a steel baton about eighteen inches long. "This looks like something I saw a police officer use once on TV. This will have to do. Let's go."

Helen cracked open the hotel room door, peeked into the hallway and motioned Clair to follow. They avoided the elevators and crept down the hall in the opposite direction. All was quiet and serene. At the far end of the hallway, they found the stairs and descended as quickly as their aching bodies would allow. As they passed the exit leading to the second floor, the door flew open and a drunk buyer stumbled into the stairwell. Helen and Clair flattened themselves against the wall and stared at the man with panic-stricken eyes.

"Well, lookee here," he said. He was a corpulent man with a barrel chest and overhanging gut, coarse features topped off by a fake hairpiece that looked as if it had been stitched together by monkeys. "Just in time," he said in slurred speech. "A threesome with two lovely gals." He swayed forward and, with a large, hairy hand, pinched Clair's ass. She cried out and stepped back, grabbed the railing to prevent falling down the stairs.

Helen struck the man on the side of his head with the steel baton. His legs crumbled and he fell to his knees, still conscious.

"Hey, what—"

Helen struck him again and again until he slumped to the floor, unconscious. Clair looked on horror-stricken. "Mom, how could—"

"No time now. Let's go." She grabbed a shaken Clair by the elbow and they crept down the stairs, both women breathing noisily. Clair thought her heart would explode.

At the first floor, Helen eased the door open and peeked into the lobby. People were milling about. She recognized some of the buyers from the show and auction.

"The lobby's full, damn it," she whispered.

Clair glanced around furtively, and peeked through the exit door. "We've got to go back up, find another way out."

They climbed the stairs to the second floor. The man Helen clubbed was lying in the same position in front of the door. Together, they rolled him over to clear the passageway.

An alarm bell rang. Clair gripped Helen's arm. "What is it?"

"Maybe a fire. Most likely, somebody found Melissa."

"Mom, what are we going to do?"

"Follow me." They ran into the hotel corridor. Doors flew open and men and women, some fully dressed, some partially dressed ran to the exit. Helen and Clair ducked into an open room.

"Take your clothes off," Helen said.

"*What?*"

"They're a dead giveaway. Most of these people are buyers. They'll recognize the gowns."

"They already saw us in the hall."

"They're concentrating on the alarm. Nobody paid any attention to us."

Both women shed their clothes and shoes. They wrapped themselves in large bath towels and swathed their heads in smaller hand towels to hide what part of their faces they could. Helen found a pair of men's and a pair of women's shoes in the closet, and she and Clair slipped into them. The men's shoes swamped Helen's feet, Clair's fit.

"I'll never go far in these shoes," Helen said.

"Mom—"

"Let's go, quick now."

Looking like women who had stepped out of the shower moments ago, they joined the tail end of the exodus leaving the second floor and followed the herd to the exit.

The stairwell was clogged with people, most of them calm, some in an agitated state. Few talked, involved as they were with a quick departure from the upper floors. They descended the stairs to the first floor, Helen and Clair among them. On the first floor, the crowd disgorged into the lobby and milled around. The buzz of conversations sounded like a disturbed bee's nest.

The alarm stopped ringing. Attendants stood on desks and chairs and peered around the lobby but the room was swollen with people, making it easy for Helen and Clair to hide. They bent their knees to keep their heads from showing above the packed crowd.

"They know," Helen whispered to Clair. "There's no fire. They're looking for us."

"What do we do now?"

"Let's work our way to the side door."

They wended their way slowly through the crowd to the door but found a burly male attendant guarding it.

Harry Phieu stood on top of the reception desk and scanned the room. His eyes flashed when he saw Helen and Clair. He jumped down and elbowed his way through the crowd. "Out of the way," he growled. People scrambled to clear a path but the lobby was so crowded it hindered his progress.

"Werner," he yelled. "Over here." He pointed in the general direction of Helen and Clair.

Werner wended his way through the crowd from the opposing end of the lobby. Harry and Werner had Helen and Clair sandwiched between them, bottled up by the crowd. The two men inched their way forward over the curses and groans of the people they pushed aside.

"Mom, what do we do?" Clair asked, a touch of panic in her voice.

Werner reached them first. Helen aimed a kick at his groin but Werner adroitly sidestepped it and took the blow on the side of his leg. He cursed Helen and struck her in the face. She yelled to Clair "Get out!" and charged Werner, scratching and biting. The two fell to the floor. In the confusion Clair yelled "Fire!" and that started the stampede. People screamed and ran toward the exits. They rudely shoved aside everybody in their path and rushed out of the building, Clair among them. She risked one glance back before departing. Werner and Helen were struggling and Harry Phieu was lost in the crowd.

For the second time, Clair had escaped the Retreat.

TWENTY-ONE

Marshall

The racist bastards! That had to be it. These Southern Georgia rednecks hate niggers; that was the reason he was being held captive. Dirty sons of bitches. White trash. Jesus Lord, why had he fought Helen when she tried to talk him out of detouring to this ungodly place? If he had only listened to her, by now they could have been safe and comfortable in their motel rooms in Ft. Lauderdale.

Marshall grudgingly admitted to himself that just two days ago he would have laid the blame for their predicament on Helen's broad shoulders, made her the scapegoat. That he hadn't this time was testament to the live or die situation he now faced.

Minutes before, he had come down from his drugged state. His head was crowded with an overload of details and his ability to think clearly was compromised by sheer fright.

Where were Helen, Clair and Heather? From the little he had heard bandied about, the women were to be become slaves. White slaves. The term unaccountably made him giggle, not that there was anything to giggle about. But *white* slaves? When Helen and Clair were anything but.

As soon as the nonsensical image drifted away, the realization of his plight made Marshall inwardly cry out to God and plead for mercy. Yet, no matter how much he besieged God, the man upstairs wasn't listening. Not today. Not ever.

Unanswered pleas were nothing new to Marshall. He was accustomed to getting fucked over. Goddamn it, he just knew God was an uptight white man who despised blacks as much as these Georgia peckerheads.

The heavy leg irons anchored to the wall and attached to his ankles irritated his skin. He eased the cumbersome iron shackles up his legs and rubbed his ankles. The leg irons were rusty and looked as if they had been last used in the Civil War. Their short chains impeded his movement, allowing him to turn no more than a foot in any direction. His hands were cuffed so he couldn't use them for anything except scratching his itchy stomach. He foolishly struggled against his bounds as if the intensity of his frustration alone could snap them apart. Thwarted, he emitted a string of loud curses.

"Hey, knock it off, over there," an annoyed person called from across the room. "Let me sleep." By the dim light emitted from the single bulb hanging overhead, Marshall saw he had the company of three other men. The man tied up next to him was the town's lawman. (What was he doing here?) Two others, opposite him in the narrow room, sat leaning against a wall: a teenage boy quietly sobbing, and the third man, a white-haired senior, the one who had told him to shut up. All three looked as unkempt as Marshall and stank to high heaven. Marshall twitched his nose until he noticed that he smelled as bad as the others.

"Jesus, God," Marshall cried out, "they're going to lynch me."

"Hey, take it easy," the lawman next to him said.

Marshall openly wept. "You don't understand," he asserted between sobs, "they hate black people. That's why I'm going to die."

The lawman looked exasperated. "Look, both of you" – this aimed at Marshall and the wailing teenager across from him – "losing control's not going to help. Besides, this got nothing to do with race. Nothing at all."

Marshall detected a note of resignation in the lawman's voice. It further alarmed him. "What's going to happen to us?"

The lawman paused as if debating whether to share bad news with men already teetering on the edge.

"C'mon, Mister, tell us," the teenager pleaded. Hands shaking, he wiped his runny nose with the sleeve of his shirt.

"They're going to use us as quarry for hunters."

Marshall didn't understand. By the expressions on their faces, neither did the white-haired senior and the teenager. "What do you mean quarry? What hunters?"

The lawman groaned. "There's going to be a hunt tomorrow morning. Maybe four or five hunters. These guys won't be shooting quail or deer or rabbits. They'll be trapping and shooting us instead."

Marshall felt his flesh crawl. He slumped against the wall and gasped for breath.

The senior across the room leaned forward and his chains rattled. "You're telling me the hunters are going to bag us like deer."

"That's exactly what I'm telling you."

The teenager joined Marshall in a chorus of convulsive gasps and whimpers. The white-haired senior looked angry. "What kind of animals are we dealing with?"

The lawman shifted around. "Look, there's no sense in getting pissed off. That'll accomplish nothing. Let's save our energy for figuring out a way to get out of here." He glanced at each man in turn. "Let's start by calming down. Tell you what, why don't we introduce ourselves. I'm Billy Ray Poynter, the former police chief for Wicked Stop, emphasis former."

"I'm Randolph Dodge," the white-haired senior said. "The Retreat is holding my wife and granddaughter hostage. By now my granddaughter might already be on the way ... somewhere to become some rich man's slave. God knows what's happened to my wife."

Billy Ray shook his head. "I know you're hurting. We're all hurting. But let's concentrate on escaping and nothing else." He hesitated. "Anybody got a watch?"

"They took mine," Dodge said. "Me, too," echoed Marshall. The teenager shook his head.

"Okay, I estimate it's about 3:00 a.m. Daylight will come about 7:00 a.m., give or take. The hunt starts shortly after. So we've got four hours to hatch an escape plan. Let's not waste any time feeling sorry for ourselves or worrying about our families. Not if you want to see them alive, again."

That quieted the room.

Marshall breathed deeply to calm himself. "I'm Marshall King," he said in a tremulous voice, fighting to keep himself under control.

"And you?" Billy Ray nodded in the direction of the teenager. "I recognize you. You're the kid I brought back to the Retreat with his girlfriend."

Marshall pulled as far away from Billy Ray as he could get. "You're with them?"

"I was. No longer. What in hell you think I'm doing down here in chains if I was with them?"

"I'm Steve Lawson," the teenager said. "The Retreat got my fiancée." His face brightened for a moment. "We were planning to get married tomorrow in Tallahassee. My family's waiting for us down there."

The lawman perked up. "Do they know you're here?"

Steve shook his head. "Naw, this was kind of an unexpected stop. You see, my girl and I, well, we thought this place would be a good a place as any to have a honeymoon before the honeymoon. The Retreat offered us a great deal, real cheap." His voice turned bitter. "We really got sucked in."

Marshall felt a flash of sorrow for the kid, could feel the anguish he was experiencing. "How old are you? You don't look old enough to get married."

"I'm nineteen, Dawn's eighteen. Old enough to make up our own minds." He sounded resentful of the question.

Marshall remembered something. "My son's in Ft. Lauderdale, Florida, waiting for us."

Billy Ray turned to face him. "Will he get worried enough to come after us?"

"Sure, if he knows we're here." Another thought crossed Marshall's mind. "You know, when we were in the car driving down here, my wife Helen called Justin, told him where we planned to spend the night."

That piece of good news energized Billy Ray. "So he knows where we are?"

"I think so, I hope so."

Billy Ray slumped against the wall. "Only problem is, he may not get here in time."

"Justin will call the state cops if he smells anything suspicious."

"Shit," Billy Ray said. "That's what I was afraid of."

Marshall was irritated. "Afraid? Why should you be afraid? That's what we want, isn't it, to get the police all over this place?"

"It's not that simple," Billy Ray answered. "Some of the state cops are in the pocket of the Retreat."

Marshall's throat choked up. "Jesus, help us!"

A gloomy silence descended upon the four men with the palpable feel of a smothering coat.

Billy Ray checked each of the men. "Is anybody here still under the influence of the drugs they gave us?"

The others either shook their heads or said no.

"Okay," Billy Ray said, "at least we're clear-headed."

Marshall shifted around uncomfortably. He swiped at his sweaty face with the back of his hand. "Where are we?"

"My guess," Dodge said, "is the basement under the lobby. Notice no windows. And feel how damp and cool it is."

Billy Ray concurred. "Makes sense."

"I'm also guessing that we'll never be able to break these chains."

Marshall snorted. "No kidding."

Billy Ray said, "Probably our first, maybe our only chance, will be to make a break for it when they unshackle us and bring us up to wherever the hunt's going to take place."

Dodge nodded. "I heard one of the attendant's say the Retreat got a few hundred acres, most of them wooded. Maybe once they give us a head start we can escape the hunters, find the highway."

Billy Ray sighed. "Not a chance. They'll have attendants posted throughout the woods and at key escape points. Besides, there's no highway anywhere near the Retreat, and as I recall, not even a dirt road where the hunt takes place. Nothing but heavily wooded country with thick underbrush."

"What can we do?" Steve asked.

"We're going to die," Marshall whimpered. "Nothing we can do. Lord's already made up his mind."

Billy Ray slapped his manacles together. They clanged and got everybody's attention. "No more talk like that. It doesn't help."

An uneasy silence gripped the room. All four men retreated to their individual thoughts. Marshall's were predictably disconsolate.

Dodge broke the silence a few minutes later. "There

is one way."

"What's that?" Steve asked, desperate for a solution.

"When they free us from these leg irons to take us to the hunt, one of us makes a break for it, distracting the attention of the attendants. The rest break away in the opposite direction."

"Good idea, except for one thing," Billy Ray said. "The one who breaks away first is going to get shot, probably killed before he gets ten feet away. The attendants taking us out will all be armed."

"Will they use their guns on us?" Dodge asked.

Billy Ray shrugged. "Probably. Most of them got nothing to lose. They're all escaped criminals dodging the law. It's in their interest to keep everything bottled up inside the Retreat."

"What other choices do we have?" Dodge said.

An uncomfortable silenced followed.

Well, then," Dodge continued, "all we need is a volunteer to make the break."

Marshall pressed himself against the wall. "Don't look at me."

"I'm too young," Steve said. "One of you older guys can do it."

"Look," Billy Ray said, "this is not a practical—"

"I'll do it," Dodge said.

The heads of all three men converged in the direction of Randolph Dodge, the white-haired senior.

"Why are you volunteering?" Marshall said, wide-eyed, finding it hard to believe that some people are selfless.

"Because I'm dying of cancer."

TWENTY-TWO

Gilbert

Mildred and her son Gilbert were relaxing in the living room of their penthouse suite. Gilbert sat back in his rose-colored Damask chair, martini in hand, the Chihuahua Pootie resting in his lap. The dog sighed contentedly.

Mildred, seated opposite her son in a brocaded easy chair, eyed the drink in his hand. Gilbert knew she didn't approve of his drinking anything stronger than his usual evening glass of sherry, given that his father was an alcoholic.

A silver service stacked high with bottles of liquor and a bucket of ice stood between them like a silent barrier. Gilbert, mindful of his mother's feelings, but so emotionally drained from the rigors of the auction, needed his martini. He sipped it while Mother looked on disapprovingly.

"It's 3:30 a.m., Gilbert. Not exactly the time to be drinking."

"Mother, it's been a tiring night. The auction and all. Allow me the luxury of taking one drink to help me relax." He stroked Pootie whose eyes closed in relaxed contentment.

"It's time to go to bed."

"A splendid idea. Tell you what, let's go over the financials, one more time, then it's beddy-bye time for both of us."

"Oh, my God, not the financials again," Mildred said and smiled to indicate she didn't really mind. She picked up the sales forecast she and Gilbert had drafted to predict dollar income for the auction, and read over the realized dollar figures she had scribbled in during the auction.

"Bottom line is we took in sales of $3,900,000 against a forecast of $2,650,000 with a breakeven of $900,000. Our best auction yet. A profit of $3,000,000."

Gilbert opened his mouth to speak but was cut-off my Mildred. "Oh, I almost forgot, we can add the $100,000 from the hunt to the total. That makes it $3,100,000."

Gilbert closed his eyes. "What a wonderful number, $3,100,000. Profit. Sheer profit." He rolled the number around as if it were a gourmet delicacy he was tasting.

Then, out of nowhere, Gilbert's face darkened.

"What's wrong, Sonny?"

"The virgin. We had a bid of $950,000 from Achmed Habi-Ban of Saudi Arabia. But we had to sell to Harry Phieu for $500,000. A loss of $450,000. Harry conned us."

Mildred wagged a finger at Gilbert. "Nonsense, we had a deal with Harry. Besides, one mustn't be greedy."

"You're right, of course, Mother. Nevertheless, it hurts. You know how hard I work to keep the Retreat afloat." Gilbert closed his eyes and pressed the martini glass to his forehead.

"And you do so magnificently. I'm certainly not complaining."

Gilbert opened his eyes and patted the back of his mother's hand and felt the dampness of the cream she used to cover her liver spots. "I can always count on your steadfast support, Mother. That's comforting."

"Family's important. In the final analysis, it's the only thing we have."

"How true, how very true." Gilbert's face clouded over again.

Mildred, ever so sensitive to mood changes in her son, said, "What's the matter now, Sonny?"

"It's that dreadful Clair King girl, the one that escaped. She's blighted what otherwise might have been a magnificent auction."

"Not to worry, we'll find her. We have the roads blocked and there's nowhere she can go. Not through the woods certainly. She's unfamiliar with this country."

"True, how true." The strain eased from Gilbert's face.

Somebody rang the suite's melodious doorbell. Pootie jumped off Gilbert's lap and sprinted to the door.

Gilbert and Mildred turned to face each other.

"Who could that be this time of the morning?" Gilbert said. He was understandably suspicious. Unexpected visitors, particularly those who come calling in the dead of night, normally came bearing bad news. Pootie growled in her ridiculously thin voice.

Mildred said, " I don't know who it is, but I'll get it."

Moments later Mildred walked back into the living room followed by Dahesh Rantoon, the buyer from India. Mildred had her face fixed in a frozen imitation of a smile, the kind reserved for anybody she disliked but was required to do business with. Pootie followed, yipping at Rantoon's feet.

"I'm glad you're still up," Rantoon said in his sing-song Indian accent, paying no attention to the dog. He bowed slightly. "There's something of considerable importance we have to discuss." His command of the English language invariably impressed Gilbert who considered Rantoon his most educated and refined buyer, a significant cut above some of the brutes he was forced to deal with in this sordid business.

Werner once confided in Gilbert that the Retreat staff called Rantoon Mr. Bones. Indeed, he appeared to be little more than a barely fleshed-out skeleton. He gave the appearance of somebody in the terminal stages of a ravaging cancer, but contrary to his appearance, Mr. Bones possessed an amazing vitality. He slept only four hours a night and hurtled through the remaining twenty hours with boundless energy.

Gilbert rose and greeted his guest. He was accustomed to handling the outré needs of buyers, a group that tended to be high-strung and insecure. But of course, that was due to the nature of their business.

"Please sit down," Gilbert said and pointed to a chair next to his. He sounded tired and in the light reflected from the muted Stiffel floor lamps his face was pale and drawn.

Mr. Bones sat down on the edge of his chair as if poised to leap from it at the slightest provocation. His tense behavior signaled bad news coming.

Gilbert snapped his fingers and Pootie jumped onto his lap. Gilbert crossed his legs and plucked at the razor-sharp crease in his pants. "And how may I help you, Mr. Rantoon?"

"The lovely young lady I bought earlier to–"

"Is there something wrong with her?" Gilbert asked, alarmed.

Mr. Bones shook his head. "Not at all. She's a delightful prize. I've spent the last two hours with her ... testing her skills. If anything, I must compliment you on your taste."

Gilbert, relieved, bowed his head slightly. "Then, what may I ask, can I do for you?"

"The $250,000 I bid for her..."

"Yes?"

Mr. Bones sucked in his breath. "I don't want to pay it."

For a moment, Gilbert thought he had heard wrong. Then Mr. Bones's words sunk in and the blood drained from Gilbert's head. He felt light-headed. "You don't want to pay it," he repeated, as if by echoing the words he could make the meaning sink in.

"Yes, exactly." Mr. Bones smiled but his eyes were as hard as sapphires. So out of character for this genteel Indian Gilbert had been dealing with for three years.

Mildred stared at Mr. Bones as if he were an apparition. "That's crazy–"

"Let me handle this, Mother." He turned to Mr. Bones and glowered. "Sir, you made a commitment. You've been here many times before as our guest. You know the rules. A bid is a promise to pay in cash or negotiable securities before one leaves the Retreat. No exceptions."

Mr. Bones cleared his throat. "I'll politely request that you make one now."

"I'm afraid that's impossible."

"If you'll indulge me, Mr. Phester, let me tell you why it isn't."

Gilbert frowned. His hands inched toward a hidden electronic alarm alongside the chair that would bring Werner or Bobby running. "Go ahead. I'm listening."

Mr. Bones took a deep breath again. "It has to do with the secret deal you cut with Harry Phieu."

Gilbert thought he would faint. Pootie jumped up and licked her owner's face.

"Pardon me?" Mildred said in a haughty tone. Her eyes threw daggers at Mr. Bones. "How dare you accuse us of anything underhanded?"

"Please, Mrs. Phester, hear me out. I went backstage before the auction, hoping to get an advance peek at the girls for sale, feeling that as a long-standing customer I could take that liberty. I was there, on the other side of the curtain when you and your son were discussing the deal you made with Harry Phieu."

Gilbert recalled the rustling curtain the night of the auction, the darkened figure of a man escaping through the back door of the theatre.

"You were spying on us," Gilbert said with both shock and resentment.

Mr. Bones cringed. "I was doing no such thing. I merely happened to be in the right place at the right time." His eyes revealed his true feelings; they flashed alternately between anger and greed. Both emotions were real. Mr. Bones did stand to cheat Gilbert of his hard-earned money. But his position was risky, to say the least. Gilbert's reputation for punishing thieves and grifters was as well known among buyers as among the Retreat's staff.

"And if I refuse to honor your ... request?"

Mildred's mouth stretched into a thin line. "Call it what it is, Sonny: blackmail."

"If you refuse, I'll let the other buyers know about the arrangement with Phieu. And that, Sir, will be the end of your business."

A stunned silence greeted this statement.

Mr. Bones cleared his throat. "There's something else."

Gilbert seemed to shrink within himself, to ward off yet another blow.

"I also want an additional $100,000 in cash before I leave tomorrow."

Gilbert rose unsteadily from his chair. His face was ashen. "How dare you?"

Mildred was more to the point. "You son of a bitch." She took a step toward Mr. Bones, her eyes smoldering with resentment.

Gilbert restrained his mother by throwing up an arm before her advance. "Not now, Mother."

"You Indian goon bastard," Mildred said, her eyes drilling holes in Mr. Bones. "Piece of foreign trash."

Mr. Bones stepped backward. "Please, let us not get physical, Mrs. Phester. Think it out. You have no choice. It's either the money or I tell everybody."

"And suppose we try to stop you?" Gilbert asked.

Mr. Bones whipped out a snub-nosed thirty-eight revolver from the belt underneath his T-shirt. "There'll be none of that." The hair on Pootie's back stood on end. Gilbert held the dog firmly as she yapped and tried to leap off his lap at the Indian.

Mr. Bones glanced at his wristwatch. "It's now 4:00 a.m. I'll give you until noon to deliver the money to my room. I'll be waiting there ... with this. Do not send Werner or Bobby. Be there yourself or send your mother. Anybody else enters the room and I start shooting, and then I call the FBI." He waved the handgun menacingly in the air. Then stepped back to the door and slipped out of the suite.

For the first few moments after Mr. Bones left, Gilbert and Mildred sat quietly and stared at each other. Then Gilbert leaned over and placed his head in his hands. "My God, Mother, I'm going to be ruined."

Mildred rushed to her son's side. She held him in her arms and crooned soft words to him as she had so many times in the past when Gilbert felt threatened. After a few moments, Gilbert quieted and regained his composure. His eyes had a steely look about them.

"That settles it. Rantoon must die before noon, preferably sooner rather than later. Agree, Mother?"

"Agreed. And I know exactly how to do it, Sonny. Leave it to your dear mother."

Pootie barked.

TWENTY-THREE

Helen

After capturing Helen and leading her to the hot boxes, Mildred and Werner made a nasty joke of it. "If you're like most women and want to lose weight," Werner said, "this is the place to do it." He gripped Helen's arm and jerked her forward to what appeared to be a row of six coffins standing on their ends, all constructed from four-by-fours with sturdy wooden doors running the length of the boxes.

Except they weren't coffins. Or, if they were, they contained not corpses but living, breathing people. Helen's heart threatened to blow a hole through her chest when she heard distinct groans emanating from inside one of the boxes. She tensed up and resisted Werner when he tugged her forward. He slapped her face and she cried out.

"You and that whore daughter of yours have caused me no end of problems. Now it's the hot box for you, bitch."

Helen, terrorized, searched for a way to escape Werner's clutches and found none. They were struggling outside in a clearing about one hundred yards behind the Retreat, the area dimly lit by reflected light from the hotel, but mainly from a string of overhead lights strung over the hot boxes and supported by two poles. A swarm of insects buzzed the lights, their bodies snapping and sizzling against the heated bulbs. The air was so heavy with humidity it brought to mind the sauna of Helen's women's club back in Cleveland.

Except this was no woman's club. She had a black

eye and swollen nose to show for her struggle with Werner. The tissue around her eye was inflamed and purple. She was drenched with sweat and exhausted from fighting. Helen recalled with humiliation and fear how Werner had captured her in the Retreat's lobby, punched her out in a fit of anger, dragged her outside near the pool and called Mr. Phester. Minutes afterward his mother arrived and they escorted Helen to the hot boxes.

"I talked with Gilbert," Mildred said. "He wants her locked up in the hot box. But don't hit her again. Harry will have the devil of a time selling her to his client if he thinks her face won't heal properly."

"I'd prefer to kill the bitch." Werner rubbed his cheek where Helen had left deep scratches.

"You're not listening, Werner. The purpose of the hot box is to knock the fight out of her. We can't harm the woman any more. She now belongs to Harry Phieu. Bought and paid for. He's mad enough at losing the daughter. And he hasn't yet seen the mother since you beat her up. Harry's not going to be happy about that."

Werner dodged the reference to Harry Phieu. By the look of fear in his eyes, Helen gathered that Werner was not anxious to cross the big man.

"And," Mildred continued, "if we don't catch the daughter, Gilbert loses a lot of money. You know what that means."

Like every attendant or worker at the Retreat, Werner was scared to death of Gilbert. "Don't worry, I've got Bobby and a crew of people searching for her. She won't get far. She didn't the last time."

"She better not," Mildred warned. "Gilbert won't be happy ... and neither will I. Wouldn't want to lose an able-bodied cocksman like you." She tittered and pinched Werner's ass while Helen looked on in disbelief.

Werner, embarrassed and showing it, angrily swung open one of the hot boxes and squeezed a balking Helen inside. Helen broke down and sobbed.

"Enjoy yourself, bitch," Werner snarled. He slammed shut the door and slipped a padlock on the latch and locked it. Helen screamed and clubbed the door with small fists until her knuckles bled.

"Werner, for God's sake, let me out of here." Her voice was clogged with fear. "I promise not to run away."

"If I have my way, bitch, you'll die in there."

"Mrs. Phester, please help me."

"Too late for that now," Mildred said in an unemotional voice. "If you behave, we'll let you out later."

Helen listened to the diminishing sounds of Mildred and Werner talking as they returned to the Retreat. She yelled after them, pleading, but nobody answered. Then silence descended, broken only by the sounds of chirping crickets and Helen's strenuous breathing.

Now, hours later, the pain was excruciating. Helen didn't know exactly how long she had borne the heat and cramped conditions of the hot box, only that at first light of dawn it was becoming unbearable. Her back spasms were so violent she had to bite her tongue to keep from crying out. She couldn't sit or lie down to rest, couldn't stand erect. There wasn't enough room to do either. All she could do within the claustrophobic boundaries of the hot box was stand in a crouched position with her legs bent at the knees, her back and knees pressing into opposite sides of the box. The air was stifling. She couldn't get enough oxygen into her lungs and hyperventilated, almost passing out. Struggling to contain her panic, she searched desperately for some light and found a few places where the wood was warped sufficiently to allow in air.

Her thoughts seized on Roger as if he were a lifeline. Images of one stolen Sunday afternoon flooded her memory. Marshall was in Baltimore attending an NFL football game with an old college chum. Clair was away at college and Justin out of town for his company. Helen sneaked Roger into her home (Marshall's home as well, she reminded herself with the sting of guilt).

That afternoon she had felt indescribably sensuous. Apparently so did Roger. They locked bodies in a four-hour sexual marathon, a frenzy that left them both spent and weak and Helen bruised and sore. She climaxed so many times they merged into one unending wave and she momentarily fainted. Actually passed out.

Reveling now in the memory, a surge of rapturous pleasure filled her body as she relived that unforgettable Sunday afternoon and crowded out the horror of her imprisonment.

"Who are you?" a faint voice came from the adjacent box.

The voice shattered Helen's fantasy and she gasped. Whoever it was knocked faintly on the wall of her hot box.

"Are you okay?" the voice asked.

"Yes, I think so. Were you one of the guests?" Helen asked.

"I'm Mrs. Dodge, the grandmother of ... they took my..." The woman faltered and started to cry.

"Your daughter? Is she here at the Retreat?"

"She's at the hotel. They've sold her. And my husband ... I don't know where he is. He's got cancer. We don't know how much time he has left."

"Oh, no." Helen thought of Clair and prayed she was free and unhurt. "At least your daughter's not suffering in this Godawful coffin."

"I don't think I can last much longer," the older woman said with a plaintive tilt to her voice.

"Is there anybody else in these boxes?"

"No, not that I know of."

"How long you been here?"

"They brought me in an hour or so before you."

"What did you do?"

The older woman sobbed. "I tried to sneak out of the hotel."

"With your granddaughter?"

The old woman's voice broke. "No, without her."

Helen said nothing.

"I'm so ashamed," the older woman said between sobs. "But I was scared."

"I understand. You did what you felt was necessary."

"I want so much to see my husband and daughter again."

"Don't worry. My daughter escaped. She'll bring back help."

"There is no way. They're too powerful." Helen heard the resignation in the older woman's voice.

Damn it, I won't give up, Helen thought. She probed every part of her tomb but discovered no crack in the door or box she could pry apart. No weakness in its construction. Perhaps the older woman was right, after all. Perhaps there was no way out. Helen slumped against the wall of the box. Tears puddled in her eyes. Helen was ready to give up, felt utterly helpless and in the hands of a world gone mad.

TWENTY-FOUR

Mildred

Mildred was bone tired. So tired, that for the first time since grade school, the very thought of sex was repulsive. Which, for Mildred, was unheard of, given that thoughts of sex occupied her time and attention as often as that of a horny teenage boy.

Mildred had been up all night and she felt the weight of every one of her sixty-seven years. The stress of the show and auction had been bad enough. Add to it the escape of that horrible King girl and the blackmail attempt by that treacherous Indian, Mr. Bones, it was a wonder she could function at all.

But the grande dame had what was once referred to as an iron constitution, and there was one more task to complete before calling it a night. Duty called and damned if Mildred Phester was going to neglect her duty because of a few minor aches and pains.

Duty to her son, that is. Poor Gilbert had been so upset at Mr. Bones's clumsy blackmail attempt. Mildred felt the need for her personal involvement to stop the skinny Indian before he spilled the beans to other buyers about Gilbert's private deal with Harry Phieu.

That would be her first call. To alert Harry Phieu to the danger and enlist his aid. To persuade him to accompany him to Mr. Bones's room. She intended to lure the son of a bitch out, then turn Harry loose and encourage him to tear the Indian to pieces.

In the corner of her mind, a vagrant thought intruded. She had nothing sexual in mind, but Mildred was astute enough to realize that, given nature's urges and the size of Harry's hidden member, anything could happen. The sight and feel of that monster pressed tightly against Harry's pants might be enough to recharge her depleted sexual batteries. Who knows?

She tapped on the door of room 412. "Harry, open up. It's Mildred. I need to talk to you. Urgently."

Mildred heard a muffled sound coming from inside the room.

"Harry, is that you?"

Thumping noises now.

She peered around. Nobody was in the hall. Mildred removed a universal passkey from her purse and unlocked the door and looked around. She was shocked to find Melissa lying on the floor of the closet, bound and gagged.

"What happened?" Mildred said, alarmed. She untied Melissa and helped her sit up. "Are you all right, sweetie?"

Melissa coughed. "The goddamn King women ganged up on me." Her voice was hoarse from the gag.

"Where's Harry?"

"He hasn't been here all night, probably bedded down with one of the other attendants." Melissa's face clouded, then turned a bright pink. "All I know is I want to get my hands on those two ... conniving bitches. They tied me up, left me to choke to death."

Mildred, only half-listening to Melissa, her mind racing ahead, came up with an idea. "Tell you what, sweetie, I need a favor, then we'll both hunt down the King girl. We already have her mother." She explained that she needed Melissa to help ambush Mr. Bones.

Melissa managed a shaky grin. "Happy to help. I don't like that creepy bastard. But does Mr. Bones have the girl he bought in his room?"

"Dawn, that's her name. No, she's back in the dorm with the other girls, ankle straps on. Where they'll stay until they're drugged again and prepared for departure later today."

At the door to Mr. Bones's room, Mildred positioned herself against the wall out of sight and Melissa knocked. "Mr. Rantoon, it's Melissa," she said in a sultry voice. "May I come in?"

"Who is it?" an alert voice answered, coming from the other side of the door, sounding cautious.

"Melissa. You know, the one who works for Werner. The blonde with the ponytail."

"What do you want?" Suspicious now.

Melissa's voice turned throaty. "It's embarrassing to admit ... but I find Indian men attractive. I'm one of your many admirers. Can you spare me a half-hour of your time? I promise you won't be disappointed."

"How come you never told me before?"

"It's against the rules for attendants to fraternize with guests. But I find you so attractive I can't resist anymore."

Mildred stifled a laugh.

Melissa's admission was greeted at first by silence. Finally, the door cracked open and Mr. Bones peeked outside. He held a thirty-eight revolver in his hand, the same one he'd used to threaten Gilbert and Mildred. Melissa thrust out her breasts and captured Mr. Bones's eye. He smiled and opened the door all the way in a welcoming gesture. Melissa and Mildred charged into the room and tore into the skinny Indian like attacking eagles, knocked him backward. With nails as sharp as talons Mildred flailed at his face. The gun flew out of his hand and thumped on the carpeted floor.

Mr. Bones twisted out of Mildred's reach and grabbed his cell phone now resting on the bed. Before he could use it, Mildred ripped it out of his hand and Melissa stomped on it hard, flattening it, tearing its electronic guts out. Mildred kicked Mr. Bones in the testicles. He made a whoofing sound like air escaping from a slit tire and doubled over.

The fight, if you can call it that, was over in an instant. Mildred slumped against a dresser and panted, exhausted from the pitched battle. She sat down on the room's double bed to catch her breath. Melissa stood over Mr. Bones triumphantly, one of her legs planted on his supine form like a hunter getting her picture taken after bagging a lion. Mr. Bones, doubled over in a fetal position on the floor, inhaled in large rasping breaths.

As if to emphasize the ladies' victory, Melissa walked over and slammed shut the door to the hotel room.

That was a mistake. Mildred saw it immediately, but by then it was too late. With both women temporarily preoccupied, Mr. Bones squirmed on the floor like a wiggle worm and snatched the gun. He propped himself against a wall and pointed the gun at Mildred and Melissa. His eyes shimmered with desperation.

"I'll kill you both if I have to."

Mildred shook a fist at the Indian. "I'm going to get you, you thieving son of a bitch. This isn't over."

Melissa, young and inexperienced, made a foolish move; she lunged for the gun. Mr. Bones fired and a slug tore into her knee, shattering it. She shrieked in agony and fell to the floor. Mr. Bones, clutching his stomach, his eyes wild, staggered backwards to the doorway of the room.

"I still want my money. You" – he waved the gun at Mildred – "come with me. We're going to get it together."

Mildred said over the noise of Melissa wailing, "I'll die first."

Mr. Bones cocked the thirty-eight. "Then you'll

die."

Bastard means it, Mildred thought. "Okay, I'll go get the money. You wait here."

Mr. Bones, on edge because of Melissa's howling, shook his head and raised his voice to be heard over the din. "No, we leave the Retreat together. Now! Quickly! You'll call Gilbert later and have the money brought to us."

"But—"

Mr. Bones pointed the gun at her head. A crazy light glittered in his eyes. "No more talking. We go now."

Mildred stumbled out of the room with Mr. Bones behind her, prodding her spine with the thirty-eight. A few guests peeked out of their rooms to see what the commotion was. Mr. Bones pointed the gun at them and they retreated and locked their doors behind them.

Thirty seconds later the alarm clanged. Probably from Melissa. Mildred and Mr. Bones were pushing through the door from the stairwell leading out of the building when they heard attendants shouting and feet pounding the stairs. Mr. Bones, his eyes wild with fright, backed off from the stairwell into the hallway, turned and ran the other way. Mildred scooted downstairs as fast as her worn out old knees would allow. When she met the attendants rushing up the stairs she yelled out "fourth floor," then stopped to get her breath. It was then she realized a Mr. Bones on the loose posed an immediate threat to Gilbert and her.

TWENTY-FIVE

Clair

The Retreat's attendants were searching for Clair in the wrong places. Earlier, when the alarm had sounded and hotel guests poured into the lobby, she broke from the milling crowd and raced out of the hotel, reluctantly leaving her mother to do battle with Werner. Clair dodged her pursuers yet again by doubling back through a side entrance. Under cover of the crowd she searched for her mother without luck. Too late. Werner had captured her.

Clair sneaked into the restaurant's kitchen, closed for the night, and into the safe confines of the kitchen's large walk-in pantry where she hid and rested for several hours behind stacked boxes of canned goods. In the concealment of early morning darkness, she crept back into the kitchen, heard voices and ducked behind a large stand-up freezer.

"...hotter than a white boy's ass out there, even this early."

"Werner put another one in the hot box. Gots themselves two older ladies in there now. That Werner one mean motherfucka."

Clair peeked around the corner of the freezer and saw two black men in white chef's uniforms.

"Shh," the other black man replied. "Doan let anybody hear you talkin' like that. Never know who be hearin' you."

"Yeah, you right."

The hot box. Whatever it meant it sounded awful. Was her mother one of the ladies in the hot box? And if not, where was she and her dad and Heather? She

195

prayed with all her heart they were safe.

Clair choked up at the thought of never seeing her family again. How she wanted to ... punish Mr. Phester and his corrupt gang of thugs, yes punish them, a word that two short days ago was noticeably absent from her vocabulary. Not that she sought revenge, she hastened to assure herself. What she wanted was justice; to bring these horrible people before the law so they could never again commit atrocious acts of cruelty.

She was especially frightened of Bobby. A shiver of revulsion crawled through her body at the image of his hulking presence. He embodied everything she disliked and feared in this world: senseless violence, vicious cruelty, the infliction of abject suffering upon others.

Clair tuned out further negative thoughts and her mind drifted to Billy Ray Poynter, Wicked Stop's lone lawman. Ex-lawman, that is. She hoped he hadn't been harmed, found to her surprise that she wanted to see him again under more pleasant conditions, if such a thing were possible given his fugitive status and her capture.

"Got the hunt this morning. About five poor fools goin' down."

"Yeah, best we keep inside, away from the honkies. Doan want them fat white hunters chasin' us for their lunch."

The other chef slapped his sides and guffawed. "Don't worry, them boys doan like dark meat."

What was the hunt? Clair was tempted to risk exposing herself and ask the chefs. They sounded like decent men. But she couldn't take the chance. Not if she wanted to stay alive. She was her parents' last hope, and probably Heather's.

The moment the two chefs got busy cooking breakfast, Clair sneaked back into the walk-in pantry. At the entrance she remembered seeing a row of attendants' blue and white uniforms, found them and slipped into one.

Then, as if she belonged in the Retreat, she boldly strode through the kitchen, nodding at the chefs as she passed, and walked out of the building and into the pool area. They threw her only a cursory glance, acted as if she were one of the staff.

Clair picked up a long pole with a screened catcher at its end and began skimming leaves and dead bugs from the pool. She worked her way around to the opposite side facing the back of the property, preparing to make a dash for the woods and hunt for the hot boxes, when another female attendant coming from a bathhouse walked up to her.

"Do I know you?" she asked, squinting at Clair suspiciously.

Clair stuck out her hand. "I'm new here. Just started yesterday. My name's Monica."

The attendant's face lit up. "Not the infamous Monica, the one who likes cigars in private places?"

Clair laughed. "Hardly."

"I'm Marilyn. Tell you the truth, I only started working here a few weeks ago, myself."

"Nice to meet you."

"What area you working in?"

Clair thought fast. "I haven't received an assignment yet. Right now I'm running an errand for Werner ... Say, maybe you can help me. Werner told me to check the hot box, but he never told me where it was. He scooted off before I had a chance to ask him. You know how busy he is."

Marilyn shook her head in sympathy. "Geez, the guy can't stop for a minute. But you know, I'm surprised he sent you out there. That's off limits for most of us."

Clair thought fast. "Yeah, that's true, but Werner

wanted me to take a peek from a distance, you know, make sure everything is okay. He told me not to get too close."

Marilyn gave Clair the once over. "Say, is he getting in your pants already?"

Clair giggled and batted her eyes. "Can't tell you that."

Marilyn grinned. "Okay, I get it. I won't ask anything else. None of my business anyway. But watch out, he hits on all the girls." She leaned over and whispered. "What have they got on you?"

"Got on me?"

"Yeah, you know. Like myself, I'm wanted for a burglary rap in Palm Beach. I owe Mr. Phester for giving me a job, keeping me out of sight until it cools down. How about you?"

Clair curled her finger, signaling Marilyn to get closer. "Manslaughter."

"Jeez, the big time. What—"

Clair grabbed the attendant's arm, a serious look on her face. "Don't tell anybody. Right?"

"Right, sure."

"You were going to give me directions."

"Oh yeah. Hey, look, take that path."She pointed to an area behind the pool. "You'll come across what you're looking for in a clearing pretty quick."

Clair thanked her and started to walk away.

"Oh, Monica, one more thing."

She turned around, apprehensive. "Yeah?"

"Keep your eyes open for that Indian, the skinny dark-skinned guy who tried to rob the hotel this morning."

"What Indian?"

"Didn't you hear the alarm?"

"Oh, sure."

"Well that Indian guy, Mr. Bones I think they call

him, tried to rip off the hotel during the auction last night."

"You mean the white slavery thing?"

Marilyn put her finger to her lips. "Don't let Werner hear you talk about the auction. It's forbidden for staff to even mention it. White slavery's illegal, you know." She smiled and winked conspiratorially at Clair.

"Marilyn, I've got to run before Werner gets on my case."

"Sure, well, see you soon."

Clair followed the path and within minutes came upon the hot boxes. When she first saw them, the breath caught in her throat. A cry of "Mom," ripped from deep inside as she raced up to them. In a panic she knocked on the doors of each of the hot boxes until she heard coughing come from one of them. "Mom," she yelled. "Mom, is that you?"

"Clair?" came the faint reply.

Clair split her fingernails as she tore at the lock. "Mom, I'm coming, hold on," she cried.

Helen wept. Her cries ripped Clair's heart out, made her redouble her efforts. She pulled, tugged, hit and kicked the door until her fingers bled and feet went numb. Frustrated, she stepped back and tried to clear her head.

"Miss, I can help."

A deathly-thin brown-skinned man with an Indian accent appeared from behind the hot boxes. His clothes were torn, wrinkled and dirty as if he had been wrestling in the dirt.

A startled Clair jumped away. "Dear God, who are you?"

"My name is Rantoon. Informally, Mr. Bones. More important, I know who you are."

Clair's gaze darted around to find a swift avenue of

escape.

Mr. Bones's lips twitched in a tremulous imitation of a smile. He had a revolver ticked inside his belt at the waist. Clair's eyes flicked from the handgun to Mr. Bones's face and back again.

"My dear, you don't have to be frightened of me. I remember you from last night. You're the charming young lady who escaped Harry Phieu's clutches. How brave and how smart you must be."

Clair recalled what the attendant Marilyn had told her at the pool about Mr. Bones. "You're one of those buyers, aren't you?"

"Yes, I was a customer of the Retreat. No longer. But enough of that for now. Let's free your mother."

A feeble voice emerged from the hot box. "Please, please get me out."

Mr. Bones disappeared behind the hot boxes and reappeared moments later. He held up a small crowbar. "I found this in an open tool shed behind the pool on the way out here."

He slipped the crowbar into the door latch and tugged at it until the latch popped open. The door swung wide and Helen staggered out of the hot box and collapsed. She was barely conscious, her clothes filthy and torn. Sweat-caked dirt covered her face. One of her eyes was swollen shut and her nose was puffed-up from the beating Werner administered. The smell emerging from the hot box made Clair gag. Tears filled her eyes when she imagined the horror her mother had experienced. She held Mom's head in her lap and stroked her head. Mr. Bones poured tepid water from a nearby spigot into a battered canteen that Clair guessed had been used to ration water for those in the hot boxes. He held the mouth of the canteen to Helen's mouth. She sipped the water through parched lips.

"Mom, are you okay? Your face..."

Helen patted Clair's hand. "I'll be fine dear."

But she wasn't behaving fine, and her lassitude alarmed Clair. "Are you injured elsewhere?" Clair's eyes raced across her mother's body, searching for other wounds.

Helen's lips twitched. "I seem to hurt everywhere. ... Maybe it's the heat."

Clair removed the blouse of her Retreat uniform – she was wearing nothing underneath – and fanned her mother. Mr. Bones tried to avoid peering at Clair's swaying breasts.

"A ... woman in the next ... box," Helen whispered in a hoarse voice.

Mr. Bones used the crowbar to pry open the door to the adjacent hot box. He reached inside and dragged out a recumbent older woman. He took her pulse and leaned over her mouth and nose to see if she was breathing. He shook his head. "She's gone."

Helen lifted her head and peered at the woman. "Mother of mercy." Tears crowded the corners of her eyes. She recognized her as the elderly woman whose husband had tried to signal Marshall and Helen when they first arrived at the Retreat.

Mr. Bones stood and wiped his hands along the seam of his pants. "If I might suggest, ladies, now is the time for us to make our way out of here."

Clair said, "You ripped off Gilbert Phester, didn't you?"

Mr. Bones smiled ruefully. "You could put it that way. In any respect, I must confess I tried to pull a fast one on him and his evil mother, and was called on it. I managed to barely escape their clutches, was hiding out in a ravine behind these torture boxes when you came along."

"Why should you help mother and me?"

"Indeed, my dear, why not? You and your mother

on the run will create a diversion which may allow all of us to escape."

Clair didn't trust Mr. Bones, but her choices were limited. She shrugged into her blouse. "Do you have a cell phone? We can call the police."

Mr. Bones smiled remorsefully. "I was foolish enough to lose it in a fight."

"Do you know any way out of here?"

"I think so. I've visited the Retreat many times, enough to know that taking the only road leaving the Retreat through the town of Wicked Stop is a trap. From which many attempted escapes have been foiled."

Clair shivered, remembering her failed attempt, the state cop on Gilbert Phester's payroll. "What's your idea?"

"There's only one way. Through the woods."

"How far would we have to go?"

"I'm not sure. But if we head away from the Retreat, we'll eventually find an outside road." He pointed to the tree line about one hundred yards distant.

"Mother's not in any condition to walk a long distance."

Mr. Bones sighed. "It's our only chance. Unless you can think of something else." His hand on the revolver, Mr. Bones glanced around him in nervous twitches, as if expecting an assault at any moment. "We don't have much time. I'm sure Werner and that brute associate of his, Bobby, are searching for us right now."

Clair, frustrated, lifted her mother to a sitting position and offered her more water. Helen greedily drank it and asked for more.

"Careful," Mr. Bones warned, "in her condition she'll throw up if she drinks too much or too fast."

From someplace nearby, gunshots rang out. Mr.

Bones dropped to the ground and cowered.

"What's that?" Clair asked, frightened.

"Gunshots. The hunt has started."

"What's the hunt?"

Mr. Bones explained while Helen and Clair stared at him in wide-eyed horror.

Clair said, "The shots came from the direction of our escape route."

The expression on Mr. Bones's face clearly showed his frustration. "We can try to flank them."

A random thought of monstrous proportions crossed Clair's mind. "Is my father there, in the hunt?"

"I have no way of knowing, since I don't participate in that barbaric sport."

Helen's lips quivered. "Marshall, is he...?"

"He may be in danger, Mom. We've got to find our way there somehow and see if we can rescue him."

"That's ridiculous," Mr. Bones said. "If he's ahead of us in the woods, and that's not at all sure, he'll be surrounded by hunters and attendants. All of them armed. Do you want to be killed?"

Clair's laser-beam gaze could have cut Mr. Bones in two. "He's my father. We're going." Her nostrils flared in defiance.

"Count me out. I'm not ready to die." He took his handgun and crowbar and trudged behind the hot boxes and into the ravine beside it.

He re-emerged moments later, saying in a firm tone, "Damn it, I can't leave you and your mother alone. They'll kill you for sure. Besides, I have another plan."

Clair instinctively reached over and caressed his cheek. "You're not like the others, are you? The buyers or the people who work at the Retreat."

Clair could swear Mr. Bones was blushing, but of course it was hard to tell since his natural coloration hid it.

"You're quite a man, Mr. Bones."

"I second that," Helen said in a weak voice. "Thanks for rescuing me."

"There's another possibility," Mr. Bones said. "If we can wound or isolate one of the hunters and get his cell phone, we can call outside for help."

"What are the chances?" Clair asked.

"Admittedly remote. If not that, I can always try to wound a hunter, scare the others off."

"Isn't there any other way?"

"Young lady, I've run out of options. We've got to make a run for it."

"I'm concerned about Mom's ability to walk any distance."

"Don't worry about me," Helen said, her voice stronger now. "I can hold my own."

Mr. Bones patted Helen's shoulder. "Good lady." He said to Clair, "If we can't find a cell phone, we still can reach civilization before nightfall. Assuming we don't get caught."

"Let's not think that way," Helen said.

Clair wiped the sweat from her face. Although it was early morning, the humidity hung in the air like low hanging rain clouds. "I suppose there's no other way."

"Believe me, there isn't. Shall we go?"

Clair lifted Mom to her feet and forced back the tears that threatened to come at the sight of how weak she was. She knew the chances of Mom, Dad, Heather and her getting out alive were slim. Still, they had to try. Clair and Helen, with Mr. Bones leading the way, staggered forward in the direction of the gunshots.

TWENTY-SIX

Justin

Marshall hadn't raised a dummy, not by a long shot. Justin had no intention of walking into the Retreat alone, not after the guy he spoke to at the front desk, Werner or whatever his name was, some Germanic type, had lied to him, said his mother and father hadn't stayed there. Bullshit! Justin didn't know what the Kraut was trying to pull, but by God, he was going to find out. He flicked open his cell phone and dialed a number.

"State Police."

Justin deepened his voice. "I need to talk with somebody in command. My name's Justin King."

"What's the problem, Mr. King?"

"I believe my mother and father are being held captive at a resort hotel in your area called the Retreat."

"What makes you think that, sir?"

Justin's patience was wearing thin. "Look, I don't have time for idle chatter. I've spent the night driving up from Florida. I need somebody to accompany me to the Retreat to find my parents ... and now!"

His command was greeted on the other end of the line by silence, then, "One moment, sir." Justin heard some muted voices in the background. The dispatcher came back on the line. "Where are you now, Mr. King?"

Justin named the motel where he had stopped to make the call.

"We know where that is. Trooper Cody will meet you in the motel's parking lot in ten minutes, sir. He's on the way now."

Justin hung up and glanced impatiently at his

watch. 6:10 a.m. and unfortunately, no time for breakfast. His prodigious stomach growled in protest. He stepped out of the motel office and paced in front until the trooper pulled in minutes later.

The trooper climbed out of his patrol car and swaggered over to Justin in that tell-tale manner many cops have of walking and showing their authority at the same time. "Mr. King?"

Justin threw him his stern look, one designed to let the trooper know he meant business.

The trooper didn't look impressed. "You have a complaint against the Retreat, the resort at Wicked Stop?" His Southern accent was so thick Justin barely understood him.

"They're holding my parents."

The trooper hooked his thumbs inside his belt. "What makes you think so?"

Justin told him about his conversation with Werner and how he tripped himself up by mentioning Helen.

The trooper listened impassively. "Okay, let's go up there. Follow me in your car. I'll lead the way."

Something held Justin back. "Is it necessary that I go?"

"I don't know what your parents look like, Mr. King. Best you come with me."

Reluctantly, Justin slid behind the wheel of his car and followed the trooper on the journey into the countryside, past the town of Wicked Stop and onto the grounds of the Retreat.

Both men parked in the Retreat's parking lot. Justin recognized his father's Lincoln Town Car and pointed it out.

The trooper indifferently looked the car over and hitched his pants. "Follow me."

Justin was apprehensive. "You familiar with this

place?"

The trooper ignored the question, kept his eyes focused on the path and ambled up the horseshoe driveway, past the water fountain and into the hotel with Justin in tow.

In the lobby Justin showed his mean face, the one meant to let people know he was no pushover. Nobody was going to take advantage of Justin King.

A tall blond-haired man with an engaging smile walked up to Justin and stuck out his hand.

"I'm Werner. Welcome to the Retreat. You must be Mr. King."

Justin's face clouded over. He ignored the proffered hand, instead pointed at Werner and turned to the trooper. "This is the guy I told you about."

"Gentlemen," Werner said in a low voice, "shall we go into a private room to have this discussion? I don't want to upset our guests' breakfast." Werner waved his arm to include the people in the lobby, including a few who were glancing apprehensively at the state cop and the angry Justin.

"Sounds like a winner to me," the trooper drawled. "Let's go."

Werner led them to the reception room off the lobby. Justin marched in with his hands on his hips.

Werner closed the door and turned around. The smile was gone, replaced by a frown of concentration as he examined Justin. "Now, what were you saying?"

The trooper removed his wide-brimmed campaign hat and wiped a sweaty bald head. "This here boy says you holding his ma and pa. That right, Werner?"

Werner beamed. "You mean Mr. and Mrs. King, right?"

"You know damn well that's who I mean," Justin said, really pissed off now, full of false courage with the trooper at his side. He was ready to give this Kraut a piece of his mind.

"Oh hell," Werner said, "sure we got them."

Justin couldn't believe his ears. "You got them?" he asked, a dumb expression painted on his face.

"Why of course." Werner rewarded Justin with a chuckle and another blazing smile.

Justin's face was a kaleidoscope of conflicting emotions. It flashed surprise, then disbelief, then realization.

Justin whirled around to face the trooper. "Arrest this man."

The trooper planted his feet apart, ticked his thumbs inside his belt and stared hard at Justin. "Shut your mouth, nigger."

"You..." he pointed a finger at the trooper. "You said–"

"I said shut your mouth, nigger," the trooper snarled. He unholstered his Glock and pointed it at Justin's face. "You are a nigger, ain't you?"

"Indeed he is," Werner said. "At least part nigger."

"Then he's all nigger to me."

Justin blanched. His heart skipped several beats, his knees weakened. Gone in an instant was the arrogant attitude that so well defined him. In its place was a cascading fear and the growing realization that he was in trouble. Deep, deep trouble. He mustered enough bravado to say, "Goddamn it, I want out of here," and strode toward the door. The trooper reached out and pulled him back by his belt loop. Justin's resistance faded once he turned and saw the hate stamped on the trooper's face.

"What ya'll want to do with this here boy?" the trooper asked Werner.

Werner picked up a room telephone and dialed a number. "Mr. Phester, I think I have another candidate for the hunt. Can you come down to the reception room off the lobby?" He listened for a moment more and winked at Justin.

Justin was afraid to ask but felt compelled to. "What's the hunt?"

Werner chuckled again, but otherwise said nothing, just smiled.

"Need anything else from me, Werner?" the trooper asked.

"Nothing, Cody. You've been a big help as usual. Mr. Phester's going to be pleased. You can expect a little extra something in your paycheck next month."

"Good enough, Werner." The trooper put the campaign hat back on his head and positioned it. "Let me know if there's anything else ya'll need." He swaggered out of the room.

"What's going to happen to me?" Justin asked in a visibly quivering voice.

"Shut up."

Moments later Gilbert entered. He circled Justin and evaluated him.

"Is this our candidate?"

"This is King's boy. You know, the fat old man. His wife's in the hot box. Think he'll do all right for the hunt?"

Justin broke out in a cold sweat. He tried to conceal his shaking hands by pressing them against the sides of his pants.

Gilbert looked doubtful. "Like father, like son. Both of them blubbery whales. Question is whether this young man is too fat to give our hunters a run for their money." Gilbert spoke as if Justin were not in the room. Justin, only now beginning to understand the full implications of the hunt, shuddered.

"We can't have our hunters disappointed in the quarry. The hunt must be worth their time. Particularly for the money they're paying. We want their repeat business."

"Yeah, sure, Mr. Phester, but of the four guys we got for the hunters, one of them, this kid's old man is so out of shape he'll probably have a heart attack out of the gate. One of the others, the real old guy with the white hair, looks sick. Don't know how long he'll hold out. At least this kid's young."

Gilbert tossed the idea around. "Hmm, you have a point ... All right, include this young man ... Now, if you'll excuse me, I'm going to have breakfast with the hunters." With that he wheeled around and left the room.

Werner made another call on his cell phone. "Bobby, get down here, the reception room."

By now Justin's face was ashen and his breath came in short spurts. He eased himself into a chair and squeezed the arms as if they were lifelines.

Bobby swung open the door and paraded into the room. Justin took one look at Bobby's size and the brutal vacant look in his eyes, magnified by the thick lenses of his glasses, and felt as if somebody had gripped his heart and was squeezing the life from it. He was as scared now as he'd ever been in his entire life.

Bobby was pissed. He shook an accusing finger at Werner. "You told me I could screw one of the girls."

"Hey look, Bobby, we got enough problems right now." Werner jerked his head in Justin's direction. "This moron's sister escaped and we got to get ready for the hunt. I'll promise you this, we get the hunt off in good shape and I'll see what I can do with Melissa or one of the other girl attendants to get you taken care of."

"They ain't gonna give me jack shit, you know that. Fuckin' women are scared of me. And if I make them do it, Mr. Phester will kick me out. How about the girls we sold? One of them."

Werner wore a pained expression on his face. "That's just it, Bobby. They don't belong to us anymore. They've all been sold."

"Shit, I'm horny enough to screw a rattlesnake if I could corner it."

Werner looked scared, like a guy trying to stop a runaway bull with a rolled-up newspaper. "Tell you what. We find Clair, the girl who escaped, you can get a crack at that."

Justin's skin crawled.

Bobby's eyes brightened for a moment, then faded. "That ain't gonna work none. She been sold to Harry Phieu. ... Shit!" His eyes found Justin and a light clicked on. "Stand up, fat boy."

Justin rose ponderously to his feet.

Bobby circled him while Justin held his breath. Bobby's hungry eyes roamed Justin's body as if he were a meat inspector examining a side of beef. He walked behind Justin's open-back chair and stared at Justin's broad ass. He licked his lips.

Justin's legs gave out. He fell into the chair and silently beseeched God to rescue him. But God didn't answer. No matter how low Justin scrunched down he couldn't escape Bobby's fierce gaze.

"How about I get me a quickie with this fat ass?"

Werner snapped his fingers; he had found the answer to his problem. "Like the old days in the Milwaukee lockup, eh, Bobby?"

Bobby shrugged his shoulders. "Ass is ass. Gonna get me some now." With reflexes so fast it stunned Justin, Bobby grabbed him with his enormous hands and lifted him from the chair. Justin screeched in protest.

"Wait a second," Werner said. "Let me gag him."

Justin squalled like a baby and Bobby slapped his face. "Shut up, sissy, or I'll tear your fuckin' head off."

Justin, terrified and openly sobbing now, dropped his head as Werner gagged him. The sobs were reduced to an unintelligible choking.

Bobby grabbed Justin's khaki pants at the belt and yanked them down. The buckle raked Justin's protruding stomach and made him squeal.

"Shit, this boy's got an ass on him as big as a hog." As Bobby stared at it his eyes shone with a strange light and his breath came fast. He unbuckled and dropped his pants and bent Justin over the back end of a sofa. Justin's ass stuck high in the air and, knowing what was coming, he tried desperately to protest through the gag. Bobby spread the cheeks of Justin's ass and lunged forward. Justin shrieked and tried to wrench away from Bobby, but he was pinned down. The pain was excruciating. Bobby gripped Justin by the waist and pumped furiously. Justin's whole body shook with rage and pain and humiliation. Moments later Bobby stiffened and came. Then he pulled out. Justin collapsed on the floor, tears streaming down his fat cheeks, his eyes wide with terror and outrage and hurt.

"Okay," Werner said, "that's enough for now. Let's bring him out to the others for the hunt."

"You owe me one of them girls, Werner."

"Yeah, yeah. Don't worry."

Bobby lifted Justin to a standing position and yanked off the gag. "Don't make a fuckin' noise or I'll rip your throat out."

Justin's eyes stung and his guts were on fire. He wanted to double over from the pain. He felt as if he had been repeatedly kicked in the balls and the stomach. He clenched his teeth and stifled an emerging scream.

Werner opened a gun locker in an alcove behind the lobby's main desk and picked up an automatic rifle and a handgun. He tossed the handgun to Bobby who tucked it underneath his belt. The three men left the hotel through a side door out of sight of the buyers in the lobby, with Werner leading the way, Justin stumbling along in the middle, followed by Bobby prodding Justin when he fell off the pace. They traversed a meandering path through woods to the back of the Retreat's property until they came to a clearing about half a mile from the hotel. Here they found two male attendants with holstered guns, standing over four men in chains and shackles. Justin was shocked to see his father among them. He had never seen his father looking so pale and haggard. His clothes were filthy and torn.

"Jesus, Dad, they've hurt me," he whined.

Marshall glanced up at his son with lifeless eyes, the eyes of a defeated man. "They're going to ... going to..." Then, as if the realization of who was talking to him hit home, his eyes widened in surprise. "Justin, it's you." He rose on shaky legs and embraced his son, circling his arms with the shackled hands over Justin's head and around him in a bear hug.

Justin sobbed. His whole body shook.

"How did you get here? What did they do to you?"

Justin looked up with eyes full of tears and pointed a tremulous hand in Bobby's direction. "He ... he ... oh, it hurt so much, Dad."

Marshall caught on right away. He turned to Bobby, enraged, and shook his fist. "You ... you scum." He was immediately taken aback by his outburst, his sudden boldness, and cowered in fear.

Bobby smirked and playfully slapped aside Marshall's hand. "Better watch out old man, your ass looks pretty good, too."

The attendants chuckled uneasily and looked away from Justin.

"You animal," Marshall said. His eyes spat venom

at Bobby.

"Shut up," one of the attendants warned and cuffed Marshall on the back of his head. Marshall uncharacteristically took a feeble swing at the attendant's hand. The attendant shoved Marshall to the ground.

Werner grinned. "Well for Christ sake, look what fat old man's suddenly grown a pair of balls."

Bobby ignored Marshall and shoved Justin, who plopped on the ground with the other men, curled into a fetal ball and held his hands over his head in a protective gesture. Marshall dropped to the ground and cradled his son in his lap.

Werner glanced around nervously. "The hunters. Are they in position?"

One of the attendants shrugged his shoulders. Werner snapped open his cell phone and called Gilbert. "We've got the quarry ready, Mr. Phester."

Werner listened and nodded. "Sure thing, I'll accompany the hunters soon as I release the game." He glanced at the men gathered around him on the ground, a chilling smile creasing his face.

"Yes, sir," he said to something Gilbert told him, then flipped the cell phone closed and addressed the men on the ground:

"Okay listen up. All five of you turkeys are invited to the hunt. Not as hunters, but as the quarry." He laughed at his own cruel joke.

Steve Lawson, the teenage boy, joined Justin in a chorus of despondent crying. The old man, Dodge, the one with the white hair, tried to console both young men.

"You son of a bitching skinhead," Billy Ray said.

"Flattery will get you nowhere, redneck. Now I suggest all you morons listen carefully because the hunters are on the way and every minute you waste is one minute less head start you get."

Rapt attention now. Every head turned to Werner.

"Here's the rules. You get a fifteen-minute start. You'll be on foot, but so will the hunters."

"Do we get weapons?" Dodge asked. His face appeared ashen and the etched lines of pain on his face showed how advanced the cancer was that had invaded his body.

Werner snorted. "Sure, Dodge, you old fart, and what else can I get you? How about a jeep? Maybe an Uzi, a hand grenade?"

Billy Ray winced. "No weapons. That's not much of a chance."

"That's all you get, redneck. Unless you'd prefer to take your chances with Bobby."

Billy Ray stole a look at Bobby and averted his eyes.

"Let's get it over with," Dodge said. He and Billy Ray exchanged meaningful glances.

"Sensible move," Werner said, missing the exchange between Billy Ray and Dodge. "Bobby, unlock their chains. Everybody else stand back."

The attendants unholstered their handguns and moved away from the men on the ground. Werner aimed his automatic rifle at Billy Ray and the others and stood back.

Bobby bent over and unlocked Dodge's chains. The old man lurched to his feet and rubbed his wrists. While Bobby was distracted unlocking the chains of the other three men, Dodge snatched the handgun from Bobby's belt. A sudden spasm made the white-haired old man grasp his belly with one hand. With the other hand shaking badly he pointed the handgun at Bobby and pulled the trigger. A shot rang out, hitting Bobby in the fleshy part of the upper arm. Bobby grunted and lifted his arm, gazed in astonishment at the flesh wound like an idiot examining a bug. Werner, taken by surprise, opened fire on automatic. Several slugs tore through Dodge. He stutter stepped and dropped to the ground.

Bobby stood over Dodge, looking dumbfounded. He held his wounded arm and gazed at Dodge in disbelief. "You son of a bitch, you shot me." Bobby kicked the lifeless body.

Dodge's escape attempt was not sufficient to distract the two male attendants. When Billy Ray sprang to his feet they cocked their handguns and pointed them at him. Billy Ray was too far away from either of them to jump them. He dropped his arms in a gesture of surrender.

Justin took one look around him and his eyes rolled back is his head. He fainted.

Werner smiled. "Let the hunt begin."

TWENTY-SEVEN

Billy Ray

No matter how Billy Ray prodded and tugged Marshall, coaxing the heavy man forward, Marshall stumbled along in a daze, at a pace suitable for disabled seniors in a nursing home, not for men being pursued through the woods by vicious hunters intent upon killing them. Tears, brought about by the frustration of his predicament, mingled with sweat on Marshall's cheeks and meandered down his cheeks in broken rivulets, then dripped to the ground. Every few minutes his knees buckled and Billy Ray or Steve was forced to support him, to keep the large man from crashing to the matted floor of the woods.

Billy Ray had to give the devil his due. Regardless of how many times the old man pooped out, he got back up again and plodded forward. Marshall refused to call it quits.

Justin, was not noticeably faster. Like his father, he was too heavy for this sudden exertion, a major candidate for a heart attack.

Billy Ray cursed to himself. Not that the lawman wished problems on either of his wards, but both obese men were holding up their escape. He found it hard to believe that Clair came from the same family as these two. She was so strong, so positive, and these two men so weak, so dependent. He shook his head in disbelief.

Thinking of Clair was a momentary respite from his current troubles. He recognized his attraction to her, wanted very much to see her again. Wistfully he imagined the two sharing a pleasant hour over coffee on the veranda of a Starbucks café (to prove he wasn't *all* redneck), both of them laughing at something silly one or the other said. Normal people doing normal things in normal conditions.

Normal conditions. The phrase almost made him gag. He was no longer sure there was any such thing as normal conditions. And even if there was, this sure as hell was at the opposite extreme. What he needed, and needed badly, was a drink. His mouth watered at the thought of a tumbler of Jack Daniel's or Jim Beam on the rocks. He could smell the booze, feel the comforting heft of the tumbler, taste the delicious liquid as it trickled down his throat.

He licked his lips and with an act of sheer will drove the thought of booze from his mind. Knew that if he continued visualizing the delectable process of drinking that he would bolt. Just up and leave the Kings and Steve and run, not walk, to the nearest bar or liquor store and drown in booze.

"Take a break," Billy Ray called out. Marshall and his son Justin lurched to a halt and dropped to the ground as heavily as sacks of potatoes. Steve, exhausted from helping Billy Ray prop up Marshall and Justin, bent over, grasped his knees and sucked in gobs of air. Billy Ray kneeled down and rested on one knee. All four men were soaked, shirts and pants wringing wet and faces bathed in sweat, as if they had just stepped out of a steam bath.

Marshall panted. "I ... can't ... catch ... my ... breath."

Billy Ray checked the woods behind him and impatiently took a fast look at his watch. His voice was tense. "In about five minutes the hunters are going to be turned loose. Believe me, you don't want to be around when they find us."

"Give me a minute," Marshall said between wheezes. "I'll be ready to go."

Justin's eyes rolled back in his head. "I don't know if I can go on."

"Goddamn it, it's either go on or die," Billy Ray spat out. Justin's defeatist attitude was getting to him; he detested being around babies disguised as grown men. Particularly in times of crisis. He took a deep breath and said in a calmer voice, "Look, this ain't working. You two are just too slow. We got to split up. Otherwise the hunters will catch up and bag all four of us."

Steve leaned back against a scrub pine tree and wiped his face with the tail of his shirt. "Will they use dogs? If they do, splitting up won't do any good."

Billy Ray shook his head in frustration. "Damn it, we don't have much choice. The way we're going right now we might as well sit down here and wait to die."

"Sorry, I didn't mean anything. You're right, let's get out of here now." As if to emphasize the point, Steve rose. "Which way?"

Billy Ray pointed in a westerly direction. "These woods and fields go on for about five miles, maybe a little less."

Justin moaned. "Jesus, five miles, I can't march that far."

Billy Ray's mouth was dry. He squinted through the canopy of the forest to peer at the sun. It beat down on them relentlessly, streaming through the openings in the trees, baking the forest and everything in it. Billy Ray felt as if he were being fried in an oven, knew they couldn't hold out much longer without water, not in this heat and humidity. Not as long as they continued to march, if that's what you wanted to call it. Marshall and Justin would collapse soon enough anyway.

"Look, I've got an idea. I'm going to hide you two. That way Steve and I can move faster. We stand a chance to get away, bring back the cops. If we have to take you two with us ... let me be frank, we're all dead."

Justin sneered. "Sure, who cares about a couple of niggers? You gonna feed us darkies to the hunters so you white folk can get away."

Billy Ray felt the blood surge to his face, felt its heat. "C'mon, cut the racist crap. That's bullshit." Angry, he jumped up from his kneeling position. "Listen, city boy, you and your old man are going do exactly as I tell you. If you want to live, that is. Otherwise, you're on your own." Realizing that he was snarling at the two helpless men, he softened his tone. "Don't want to be so blunt, but there it is, take it or leave it."

Marshall made a noise that was part sigh, part sob. "Got to do what the man says, Justin. He's right. You and me'll never make it this way."

Billy Ray didn't wait for a response from Justin. "Saddle up."

Justin didn't move, looked as if he had given up. Marshall stirred, struggled to get to his feet.

Billy Ray helped Marshall stand. Steve grabbed Justin and dragged him to his feet, cursing Justin all the while. Justin protested feebly but did as he was told. The four men forged through woods thick with undergrowth until they heard a gunshot from some distance behind them.

"The hunters," Billy Ray said and froze, his eyes wide with concern.

"Jesus, God, they're going to get us," Justin said, swearing now like his father. Sweat rolled down his fat cheeks, plowing new tracks through the dirt caked on his face. Billy Ray felt a mixture of contempt and sympathy for the kid.

"Quick, up ahead," Billy Ray pointed to a rock outcrop along a ridge partially hidden by overgrown holly bushes. The four men clambered up until they reached the outcrop, dodging the needle-sharp points of the holly leaves, cursing when the points pierced their skin. Billy Ray scooted around, searching the ridge while the others stopped to gather their breath. Steve followed him. "What're you doing?" he asked.

Billy Ray said, "I used to go small game hunting around here. There's a cave somewhere along this ridge." He poked through the holly bushes.

"Here it is," he said excitedly and pushed aside a jumble of shrubs. The entrance to the cave was just large enough to crawl through. "I got caught in a bad thunderstorm. Holed up here for a couple of hours. It's really nothing more than a crawlspace for a few people but high enough to sit up. It's a good place to hide. You have to be right on top of it to see the cave entrance."

Another gunshot shattered the morning air, this one closer than the last.

"Let's get those two inside."

Billy Ray and Steve scrambled down the slope and guided Marshal and Justin back up to the mouth of the cave.

"Get in there," Billy Ray directed. "You'll be safe until we come get you. Just keep quiet regardless of what you hear. And, for God's sake, whatever you do, don't come out of the cave."

"Jesus," Justin said in a trembling voice. "The hunters will find us."

"Not if you're quiet," Billy Ray assured Justin, although he wasn't at all certain. If they had dogs, well ... But he hadn't heard any dogs barking. A sign that disturbed him. Why no dogs? It made sense on a hunt. But then again, Billy Ray had never been included in a hunt sponsored by the Retreat (thank the good Lord) and wasn't familiar with its hunting protocol.

"Don't leave us, please," Justin whimpered.

Billy Ray pointed to the mouth of the cave. "Inside! Now!"

Marshall and Justin dropped to their knees and crawled inside the cave, Justin bitching and moaning every step of the way. "I don't want to die."

"Best you keep quiet," Billy Ray hissed at Justin, "or the hunters will hear you when they close in. They're not far behind now." He dropped to his knees and peered inside the cave. "Marshall, you okay?"

Marshall's voice floated out of the cave. "We'll make it. Hurry up and get out of here. Find the cops."

"We're going now." With that Billy Ray rose to his feet and shinnied down the hill, Steve in tow.

The two hiked at a fast clip for the better part of a half-hour, their breath coming fast, hearts pumping hard to sustain the physical activity, sweat pouring from their exhausted bodies. Neither talking. After negotiating a ravine, Billy Ray climbed its banks and halted. He held up his arm to halt Steve.

The kid gave Billy Ray a quizzical look. "What's–"

"Shh," Billy Ray whispered.

Both men stood as still as corpses, breathing through their mouths to keep from making noise. Billy Ray pointed ahead of him and whispered, "See it?"

Steve combed the woods in front of him, saw nothing. He shrugged his shoulders.

"Look closer."

Steve peered ahead, searching. His eyebrows shot up. "Yeah, there's some kind of ... I don't know. A box maybe?"

"It's a blind."

"You mean, like hunters use."

"Exactly. Like hunters use."

Steve sucked in his breath, glanced about and shivered, despite the heat.

Billy Ray now understood why no dogs. Werner had positioned hunters or attendants around the periphery of the hunting area to contain their quarry.

He whispered to Steve to remain where he was and crept forward in a crouched position to examine the blind. And dropped to the ground when he heard the sound of the lever of a rifle being cocked. From a prone position, Billy Ray twisted around and signaled Steve to flatten himself on the ground.

Too late.

The crack of a rifle shattered the humid air and Steve's head exploded in a grisly mist of bone, brain and blood. His body plopped to the ground in the grotesque imitation of a rag doll being flung aside.

Billy Ray, pulse hammering in his temples, snaked his way into a trench. The rifle cracked again and dirt near his head exploded. He crawled inside the trench and climbed out the other side.

To find Harry Phieu waiting for him. The huge bald Asian had a radiant smile creasing his face. His bald head glistened with sweat.

"Today's my lucky day. I'm bagging twice my limit." He lifted the Winchester 30-30 lever action rifle to his shoulder and peered down at Billy Ray through the rifle's sites. Then lowered the rifle slightly. "Don't I know you?"

"I'm the law. Shoot me and the cops and feds will hunt you down regardless of where you are."

Harry grinned and raised the rifle back to his shoulder.

"Wait, don't!" Billy Ray pleaded. Under the cover of brush his hand clasped around a fist-sized rock.

Harry grunted. "Got something important to say, like 'Please sir, don't kill me?'"

Billy Ray tried to imitate a frightened man. He didn't have to try hard. "Something like that."

Harry's smile broadened. Clearly savoring the moment, he slowly reached up and slid his right hand sensuously along the stock of the rifle and into the trigger guard. He wrapped his finger around the trigger.

But toying with Billy Ray distracted him. It was the opening Billy Ray was praying for. He smashed the rock against Harry's knee. Harry howled with pain and stumbled backward. His hands flew outward to balance himself, the rifle clutched in one hand. Billy Ray jumped out of the trench and slammed the rock into Harry's forehead. Harry, stunned, dropped the rifle. Billy Ray scooped it up and backpedaled twenty feet away from Harry along the edge of the trench.

Harry was enraged by Billy Ray's unexpected aggressive actions. Despite the blood flowing from his forehead into his eyes, and a damaged knee, he roared and charged. All two-hundred sixty-five pounds of him, a frightening spectacle. Billy Ray snapped the rifle to his shoulder and squeezed the trigger. The rifle cracked. A spot of blood saturated Harry's khaki shirt on his breastbone and slowed his lunge. He tottered forward, held his hands over the wound and peered down at it, eyes opened wide in utter amazement, then looked up into Billy Ray's eyes. The two men stared at each other like town idiots, shocked to be in the same place at the same time and fighting for their lives, knowing that only one of them was going to come out alive.

Rage gathered in Harry's face like a rapidly approaching storm, twisting it out of shape. "You ... you," he yelled and charged Billy Ray again. This time he managed to knock the rifle sideways so the barrel was pointed over his shoulder. He fell on Billy Ray and the air whooshed out of Billy Ray's lungs.

Harry raised his arm and brought his fist crashing down. Billy Ray deflected the blow with his forearm. Harry raised his arm to strike again and Billy Ray thrust his hand forward and jammed his thumb into

Harry's eye socket. Harry screeched in agony and flew backwards. Billy Ray rolled out from under Harry and scooped up the rifle.

Harry rose on unsteady legs. By now, blood had stained the entire front of his shirt. He grasped his chest as if from a sudden bolting pain, sank to his knees and crashed sideways to the ground. Billy Ray kneeled and felt for a pulse, found one weak and fluttering, figured the big man was moments away from death.

He rose and slung the rifle over his shoulder. A sudden craving for a cold beer laced with a double shot of bourbon was so palpable and overwhelming that he wanted to cry out. He stood quietly with his eyes shut tight until the urge faded. Then took one uneasy look around him, threw a flickering glance at Harry Phieu's inert body before tramping away through the woods.

TWENTY-EIGHT

Marshall

Justin and Marshall heard the shots. Justin fell to his knees and clung to the wall of the cave and shrilled like a mortally injured animal.

"Mother of God," Marshall prayed under his breath so as not to frighten his son, "give us strength in our hour of need."

"Jesus, Dad, they're coming to get us." Justin trembled with the force of a dog shaking off water. He shut his eyes tight and sobbed.

Marshal knew that if both he and his son panicked, they might bolt from the cave in blind terror and be gunned down by the hunters. "The shot came from a distance, from the direction Billy Ray was going, not from the Retreat, where the hunters are coming from."

Between choking sobs, Justin said, "What's that got to do with anything?"

"It could be good news. Maybe Billy Ray ran into some hunters after game, real hunters, not those white goons from the Retreat. Hunters that will help us escape this hell hole."

"Maybe it means something happened to Billy Ray."

"C'mon, Son, take it easy. Don't let your imagination run away with you." But he wasn't sure himself, believed in fact that Billy Ray might now be dead or captured.

"Oh my God, don't you understand, Dad? They're going to kill us." Justin bent over, sobbing uncontrollably, drooling, snot dripping from his nose. He pissed his pants and the smell of urine permeated the cave making Marshall breathe threw his mouth to avoid the stink. Watching his son steadily lose his manhood, reduced to a sniveling baby, wrenched his heart, suffused him with an overpowering impulse to raise his fist to God and curse him for allowing this to happen.

Instead, Marshall glanced at his son in sorrow. How had Justin come to this? And immediately was struck with the punishing realization that he was partially, if not fully, responsible for his son's cowardice.

A coward. What Marshall had been all his live. A craven coward, hiding behind the cloak of racism to make excuses for his personal failings. Now, for the first time in his life, he acknowledged with regret the many professional opportunities his caustic attitude had cost him over the years.

And not only professional. As he held his convulsively weeping son, Marshall's thoughts drifted to Clair. With a wrench in his heart, he now saw how he had foolishly driven a wedge between himself and his bright, loving daughter while doting exclusively on his son. It dawned on Marshall that not once had he bothered to hide his preference for Justin, that Clair always came in a distant second in his affections and thoughts.

"Jesus, how could I be so stupid?"

"What's that, Dad?"

Marshall patted his son's arm. "Nothing, Son. Go ahead and rest now."

When Justin fell into a restless sleep, Marshall opened the floodgates of his past: how Justin attended Notre Dame for his undergraduate degree in accounting and the Wharton School for his graduate MBA, Marshall paying the full freight, while Clair struggled to pay her way through pre-med at Ohio

State. How much that must have devastated her, how terrible she must have felt. It all sunk home now with a razor-sharp stitch of guilt that sliced through his consciousness so sharp that it brought tears to his eyes.

And Helen. Jesus, he had neglected her, treated her almost like an adversary. In the clearness of the moment that sudden insight brings, Marshall understood how jealous he was of her really magnificent accomplishments as an architect. He recognized how she must have struggled to break down racial barriers to achieve her position, while he stood idly by, blaming his own lack of accomplishments on race.

Helen. Clair. Even that poor girl, Heather. God, if he had them here, right now, he'd crush them in a bear-like embrace, tell them how much he loved them, promise them the old grouch they knew so well would never again reappear.

But, of course, all that was wishful thinking.

Another gunshot ruptured the calm of the forest. Justin shot up, his eyes wild with fright. "They're coming for us, Dad." He started to bawl again.

Marshall tried smiling at Justin to reassure him, but felt his lips tremble as if they were in revolt for the lies that were about to spew forth from his mouth. "No reason to panic, Son. The shot might have nothing to do with Billy Ray. In the woods sounds carry." Marshall knew how feeble his reasoning sounded. But he had to bring Justin back from the edge of sheer terror, before he fell over the cliff into a state of babbling insanity. He patted his son's arm. "Trust your old man. We're going to be okay. Hey, has your old man ever let you down?"

Justin's sobbing eased. His eyes pleaded with his father to protect him, to tell him how this nightmare would soon be behind them, some sugarcoated bullshit, anything to ease his fear. His voice, when it emerged, was reminiscent of Justin as a child: squeaky, unsure, scared of the world. "How do you know we won't get hurt?"

Marshall wrapped Justin in his arms. "Hey, I just know, okay? I'm your old man and I know everything." He kept the tone of his voice light, fought incipient panic, prayed to God he could maintain his equanimity, enough at least to ease his son's dread of the horror that lie outside their cave and the test of their courage that might soon follow.

Marshall was amazed to find that he had reached deep within himself to tap a hidden well of strength, one he never before this moment knew existed. He was scared shitless, that hadn't changed, but instead of collapsing in the face of danger, he now thought more clearly and fought the fear that threatened to engulf him. Marshall silently thanked the good Lord for this newly found power.

"Look, Son, Billy Ray told us to stay here, but that was before we heard the shots. Maybe it means nothing, but then again, maybe it means the hunters are closer than we thought. What we're going to do is stay here until the coast is clear, then I'm going to make a break for it, just like Billy Ray did. Go in the same direction."

Justin grabbed his father's arm and squeezed. "And leave me here by myself?" His eyes were wide with fright.

"You'll be safe here, I promise. I'll be back with the police before you know it."

"Jesus, Dad, don't desert me."

Marshall's heart shattered. He gripped Justin and stared into his eyes. "Listen to me, Son. I'll *never* desert you, *never*. Do you understand?"

Marshall's resolve spilled over into his son. "I know, Dad."

They threw their arms around each other in a life-affirming hug.

"I'm so scared, Dad."

Marshall patted his son's back. "I know, Son, I know."

At least Justin had stopped sobbing, Marshall thought. "Don't worry, we're going to get out of this mess. And rescue your sister and mother. And Heather, of course. Don't you worry." He continued talking to Justin in a soft melodic way while gently rocking the boy to sleep as he had done so many times when Justin was a baby. Justin held on tight to his father and gradually relaxed.

Father and son clung to each other and, in the relative coolness and safety of the cave, Marshall fell asleep, his exhausted body demanding rest.

TWENTY-NINE

Clair

It was becoming harder to make any time. As Clair and Helen and Mr. Bones trudged through the forest, the undergrowth of weeds, shrubs and bushes grew higher and thicker, and it was often necessary to stop and clear a path before resuming their trek. A task that exhausted both Clair and Mr. Bones.

They hadn't plodded more than a couple of miles when Helen gave out. Despite being supported by Clair and Mr. Bones, her legs finally trembled and collapsed. The two lowered Helen to the ground and propped her up against a tree in the shade. Clair noticed that her mother's breathing came in hot spurts.

The heat was brutal. The trio had tried to walk under the canopy of trees and avoid open fields. But even within the forest, the air was heavy and humid and blistering hot.

"Mom needs water."

Mr. Bones screwed open the water bottle he was carrying and brought it to Helen's parched lips. She sipped until he gently tugged the bottle away. Mr. Bones wet a handkerchief and passed it to Clair who wiped her mother's brow. "She's burning up." Helen rested her head against a tree and instantly fell into a restless sleep. Groaning with the effort, Clair and Mr. Bones eased themselves to the ground next to her.

"We'll let her rest for a few minutes," Clair said, looking with concern at her mother.

Mr. Bones nodded. "Drink?" He offered Clair the canteen.

"Any other water around here?" She stared

hungrily at the canteen and licked her dry lips.

"If there is, I don't know about it. This canteen is it unless we get lucky."

Clair sighed and reached for the canteen. She drank a little and swirled it around her mouth before swallowing. Then leaned back against a tree and closed her eyes. "God, I didn't realize the world could be this savage."

Mr. Bones smiled sadly. It stretched the taut skin of his face and made him appear more skeleton-like than ever. "My dear, savagery is the way of the world. You Americans, at least your generation of Americans, do not understand this. If I can be so bold, you think thousands of years of history do not apply to you."

"We're not really that naïve, are we? Isn't that an exaggeration?"

"Even the most rudimentary examination of history will reveal man's inhumanity to man. It's never changed. From the days of the cave men to these heady days of cyberspace and rockets to the outer stars, killing has been the one thread of human history that's remained constant."

"I thought all of that ... war stuff was behind us, that we're living in a golden age of peace, a time where the nations of the world are coming together to form a world government."

"Like here, like now?"

"I see your point. But what's happening at the Retreat, selling women into slavery and prostitution, it's unreal. It has to be an exception."

"There's nothing unreal about what we're facing now and the harsh reality of Gilbert Phester. Or that brute Bobby." The smile dropped from his face and he hugged himself as if to ward off evil images. "And I'm almost ashamed to say, my own profession."

"White slavery."

"Indeed, white slavery. Prostitution. Indentured servants. It goes by many names. It's been with us since time immemorial and it's not going away anytime soon, if ever."

Clair's brow wrinkled. "Why are you so cynical?"

"Because of my background. I'm as captive to it as you are to yours."

"I don't understand."

"You're an upper middle-class American which, by definition, is somebody who hasn't felt the brutality of the world." Mr. Bones folded his legs underneath him. "I come from the subcontinent, from an Indian family living in the Kashmir. When I was twelve my parents were killed in brutal assaults by Pakistanis. I had to steal food, sell my body, to survive. I lost my brother, murdered by bandits. My two sisters were sold into prostitution thirty years ago. I've never seen them since, and don't know if they're dead or alive."

Clair touched his arm. "I'm so sorry."

"Thank you for that, but it's not the point. The life I've led is not unusual. Possibly four or five of the six billion people on this planet lead lives comparable to mine." His voice was free of rancor.

"I find that hard to believe."

"As I knew you would."

Clair examined Mr. Bones. "You speak English beautifully. You must have risen above your environment."

Mr. Bones gave Clair a cursory smile. "I won't tell you how, but I managed to scrape together enough money to come to the states and attend Northeastern University on a needs scholarship. After graduation I spent some time in the states before returning to India, so I understand your language and customs well."

"Well enough to twist them around to suit your awful business." Clair reddened. "Sorry, I shouldn't have said that."

"No offense taken. As to your comment, if it isn't me, there are many behind me willing, indeed anxious, to take my place. White slavery can be a lucrative business."

"You don't sound especially repentant."

"That's because I'm really not. I said before I was '*almost* ashamed,' to be in this business, not 'ashamed.' I've made my living, and a good one from it for eighteen years."

"I find your blasé acceptance of slavery hard to understand. The misery it creates. When I think of what might yet happen to Mom, Heather and me..."

"That's right, you don't understand, although it's all around you. Cruelty and degradation form the boundaries of the human experience. Murder, rape, genocide. In fact, the history of your country is a picture of bloodshed and persecution. From destroying whole tribes of Indians to lynching blacks. And, of course, your wars. Of which you've had many."

"None of that makes white slavery right. Or any other crime."

"What you don't see, the point you're missing, is that crime will always be with us and killing is as natural as breathing. Someday, even you Americans in your own homeland will have to kill to survive."

"I don't know if I could ever kill anybody."

"Not even to save your mother? Your father?"

"I just ... don't know."

"You may have to, and that time may be soon. Perhaps as quickly as today or tomorrow, if we are to escape."

The blood rushed from Clair's face. "I hope – pray – you're wrong. I don't know if I'm strong enough."

Mr. Bones gave Clair a knowing grin. "You see what's happened to you, of course?"

"What do you mean?"

"I would venture to guess that just a few short days ago, before you entered the Retreat and all the horrors it's held for you and your family, you never would have said about killing, 'I don't know if I'm strong enough.' You would have dismissed the possibility outright, would have felt positively nauseous at the very thought. The horrible events you're immersed in are shaping you. Even though you're unaware of it."

"I'm not so sure."

"There was an English philosopher, Hobbes, I believe, who said something like 'Men's lives are nasty, brutish and short.' He was describing the typical human condition."

"You make living sound so ... so base. Like animals grubbing around killing each other for food and shelter."

"You've put your finger right on it. The exact thought. Animals killing each other. Beneath the thin veneer of civility, that's what humans are and what they do best."

"I don't buy it. Whatever happened to love, to trust?"

"There is an old Italian proverb, 'To trust is good, not to trust is better.'"

Before Clair could issue a sarcastic reply, the sound of a gunshot startled them and ended their introspective conversation. Helen, leaning against a tree, groaned and rose to a sitting position, fear blooming in her eyes.

"Where did that come from?" Clair asked.

Mr. Bones crouched on the ground. His eyes darted every which way and his nostrils flared. "We better go now."

Together they lifted Helen. Her eyes were unfocused and she mumbled incoherently. The three pushed deeper into the forest, Helen in the center, supported by Mr. Bones on one side, Clair on the other. Nobody spoke. There was nothing further to say.

THIRTY

Werner

When Billy Ray shot and killed Harry Phieu, the hunters, not more than a few hundred yards away, heard the gunshot and rushed to the point of its sound, impatient for the kill, expecting that a fellow hunter had cornered one of the prey.

Werner, already jittery and riding an adrenaline high from gunning down Dodge, was first on the scene. He searched the area knowing that Harry had staked out the same part of the woods during the last hunt, had bagged a kill, a young guy about nineteen. Not an easy feat since the kid had been unusually fast on his feet, with the moves of a pivoting running back in the NFL. So Werner was on the lookout for Harry standing over the body of Billy Ray, or that old fat nigger or his chump nigger son. Maybe both.

What Werner really wanted to find was a dead-as-a-doornail Billy Ray. He hated that son of a bitch with an undying passion, recalled all the times Billy Ray had barbed him, figuratively spit in his face.

He was equally afraid of the lawman, knew intuitively that he'd be a hard man to bring down. Despite Billy Ray's boozing, Werner wasn't at all sure how a face off against him would turn out.

What he found shook him to the core: the body of Harry Phieu lying in a ditch, a gunshot wound to the chest, one eye gouged out. Deader than Werner's highly touted philosopher, Nietzsche.

Werner sucked in his breath and dropped to a crouch, waited motionless. When he was reasonably certain Billy Ray wasn't hiding in the woods and taking a bead on him, he rose to his feet and futilely searched the area, looking for Harry's Winchester 30-30. What he discovered was the grisly remains of Steve a few yards away. But no sign of Billy Ray or the two King men.

The four hunters came running up, panting, out of breath.

"Holy shit." The first hunter on the scene was a tall well-built guy with broad shoulders. The best in-shape of the bunch. He stared with horror at Steve's body, then Harry Phieu's.

Werner told them the kid was one of the guys they were hunting. The hunters paid scant attention to his corpse, gravitated instead to Harry Phieu's body.

"My God," the second hunter whispered. He was a fifty-year old businessman gone to fat, and one of Gilbert's long time flesh peddlers. "That's Harry Phieu. Who killed him?"

Werner was about to give him some cock and bull story when the third hunter, another white slaver and a mean bastard with a mouth to match, crooked his rifle in his arm. "Know what this means, don't ya? One of these guys we were huntin' killed Harry. And Harry was one strong and smart son of a bitch. If Harry Phieu came out second best, no tellin' where we'll wind up. This whole huntin' thing don't look none too good to me right now."

"You're saying one of the guys we were hunting killed Harry?" asked the first hunter.

"Who else could have done this big guy in?" the third hunter replied. "His mother? For Christ sake, wake up and smell the blood."

"Goddamn," the fourth hunter said, "whoever killed him is still on the loose. Could be around here, drawing a bead on one of us as we speak." He licked his lips and glanced around him nervously, living up to his reputation as a worrier that had earned him the nickname "Nervous Nellie."

The other hunters cocked wary eyes in every direction. All Werner saw was a forest of trees and bushes. Nothing to worry about, he kept on repeating to himself as he stood there dripping sweat, nothing to worry about. Besides, can't let these guys get spooked. If they split, there goes the hunt ... and my ass along with it. Sure as shit, Mr. Phester'll blame it on me. "Hey, c'mon guys, no reason to get jumpy. We'll get whoever–"

"Don't give us that bullshit, Werner," the third hunter said. "This wasn't supposed to happen. If Harry could catch a bullet so could any of us."

"Yeah, look at him," the first hunter said. "Right in the heart. Damned good shot."

"Hey," the second hunter said and snapped his fingers, "isn't one of the guys we're hunting a former lawman?" His triple chin waddled every time he spoke.

"Now that you mention it, yeah he is," the first hunter said. "Or was. Town police chief, something like that."

Nervous Nellie shuffled his feet in a jittery rhythm. "Guy like that would have a lot of training in killing people. Maybe through the cops. Maybe he once was Special Forces, Seals. Lots of cops get their training in the military."

Werner said, "Listen, I know this guy. He's a rummy. Stays drunk most of the time. Nothing to worry about. Besides, we don't know he was the one who killed Harry."

"He sure as hell ain't drunk now," the third hunter replied. "Which means the fucker's probably hunting us. Using Harry's rifle."

"I don't know about the rest of you guys," Nervous Nellie said, "but I'm getting the hell out of here."

"Best idea you've had all day," said the second hunter. "And I'm headed right to Gilbert Phester and demand my money back. ... Or else." He cocked his rifle to emphasize the point.

The other hunters grumbled their agreement and edged away from Harry's body.

"Let's haul ass," Nervous Nellie said, real edgy now. His worried gaze took in the thick woods surrounding them. "If somebody's hunting us, we're great targets, clustered around like this, yapping our heads off."

The hunters formed a single file and marched away, throwing looks of concern behind them as if they didn't trust Werner to cover their backs.

"Hey, c'mon," Werner cried out after them, in a near panic now. "I'll go after the lawman. You guys keep on the hunt. Got two fat niggers for you to bag."

The hunters didn't reply. They continued scurrying away, guns at the ready, peering into the woods along their flanks as they left, afraid that whoever shot Harry Phieu, probably that ex-lawman, would shoot them down, too.

Werner, left behind, struggled with himself, made a decision, yelled, "Hey, wait for me," and ran after the hunters. Really anxious now, goose flesh rising on his arms, he raced to catch up.

Never had anything gone as wrong as this in Werner's short but illustrious career at the Retreat, and he feared for his life. Part of Werner yearned to go back to the relative safety of the Retreat, part of him screamed to make a run for it through the woods. Both options stank, but he chose the familiar as opposed to the daring. The story of Werner's life.

The hunters made a lot of noise crashing through the underbrush. Werner accelerated until he was fifty yards ahead of them, wanting to put as much distance between them and him as possible, scared that the noise the hunters were making would attract Billy Ray if he was in the vicinity. He circled a clump of trees ... and came to a dead stop.

On the ground in front of him lay the two King women and Mr. Bones, the Indian Mr. Phester was looking for. All three appeared to be prostrated by heat exhaustion.

An idea flashed in Werner's; he saw a way to redeem himself with Mr. Phester. He pointed the rifle at the three, none of whom made any effort to resist him. The old lady was either passed out or asleep. Her daughter, the bitch who flew the coop twice and made Werner look like an asshole, was awake but leaning against a tree and appearing as if she didn't have an ounce of strength left in her.

The third person, Mr. Bones, slowly reached underneath his shirt. Werner slapped the barrel of his rifle against the Indian's arm. The thirty-eight revolver dropped out of the Indian's hand. Werner reached down and picked it up and slipped it inside his pants pocket.

Moments later the four hunters thrashed their way through the underbrush and came upon the scene.

"What the hell!" said the first hunter.

"These aren't game," Werner was quick to say.

"Who in hell are they?" the third hunter demanded to know.

Werner fidgeted. "Why don't you guys return to the Retreat? I'll take these three in myself. They're escaped criminals."

"They don't look too dangerous to me," the second hunter, the fat man, said. "Two women and a skinny old goat."

"Look," Werner insisted, "I've got to take these people in."

"Before you do, let me tell you something," Mr.

Bones said, rushing the words in his sing-song Indian accent.

"Hey, I recognize you," said the second hunter, staring at Mr. Bones. "You're one of us, a buyer, the guy called Mr. Bones. I sat at the table next to yours last night."

"None other." Mr. Bones mock bowed from the ground.

The third hunter, the cynical one, snapped his fingers. "You know, I remember now. You started the bidding last night. Saw you last quarter, too. Bought yourself a pair of pretty redhead twins. You don't look too good right now. What happened?"

"He's what happened." Mr. Bones pointed at Werner and winced as he touched the bruise on his arm.

"Wait a goddamn minute," Werner said. "What is this shit? This bag of bones tried to hold Mr. Phester up last night. He's a fucking thief."

"As I was saying before Werner rudely interrupted me," Mr. Bones continued, "his esteemed boss, Glibert Phester, pulled a fast one on every buyer at the auction last night. He prearranged with Harry Phieu to buy the virgin regardless of how many other buyers outbid him."

The hunters stared hard at Werner.

He backed up defensively. "That's a crock of shit. Fucking Indian's lying."

"Maybe," the third hunter said, "and maybe not. I never trusted that wimp Phester, anyway. Too dainty, too woman-like. Looks like a faggot."

"And I don't trust you, Werner," the second hunter added, his chins wobbling. "That phony smile."

Mr. Bones raised his hand. "I overheard Phester and his mother arrange with Harry Phieu to pay no more than half-a-million for the girl."

The cords in Werner's neck stood out. "Goddamn it, that can't be true. I—"

"Shut up, Werner," Nervous Nellie said. "Let Mr. Bones talk."

"If you recall three buyers bid $850,000 or over, one as high as $950,000. Phester sold the virgin to Harry Phieu at $1,000,000, but Harry paid only $500,000. Ask Phester to see his sales record. The man is compulsive; he records everything."

Werner advanced on Mr. Bones. Hunter number one, the strongest of the four, stepped in between them, his rifle saddled in the crook of his arm. "Keep your pants on, Werner. There's a way to settle this. We'll all visit Gilbert Phester. He owes us a full refund for the hunt, anyway. If hunt is what you want to call this sorry state of affairs."

"But—"

"But nothing." The third hunter raised his rifle to a half-alert position. The gesture was unmistakable. Werner blanched.

The other hunters slipped the safeties off their rifles, each keeping an eye on Werner who now shrugged his shoulders, telling himself fuck it, it's out of my hands. He deliberately kept his weapon pointed at the ground, knowing the hunters were royally pissed off and edgy. If what they said about a side deal between Mr. Phester and Harry Phieu was true, the whole auction could blow up in the boss's face and of course, Werner would take the fall for it. The messenger's always blamed.

Caught between the hunters and Gilbert Phester, Werner realized his only option was to blow the joint.

THIRTY-ONE

Gilbert

Despite the frigid temperature of the air-conditioned reception room adjacent to the lobby, Gilbert was sweating. His mother, sitting beside him on a sofa, was losing her composure. Werner, pale faced and looking frightened, stood behind the sofa and said nothing. Gilbert's Chihuahua, Pootie, sat at her owner's feet and snarled at the hunters. Gilbert tugged at her leash and told her to hush.

Mildred bounded to her feet. "How dare you accuse my son of cheating?"

Gilbert patted his mother's arm. "Sit down, Mother."

Mildred glared at the hunters but obediently sat down.

The hunters, with rifles in hand, stared angrily at Gilbert, ignoring Mildred's outburst. Faces set and dour, their eyes drilled Gilbert. He squirmed under their unforgiving gazes.

"The hunt was bad enough, Harry Phieu getting killed and all," the second hunter said, "but you cheating us at the auction, that's where you went way over the line." He hefted the rifle on his hip. A gesture not lost on Gilbert who fervently wished he was someplace other than the Retreat. Pootie alternately growled and whined.

"Hush," Gilbert whispered to the dog.

"I don't know about the rest of these guys," the third hunter, the cynical one, said, "but I want my goddamn money back. Both for the hunt and for the young brunette I bought last night. As I remember,

Harry Phieu bid on her. How do I know he didn't bid up the price so you could get more money from me?"

"That's a pretty shitty way to treat your good customers, Mister Phester," said hunter number two, his eyes blazing with anger. "No way do I come back here next year."

"Or any other year for that matter," Nervous Nellie added.

Gilbert sputtered something unintelligible. Mildred's face turned a deep red, bordering on purple. Her eyes radiated unadulterated hatred. Gilbert patted her arm although his heart was threatening to detonate.

"Yeah," said the first hunter. "We trusted you, Mr. Phester. Now we want our money back and pretty damn quick. We think your local lawman killed Harry Phieu, and right now it wouldn't surprise me if he wasn't having a cup of coffee in police headquarters somewhere, spilling his guts about the auction and the hunt. Which means there's not much time left."

Gilbert felt as if his stomach was caving in. Events were rapidly slipping out of his control. He had to find some way to calm the hunters before the other buyers found out. He thought fast and hatched a desperate plan.

"I'll tell you what I'm going to do for you gentlemen. I have a lot of money in my safe upstairs from the auction last night. Simply accompany me to my private suite and I'll pay what I owe you and a generous stipend besides. In cash." Gilbert stared at his mother. A signal passed between them. Pootie, restless and instinctively recognizing danger, jerked on her leash. She yipped and yapped until Gilbert muzzled her with his hand.

"What's this stipend thing?" the second hunter asked.

Glibert managed a shaky smile. "Just an extra something for your troubles."

The third hunter smirked. "You mean for not sayin' anythin' to the other buyers, right?"

Gilbert blinked. "Right."

"Exactly how much is this stipend?" the second hunter asked.

"Ten thousand dollars. And, in addition, a full refund for the hunt plus whatever amount you paid for the girls. And you get to keep the girls as my apology." Gilbert patted the sweat from his brow with a monogrammed handkerchief. "Provided, of course, you do not mention this to any of the other buyers."

The hunters looked suspicious. They put their heads together and whispered. The third hunter, appointed spokesman for the group, eyed Gilbert with distrust. "Okay, but anything goes wrong or you try something tricky on us, I'll personally blow your head off. That's a promise."

Gilbert winced. "Understood. We'll all go up together ... without the guns."

The third hunter exploded. "Bullshit, no fucking way."

"What're you trying to pull now?" the first hunter asked. His jaw muscles worked furiously.

"Please, gentlemen, I'm only proposing what's sensible. If all of us walk through the lobby, guns at the ready, the staff and other guests will become alarmed. They might call the police, even charge you."

The hunters whispered among themselves again. The third hunter, as spokesman for the others, reluctantly acceded to Gilbert's request. He told the hunters, "There are four of us and three of them, including Werner and the old lady. If any of them fuck with us, we'll gut the bastards." He unsheathed his hunting knife and flashed it underneath Gilbert's nose.

Gilbert's face turned ashen. Pootie barked and strained at her leash. Mildred shook with restrained fury.

"Where are the two women we dragged in?" one hunter asked. "Them and Mr. Bones?"

"They're being attended to," Gilbert said in a shaken but frosty voice. "That's our business. ... Are we ready to go?"

Werner deposited his handgun—the revolver he had stripped from Mr. Bones – and his rifle behind the sofa. The hunters stacked their rifles in the same spot. The party of seven plus Pootie, led by Gilbert, marched out of the reception room and stopped in front of the elevators. Guests and attendants in the lobby looked the party over with cursory interest and returned to whatever else they were doing.

Gilbert's heart raced as he pressed the elevator button. Everybody faced forward, backs to the lobby until the elevator arrived and its doors swooshed open. Gilbert and his mother exchanged meaningful glances again. At the fifth floor the party emerged from the elevator. Mildred, last out, staggered and collapsed in front of the door the elevator, on the opposite side from the entrance to Gilbert's penthouse suite.

"Mother, my God!" Gilbert screeched. "Somebody help her."

The hunters rushed forward and kneeled beside Mildred. In the ensuing confusion Gilbert, with Pootie in his arms, slipped inside his suite and locked the door behind him. He dropped the incessantly barking dog, and at a console in the foyer rang the alarm. He knew in moments armed attendants would storm the fifth floor and either kill or capture the hunters. He offered a silent prayer for his mother's safety, then picked up the house phone and called Bobby.

THIRTY-TWO

Helen

Helen, feverish but conscious and aware of her surroundings, cast furtive glances at the area around her. They were in a storage room. Spare pieces of furniture in various states of repair cluttered the floor. Clair sat next to her along with Mr. Bones, all of them under the watchful eye of Bobby.

She had overheard Gilbert's instructions to Bobby moments before he left to talk with the hunters. "Whatever you do, Bobby, don't hurt the women. They're still worth money to me, particularly the young one." He wrinkled his nose in distaste. "After they're suitably cleaned and dressed, of course. Keep them locked in this storage room and don't allow anybody in until I give you the all clear."

"What about the skinny sand nigger?"

Gilbert's cold eyes appraised Mr. Bones. "For now, leave him be. I'm not sure what we'll do with him. Just don't let him out of your sight."

"He shot Melissa in the knee. I like Melissa." Bobby repetitively flexed and relaxed his fists as if preparing for a fight.

Gilbert raised one eyebrow, apparently questioning Bobby's motives. "Don't worry, we'll find some other woman for you. Somebody besides Melissa. One that takes your fancy."

"I still don't like the sand nigger."

Gilbert studied Mr. Bones again and whispered something in Bobby's ear. Whatever it was it pleased the giant. His eyes, through the thick lenses, shone with a mixture of excitement and anticipation.

251

Gilbert walked to the door.

"Boss?"

A look of impatience crossed Gilbert's face. "Hurry up, Bobby, there are people waiting for me."

"How soon can I have one of the women you told me about?"

"As soon as this is over, I promise you. And not one, but several. Now, I must go. The hunters are waiting for me." Gilbert slipped through the door.

Bobby, apparently aroused by whatever Gilbert promised him, locked the door behind him and loomed over the two women. Mother and daughter huddled together on a love seat. Bobby's breath came in raspy spurts and his pants tented at the crotch. He pulled at his pants with bulky fingers.

Clair said, "Mr. Phester told you not to harm us. Better not cross him."

Bobby's face clouded over. "You," he said and pointed an accusing finger at Clair. "I got lumps on my head from the pickup truck you drove that hit my head." His hard-on faded and he gingerly probed the top of his skull. But Clair's words had their desired effect; he stepped back from the women.

"Don't get him upset," Helen whispered, alarmed.

Clair turned to her mother and hugged her while eyeing Bobby. "I'll get you some more water, Mom."

"Sit still," Bobby growled.

"Not now, dear." Helen's eyes revealed her dread.

Bobby sat down in a chair opposite the women and Mr. Bones and folded his hands on his lap. Helen took the opportunity to more closely study her surroundings. If she remembered correctly, the storage room they were in was attached to the reception room. If somehow they could enter the reception room, from there it was but a step to the lobby and possible escape.

But such a long step.

Helen didn't know what to do. And she was too exhausted to think clearly. She felt her forehead, realized she had a slight fever, and had in fact been slipping in and out of consciousness since Clair and Mr. Bones rescued her from the hot box.

She slumped in her seat, discouraged. They'd never get past Bobby. He was too strong and too alert and too fast. Not to mention mean. If they dared an escape attempt, no telling what he'd do to them.

God, how she wished she had followed her own instincts when Marshall insisted they spend the night at the Retreat. Some inner alarm bell had clanged and she stupidly ignored it to appease Marshall's fragile ego.

That's what comes from being too civilized, she realized. You dampen your natural instincts, those that protect every human from harm. Never expecting the worst, you ignore the marvelous warning system nature installed in you thousands of years ago. To your everlasting regret.

She stirred and her thoughts returned to family. Marshall, where was he? Was he safe? Had Justin attempted to find us when we didn't show up at the resort in Ft. Lauderdale? If so, where was he? Was he here, captured? And Heather, poor girl, what did we get that innocent child into? Twinges of guilt shot through Helen.

A thousand images crowded her mind. She squeezed her eyes shut and concentrated on Roger until, in the thrall of loving recollections, she relaxed and a warm feeling washed over her. A tiny smile turned up the corners of her mouth as she recalled lying in bed beside Roger in his apartment on rainy weekend days, preparing gourmet meals for him in the crowded kitchen of his apartment, watching daytime soap operas and laughing together at the absurdity of life. All the simple mundane things people take for granted.

And yet ... she couldn't put her finger on it but an unsettling feeling gripped her. The idea that she might never *want* to see Roger again slipped into her consciousness and startled her, made her catch her breath. It can't be ... could it?

Suppose, she asked herself, that she miraculously survived the horrors of the Retreat, would she ever be the same woman again? Could she pick-up her life where she left off? Did she really and truly want to?

She didn't think so. At least she wasn't sure, anymore. The appalling events of the past few days had shaped her thinking, made her realize that family was everything; in the final analysis it was all one had.

She had to admit that had Roger been with her on this trip he would have abandoned her in a heartbeat to save his own skin. Roger was *not* family. All she was to him, and all that she ever would be, is a sideline piece of ass, a handy pit stop to relieve his raging hormones. She intuitively knew that before today, but until now never wanted to admit it. The thought hit home with the concussive force of an exploding grenade.

What a damn fool she had been. How could she ever have thought that his touch could replace the real love and joy of her life, her family? She took a deep breath and tried to let go of Roger, or more precisely, her obsession with him. With a searing finality she realized that never again would she dare hold Roger in her arms. Understanding that he was her personal Armageddon, and if she ever was foolish enough to find herself alone with him, she would collapse and surrender to Roger and abandon her family. A sacrifice she was not prepared to make. With fierce determination she rudely shoved aside the image of Roger.

But oh how it hurt. It hurt so much. Tears flooded her eyes.

"Mrs. King, are you okay?" Mr. Bones asked.

Helen choked out a yes. Clair wiped away her mother's tears.

Bobby, restless, jumped up from his seat. "All of you, shut up."

"The woman is ailing," Mr. Bones said. "We need to–"

The backhand blow from Bobby's meaty hand caught Mr. Bones on the side of his face with the force of a grenade. Bloody teeth flew from his mouth. He dropped to the floor like a pile of clothes dropped into a hamper. Dazed but conscious, he lifted himself to a sitting position.

"You son of a bitch," Clair yelled.

"Clair, don't!" Helen cried out.

Her warning came too late. But instead of attacking the two women who cowered on the love seat, Bobby reached down and grabbed Mr. Bones by the throat and lifted him off his feet with his good arm, the one not wounded. He held his arm straight out and squeezed Mr. Bones's throat. The corded muscles in his arm bulged with the effort but held firm, his arm as steady as a steel beam set in concrete and just as large and imposing. Bobby's eyes glistened and his pants tented again.

The hanging seemed to last forever. Mr. Bones's bloodshot eyes swelled and protruded. His tiny hands beat ineffectually at Bobby's arm and he emitted mewing noises as he unsuccessfully tried to suck air into his lungs. His dangling feet tangoed in a macabre dance. Helen heard a series of dull cracks and realized to her horror that Mr. Bones's neck and Adam's apple were collapsing. When Mr. Bones's face changed from a congested red to a cyanide blue, Bobby dropped the corpse at his feet.

Helen's heart was thumping so hard she feared a seizure. She clung to Clair, and the two women gawked fearfully at Bobby. He took a step towards them, his mouth frothing, a cruel gleam in his eyes, his breath coming fast. Helen prayed silently, her lips mouthing the words.

The house phone rang and Clair had the presence of mind to pick it up. She listened for a moment and handed the phone to Bobby. "It's Mr. Phester. For you."

Bobby hesitated and stared at her open-mouthed. The maniacal look left his eyes and he grabbed the phone from Clair's hands.

"Yeah." Bobby listened and nodded his head. "Be right up." He turned to the women and shook his fist at them. "The boss wants me upstairs. Soon as I get done, I'm coming back for you two." He reached over and squeezed the nipple of one of Clair's breasts. She screamed and fell into her mother's arms. "Something for you to remember me by, bitch."

With that he gave them a twisted smile and lumbered from the room, locking the door behind him.

Clair gripped her breast, doubled over and broke out in whimpers that broke Helen's heart. She held Clair in her arms until her daughter's pain eased off. Both women avoided looking at Mr. Bones's body. Soon afterward Helen turned her attention to how she and Clair might escape.

THIRTY-THREE

Mildred

When the attendants stormed the top floor of the Retreat, the hunters met them using Mildred as a shield. Hunter number three, the mean one, gripped the old lady in an arm lock around her neck with his hunting knife pinpricking her throat.

The other hunters, standing behind Mildred and using their cell phones, called buyers who hadn't yet left the resort with their prize slaves in tow. Telling them about the private deal between Gilbert Phester and Harry Phieu. Dirty bastards! Ingrates! Despite everything Gilbert had done for them, they were turning on him as if he was a nobody, a stranger, instead of the man who had hosted them graciously over the years and made them all rich.

Werner stood well back of the hunters, sweating profusely, his back pressed against the door of Gilbert's penthouse suite, as far away as he could get from the action.

The hunter holding a knife to Mildred's throat growled at the attendants, "Back in the elevator or I'll cut Phester's mama."

The attendants backed away. One of them repeatedly jabbed the elevator button. Otherwise nobody said a word or made a sound. The hunters and attendants gaped at each other open mouthed like people and fish on opposite sides of an aquarium glass tank. The only sounds permeating the hallway in front of the penthouse suite were heavy breathing and the elevator motor humming as the elevator cab slid along its cabled pathway to the top floor.

When the elevator arrived, the doors swished open and Bobby charged out, bellowing, his eyes ablaze with fury, lips drawn back over his teeth in a snarl. Like the seas parting, the attendants jumped aside to give Bobby a clear passage. He plowed into the hunter holding Mildred and the knife flew out of his hand and clattered on the marble floor. The hunter fell to the floor with Mildred on top of him. The other three hunters, stunned, backed away from Bobby, their eyes flashing fear and disbelief.

Bobby emitted a blood-curling howl, kicked the prostrate hunter in the head and tore into the remaining three. The terrified hunters scattered in the small hallway but were unable to escape the terror confronting them. They cringed and covered their faces in abject surrender but Bobby, in a rage, kicked and punched all three until their shattered, bloodstained corpses littered the hallway.

Bobby stood over them, panting, spittle flowing from his mouth, fists clenching, unclenching in a convulsive rhythm. Mildred climbed to her feet and wheezed, rubbed her breasts where she had fallen on the third hunter.

The attendants fought one another to escape into the relative safety of the elevator, each of them muttering words to the effect that "No amount of money is worth losing your life over," and "I don't give a shit what Phester's got on me, I'm getting the hell out of here." Several hands from frantic attendants stabbed at the down elevator button. The elevator door closed and the cab descended.

A deadly quiet permeated the hallway. Bobby stood shuddering, slobbering, sucking in deep rasping breaths of air, sounding like a pilot without an oxygen mask at 40,000 feet. He removed his glasses and wiped its lenses on the sleeve of his shirt. Mildred and

Werner, frightened beyond belief, stood as far away from Bobby as possible, which to Mildred wasn't far enough.

The sound of footsteps pounding up the stairwell alerted the three. Their heads pivoted to the door leading to the stairs as it flew open and several angry buyers charged into the hallway, knives and handguns flashing. Bobby let loose a ferocious howl and slammed into them with the power of a human bulldozer on speed, knocking the startled buyers down, sending them and their weapons sprawling in every direction. Those few buyers left standing after the frightful onslaught, and now instantly terrorized, fired their handguns wildly. Bullets chipped the marble entranceway and floor, missing Bobby, Mildred and Werner.

Bobby ripped the guns from their hands and flayed the buyers, hollering like an Indian warrior scalping white settlers. Werner dropped to a crouch and slipped through the stairwell door and disappeared. Mildred hovered in a corner as Bobby grabbed one buyer from behind, grasped his neck with one giant hand, shoved his knee into the buyer's back and snapped his spine.

That was enough for the other buyers, those who still maintained control over their motor functions. They ran or crawled, shrieking, into the stairwell. Bobby pummeled the buyers left behind until no life remained in their bodies.

When he was spent and everybody lay dead or near death, he lifted his head and gazed at Mildred with a menacing look that spoke of horrors to come. "Where's the boss?" he asked in a voice as incongruously calm as if he were asking Mildred the time of day. Spittle dripped down his chin and his mouth formed an ugly scowl in harsh counterpoint to the gentle sound of his voice.

Mildred didn't know whether to laugh or scream. She cowered in a corner of the hallway, recognizing that the split between Bobby's savage behavior and the calm manner of his voice showed he was out of control..

"He's safe inside." Guessing that Gilbert had called Bobby when the hunters stormed the hallway. Assuming that he now wished he hadn't. Now, after listening to the commotion on the other side of his door, she knew her precious son would be too frightened to let Bobby in.

Bobby slapped the door to the suite with an open hand. It rattled on its frame in response.

"Yes?" A timid voice came from inside the suite, the sound emerging through an electronic transmitter in the solid oak door. Accompanied by Pootie's tinny but relentless barking.

"It's me, Bobby. Open up."

Silence, then, "Let me talk to Mother."

Bobby motioned to Mildred.

She approached the door and knocked while keeping a wary eye on Bobby. "It's me, Sonny."

"What's going on, Mother?"

Mildred's gaze swept the pile of bodies on the floor of the hallway. "Bobby took care of our problem. But I'm afraid the word's out. The buyers know."

"Oh my God! We're ruined."

Bobby scowled at Mildred. She licked her dry lips. "Better open up now, Sonny. Bobby's getting impatient."

"Are the flowers blooming?" Gilbert asked. Code words that he and Mildred had devised to query each other about impending trouble.

"They bud only in springtime," Mildred answered. A coded reply meaning imminent danger.

Bobby paced in front of the door. Every time he passed Mildred she cringed.

He abruptly stopped in front of the door and put his face near the transmitter. "Hey, boss, c'mon, I got to talk to you. Open the door."

"I'm okay now, Bobby. I don't need you any longer. Just go back down to the lobby. You've done a good job. I'll have two women waiting for you. You can have all the fun you want with them."

"That ain't what I want to see you about, boss. See, everythin's turned around right now. I killed a whole bunch of people for you, boss. I'm in trouble and need a lot of money to get away."

"And I appreciate what you've done, Bobby. Tell you what, you go downstairs, take any woman or as many as you want with my blessing. I'll have your money ready in an hour."

Bobby said "Shit, boss, I ain't waitin'," then cocked one of his mammoth legs and kicked the door of the penthouse suite. The doorframe cracked around the hinges but held. Mildred screamed. Bobby cranked his leg like a piston and let it fly into the face of the door. BOOM! Once, twice, three times. To Mildred each whack reverberated like an airplane breaking the sound barrier. Bobby swore and kicked harder with each blow to the door. His eyes started getting crazy again; they shone with a malevolent intensity that made Mildred shiver. The door finally blew open, splinters flying like shrapnel. It hit the carpeted floor with a thunderous crash. Bobby grabbed Mildred by the arm and dragged her, swearing, into Gilbert Phester's penthouse suite.

THIRTY-FOUR

Gilbert

"**W**here's my money, boss?" Bobby's voice came out reasonable, quiet, in opposition to his eyes, which alternately sparked with fire and ice.

Gilbert's face was drawn and pale. He held the yapping Pootie and petted her to quiet and reassure the dog, which was frothing at the mouth. When Gilbert spoke his lips trembled. "I promise you'll have it within the next hour, Bobby. I need to go to the bank."

"Hey boss, don't treat me like a dummy. I know you keep the money you get from the buyers somewhere around here."

"I ... I put it in the bank."

Bobby shook his head. "No way, you didn't have enough time since the auction. Besides, I know you always keep a whole pile of cash around. Got that info from Werner."

Gilbert licked his lips and stared at Bobby in dread fascination. He inwardly cursed Werner, promised himself to find the traitor and have him killed as soon as this crisis ended.

Pootie continued snarling, tried to pry herself loose from Gilbert's arms and strike at Bobby.

"Boss, shut that fuckin mutt up."

Gilbert petted and hushed the dog until she quieted. Thinking fast all the while. He sadly realized that after today, the Retreat was history. It was only a matter of hours until the place was swarming with police. His only option was to take Mother and Pootie and run. A terrible, terrible pity, but not an event that would bankrupt him. For years he had squirreled money away in a Bahamian bank account, preparing for the possibility of a catastrophic event. Always a strong possibility in this business. His offshore bank account now stood at over ten million. Add the cash from his safe, about four million, and he had more than enough to retire. A princely sum. Preferably to be spent in retirement in Buenos Aires, Argentina, a location he and Mother had scouted years before, a place where his American dollars would stretch the furthest.

Mildred asked Bobby, "How much do you want?"

Bobby cranked his head to the side and grinned at Mildred. "Now you're talkin'. How much you got?"

"How about $100,000?" Mildred said.

Bobby thought about it. "Look, with everythin' that happened here, me protectin' both of you and all, killin' all them hunters, I deserve a lot more."

"How much more?" Gilbert asked. He was regaining his composure now that they had moved from threats to bargaining, an activity Gilbert had mastered over the years.

"Say a million."

Glibert blanched. "That's excessive, Bobby. Look, I'll give you $250,000 and help you escape."

"I don't need no help. I want the million." He took a threatening step toward Bobby. The dog growled, the hair along its back stood on end.

Gilbert didn't trust Bobby, was afraid to reveal to him where he kept his cash, yet what alternative did he have? Bobby's emotions were volatile, his flash point low. He could easily crush Gilbert and his mother. Gilbert was afraid to push the giant beyond the point where he lost all reason.

Mildred jumped in. "One million sounds reasonable, doesn't it Sonny?" She flashed her eyes at her son. Gilbert picked up the message. "Yes, mother it does. It certainly does." Gilbert pasted a phony smile on his face and flashed a response with his eyes: Be careful.

"All right, Bobby, the million is yours. All in cash. But you must leave immediately afterward. Of course, on the way out you can help yourself to any girl you want in the Retreat." He winked at Bobby and gave him a wan smile.

"You got it, boss." Bobby smiled generously at Gilbert and Mildred. "Let's see the green."

Gilbert waded into his apartment, carrying Pootie with Bobby and Mildred trailing behind him. In Gilbert's lavish bedroom, Bobby looked around and whistled. "Livin' high off the hog, ain't you?"

Gilbert ignored the comment, instead flashed his eyes again at Mother who nodded imperceptibly. Near the king-sized bed Gilbert dropped to his knees and pushed aside a night table, revealing a waist-high safe sunk into the bedroom wall. With his back to Bobby and blocking the giant's view, he cushioned Pootie in one arm and twirled the tumblers until the safe cracked open. All the time his heart drumming a staccato beat, knowing that once the cash was in reach, Booby would be at his most dangerous.

Gilbert counted out a million dollars in stacks of hundred dollar bills and passed the packages to Bobby. "Go now. There's no time. The police will be here soon."

Bobby licked his lips at the sight of all the money. He looked beyond Gilbert to the safe. "How much more you got in there?"

"Bobby, you promised." Gilbert's voice exposed his fear.

"Yeah I sure did." Bobby's eyes glimmered with reptilian malice. "Now get out of my way while I check for myself."

Mildred, carrying a poker iron, which she had quietly taken from the bedroom's fireplace, sneaked up behind Bobby and swung the poker with all the strength she could summon.

Bobby, attuned to danger as only a wanted criminal and ex-con can be, never allowed himself to become so distracted as to lose a sense of his surroundings. He felt rather than heard Mildred approach and immediately whirled around and brought his arm up in a self-defensive gesture. The poker struck him on the arm and he bellowed. The packages of money dropped to the floor. With his free hand he grabbed the poker and twisted it out of Mildred's hand, dropped it on the carpet. Roaring with pain he seized Mildred by the neck.

Gilbert released Pootie. She coiled her small body and jumped up and sank her tiny razor-sharp teeth into Bobby's forearm. The same arm wounded when Billy Ray tried to escape. The same arm Mildred struck with the poker. Bobby released his grip on Mildred and grabbed the dog by the throat. He swore and held the Chihuahua in front of his face, shook Pootie until her neck broke with a distinctive crack, the kind of noise one makes when snapping a wishbone in two. He slammed her lifeless body onto the floor and drop kicked her across the room.

"*No!*" Gilbert screeched. He charged Bobby, pummeled Bobby's chest and face with tiny fists. Bobby, startled, stepped back and stared at a boss gone wild, a snarling creature he had never seen before. A boss who never lost his cool. Until now.

Gilbert collapsed on the floor and cradled Pootie's body in his arms and wept.

Mildred, teeth exposed in a ferocious snarl, attacked Bobby. She jumped on his back and wrapped her legs around his waist. She reached in front and tried to gouge out Bobby's eyes. The lady never made it. Bobby grabbed her outstretched hands and crushed them in his own powerful mitts. Gilbert heard the delicate bones in her hands crack. She screamed but held onto Bobby, her legs clenched around him in a death grip and bit his neck. Bobby, howling, danced around the bedroom trying to dislodge a now crippled Mildred but she refused to let go. Yelling curses, he rushed backwards until he crashed against the glass door of the apartment's terrace. The door shattered and Mildred cursed as an army of tiny cuts stung her. Still she clung to him like a leech to a dog's bloodstream. Bobby jumped backwards and slammed into a bedroom wall. The air whooshed out of Mildred's lungs and her grip weakened. Bobby pried her legs loose and dislodged her. She fell to the floor, barely conscious, eyelids fluttering, crippled hands held close to her chest. Blood poured out of her nose and mouth and from a hundred tiny cuts on her lacerated face. Bobby kicked her in the head three times until she stopped moving.

"*Mother!*" Gilbert shrieked in a falsetto voice. He dropped Pootie's lifeless body and rushed to his mother's side.

Bobby strode to the bed and stripped a pillowcase from a pillow. He carried it to the safe and bent over and scooped piles of stacked bills into the pillowcase, threw his million on top.

"You killed her, you monster." Gilbert sprang to his feet and clawed at Bobby's face. Unfortunately for Gilbert he succeeded in ripping open the skin underneath Bobby's left eye. Bobby dropped the pillowcase filled with bills and jumped back, tenderly felt his face and came away with blood.

Gilbert watched Bobby's face with utter fascination, like a condemned prisoner observing the testing of a rope at his hanging. Bobby's face erupted in a series of emotions, ranging from stunned disbelief to absolute rage. Something snapped in Bobby, something horrible.

Gilbert backed up on unsteady legs, trying to put as much distance between himself and Bobby as possible. The big man trembled with the force of a machine shaking its foundation, then erupted in an ear-splitting roar. He charged Gilbert, lifted him over his head with the ease of a weightlifter hoisting a rag doll, and carried him through the shattered glass door onto the terrace. Gilbert screamed his protest and ripped out clumps of Bobby's hair. Bobby, in such a furor that he felt no pain, paused at the rail of the terrace and straightened his arms overhead, holding Gilbert aloft like an Olympian hoisting a trophy. Gilbert glanced down at the concrete walk below and in that instant understood his fate.

Bobby hurled him into the air. Gilbert, falling, realized in his last few cogent moments of life, that living without his mother and Pootie would be intolerable.

He surrendered his body.

THIRTY-FIVE

Billy Ray

Billy Ray reckoned that Werner had positioned attendants at the edges of the Retreat's estate to contain the hunters' quarry. He decided that the best way to return to the Retreat without risking a confrontation was to travel the access road from the public highway leading to Wicked Stop.

It was a daring move. He didn't know if the road was blocked, gambled instead that the hunt had stretched the Retreat's manpower resources so thin the public access road would be unguarded, at least for the duration of the hunt.

There was no question in Billy Ray's mind that he had to return to the Retreat. Too many lives were at stake, not only the young women being hauled away as slaves, but also older people like Marshall and his wife who were defenseless against the likes of Gilbert Phester.

And, of course, there was Clair. He couldn't get her out of his mind. Didn't really want to, if he'd care to admit it. It wasn't so much her looks, though she was certainly attractive enough and had a dynamite body. He vividly recalled finding her naked when she tried to break out of Wicked Stop, and how one look had left him breathless. Neither was it solely her intellect, which he both envied and admired. He certainly had to consider her courage, or as his grandpa called it, "pluck." He smiled to himself at the thought. Clair was considerably younger than he was, yet she possessed a maturity beyond her years, a maturity that leveled the playing field between them. Or so he wanted to believe.

Wake up, he admonished himself, and the daydream fizzled. He could never compete on the same playing field as Clair, not in this lifetime. A chasm of differences stood between them. He dismissed the idea, writing it off to mere foolishness. How could a roughshod guy like himself with a dim future ever hope to attract a woman of Clair's caliber? Just another pipe dream that would never become reality. Not a chance.

Returning to the Retreat had not been his first thought. More than anything he thirsted to grip the neck of a bottle of bourbon, work up a thirst reading its label. Oh yes, he'd lift the bottle slowly, deliciously, to his parched lips, tip it up and let the bourbon trickle down his throat, and withdraw the bottle only to let air into his lungs, then tip it back to his lips to slake his devouring thirst.

Mustering all the willpower at his command, he drove the idea from his mind and turned his attention to what lay ahead. By going to the Retreat the best he could hope for was to be brought back to Alabama to face a murder charge. The worst: his death at the hands of Werner or Bobby.

He didn't believe the few state and local cops Phester had in his pocket would go anywhere near the Retreat. Not since Billy Ray had reported the hunt and the murder of the old man, Randolph Dodge, to the Georgia Bureau of Investigation (GBI), the state of Georgia's equivalent of the FBI, a statewide police agency known for its integrity and effectiveness at solving crimes. Especially since Billy Ray told the GBI about the crooked state cops cooperating with Phester's criminal enterprise.

Police grapevines are noted for their speed. The suspect cops soon enough would be heading for the hills. The few hundred dollars Phester paid the crooked cops every month wasn't anywhere near enough to guarantee they'd stick around and try to bluff their way out of a felony charge.

Billy Ray found the access road and jogged along it in the direction of Wicked Stop. What he didn't expect to find was the Retreat's pickup truck barreling down the dirt road toward him, fleeing Wicked Stop, jouncing on ruts and grooves, springs squeaking in protest. And he particularly didn't expect to find a panicked Werner driving.

Billy Ray was positioned thirty yards in front of the pickup truck at a u-bend in the road. He brought the Winchester 30-30 to his shoulder and shot the front tire on the driver's side. The tire exploded and spun off the wheel. The pickup truck slid to the side and caromed off a poplar tree, then bounced to the other side of the road and smashed into a thicket of bushes and came to rest out of sight.

Billy Ray cautiously wended his way through the brush, approaching the truck from the rear. He crept up to the cab and yanked open the door.

To find it empty.

"Don't move a muscle, redneck." Werner, clothes torn, lower lip swollen and bleeding exited the brush at Billy Ray's side and pointed a nine millimeter Beretta handgun at him. He cocked the hammer. Billy Ray stretched his neck to get a better look.

"I said don't move. You never did learn to follow instructions ... Now real slow, put that rifle on the ground."

Billy Ray lowered the Winchester as instructed.

"Step away from the rifle. Move slow and easy, hands behind your head."

"It won't do you any good, skinhead," Billy Ray said as he moved aside. "The cops are on their way. They'll be driving up this here road before you know it."

Werner picked up the rifle and sneered at Billy

Ray. He tucked the handgun in his belt and pointed the rifle at Billy Ray. "Show's how stupid you are, redneck. Mr. Phester's got the state and local cops in his pocket."

"I'm not talking about the state or local cops. I'm talking GBI. I called them." Werner's sneer faded. He was from Wisconsin, but since landing in Georgia he had heard about the GBI from damn near every local criminal working at the Retreat. "What're you, nuts? Don't you know your ass is on the line?"

Billy Ray grunted. "Thought you might like to know I called from the cell phone I took off of your asshole buddy, Harry Phieu, after he tried to kill me."

Werner paled. "Shit, Billy Ray, don't blame me. You crossed Mr. Phester, tried to rat him out."

"Look at you, little Mr. Innocent. You been Phester's sidekick for a long time. How many girls you help him buy? How many people you help him kill?"

Werner sneered. "Yeah, and you didn't have nothing to do with it, did you? Shit, you knew everything going on at the Retreat, the slave business, the hunt, everything else. You even brought back a few runaways. You're in this up to your ass. We go down, you go down."

"Maybe, but you're going down for murder. You killed Mr. Dodge, that old man. I was right there, an eyewitness. State of Georgia's going to inject you with lethal chemicals."

Werner's mouth tightened. "I guess you don't see me holding the gun. Only thing standing between you and a grave is my trigger finger."

Billy Ray shook his head. "You forgot old man King and his son. They also saw you kill Dodge. And they're both safe, away from here, on their way to the cops."

"Then I got nothing to lose by killing you, do I?" Werner spat out angrily. He lifted the rifle to his shoulder and Billy Ray tensed, waiting. "You don't want to do this, Werner."

"Oh yeah? Tell me why not."

"There are witnesses."

Werner, spooked, looked around. "I don't see anybody."

"I'm not talking seeing, I'm hearing." Billy Ray cocked an ear. "Hear it?"

"Hear what?"

"Just listen a second or two."

Werner strained to listen. From a distance came the sound of car engines racing and growing louder. The closer it got, the more Billy Ray thought it resembled the noise of a bunch of racing car drivers gunning their engines at a track meet.

As the racket continued to grow, Werner's mouth fell open. "What the hell!"

Werner was standing on the dirt road, Billy Ray to the side. From the direction of Wicked Stop a caravan of cars and trucks cannonballed down the road in the direction of the public highway, skittering across the curving road in an uneven line, trailing a mountain of dust behind them. Billy Ray reckoned these were the buyers and Retreat attendants making a run for it.

Earlier he had used the cell phone to call Clair, had found instead a panicked front desk attendant at the Retreat who was unaware of Billy Ray's fall from grace in the organization. So the attendant blabbed about Phester's side deal with Harry Phieu, how the buyers had found out and then stormed the fifth floor, how Bobby went bonkers in front of Phester's suite and killed a bunch of them.

As Werner gaped at the advancing army of vehicles, he lowered the rifle. Billy Ray came up close and sucker punched him on the side of his face, right on the jaw underneath the ear. The blow was enough to make Werner blank out for a moment or two. His legs wobbled and he dropped the rifle. Billy Ray scooped it up and jerked the handgun from Werner's belt.

"Like taking candy from a Nazi. I don't have the words exactly right, but you get my point, skinhead."

Werner got no further than opening his mouth to reply. The cars roared closer, their noise drowning out his words. Billy Ray lifted the rifle and waved it in front of the lead car, signaling it to stop. The driver saw Billy Ray at the last minute and stomped on the brakes and swerved to a stop. The pickup truck behind it narrowly missed a collision, as did the cars following. Windows flew open and people cussed Billy Ray.

The lead driver stepped out of his vehicle. "What the hell's goin' on here?"

"You're all under arrest," Billy Ray yelled, "Drop your weapons, get out of your cars and line up in front of me."

Werner skittered aside, but Billy Ray was faster. He cuffed him across the head with the butt of the rifle. Werner yelped, reflexively and bent over to avoid getting hit again. He remained crouched, afraid Billy Ray would clobber him again.

From the third car in line one of its occupants said, "It's Billy Ray, the town cop."

"Bet your ass," Billy Ray replied, "and the state police are minutes behind me." To emphasize his point he shot the rifle in the air.

The stampede began. Car doors sprang open, disgorging buyers and attendants, who dispersed into the woods surrounding them like ants fleeing a grass fire. To assure they didn't have second thoughts and return, Billy Ray shot the rifle two more times into the air. Moments later there wasn't a person in sight other than Billy Ray and Werner.

"Okay, skinhead," Billy Ray said and prodded Werner with the end of the rifle, "let's get moving. Back to the Retreat."

Werner stood to his full height, flexed his muscles and glared at Billy Ray. "You wouldn't be so tough without the rifle and gun."

Billy Ray showed Werner a toothy smile. He strolled up to him and threw the rifle at his feet. "Okay, skinhead, grab it."

Werner darted down and snatched the rifle. Before he could lift it more than a foot off the ground, Billy Ray kicked it out of his hands, then smacked Werner in the forehead with his open hand. Werner staggered to the side and twisted away. Not in time. Billy Ray spun him around and punched him in the abdomen. Werner doubled over, holding his gut. "Jesus, Billy—"

"Shut up." Billy Ray searched the cars closest to him, found a coil of rope and bound Werner's hands. Werner said nothing.

"You're not so tough after all are you, skinhead? Where's that superman you keep on talking about, where'd he disappear to, the one you always quote from, that German, what's his name?"

"Nietzsche."

"Sounds like Nazi to me."

Billy Ray with Werner in tow, followed the train of cars until coming to the last one, a dusty Toyota sedan. He shoved a quiescent Werner into the passenger seat and tied his feet with the remaining rope, then slid into the driver's seat, turned the car around and drove away. Werner, hands and feet bound, sat next to him and scanned the woods, silently weeping.

In the town of Wicked Stop not a soul was in sight, testament to the crisis at the Retreat. The two men reentered the woods on the other side of town and followed the winding dirt road until arriving at the perimeter of the Retreat's property. The gates were open, and they climbed the hill until the Retreat came into view.

Only one person was visible, a man floundering around at the entrance to the Retreat. Billy Ray tensed, preparing for trouble. He squinted at the man, then relaxed, couldn't believe who it was. He drove around the entrance horseshoe near the waterfall and cranked down his window to face a sweating and shaken Marshall King.

"I thought you were–"

"I came back for my family and my daughter's friend," Marshall said, out of breath and wheezing.

"Where's your son?"

Marshall hesitated and glanced inside the car at a bound and subdued Werner.

"It's okay to talk."

"Justin's safe. Exhausted but well." Marshall's voice turned bitter. "As well as anyone can be who's been raped. He's still in the cave."

Billy Ray reached out and touched Marshall's arm. "We'll get him out, soon. I promise."

A sob tore through Marshall's throat. "If only I had–"

A nightmarish scream from the Retreat interrupted their conversation. Billy Ray scrambled out of the car. "What was–"

"No time to talk now," Marshall said, rushing his words. He pointed to the Retreat, his eyes wide with fear. "That sounded like my daughter, Clair."

THIRTY-SIX

Helen

After Bobby locked-up Helen and Clair and rushed upstairs to Gilbert Phester's quarters, the women carried Mr. Bones's light body to a sofa and covered him with a spare blanket they found in a corner.

"May he rest in peace," Helen said and crossed herself.

"He helped save us. He's a hero."

"Let's make his death count for something," Helen said. "By getting out of here."

They hurriedly searched the room, seeking some way to flee before Bobby returned. The storage room they were in had no windows. Its single door led to the reception room where Werner and the hunters had confronted Gilbert Phester.

"If the hunters were in the reception room," Helen said, "there might be guns inside."

Clair, with one hand cushioning the breast Bobby had pinched, and wincing in pain, rattled the door handle. "Bobby locked it."

"What kind of lock is it?"

Clair examined the door hardware. "It's not one of those flimsy door locks like most homes have. The kind you can slip a credit card through and pop it open."

"Then it's a deadbolt." Helen groaned.

Clair tapped the door in various locations.

"What're you doing?"

Clair pressed her ear to the door and tapped again. She pulled away, her face flushed with excitement. "The door's hollow."

Helen wobbled to the door.

"Are you okay, Mom?"

"Do I look okay?"

A long-standing private joke between them. When something was wrong, they cheered each other with an "I'm okay, you're okay" repertoire, like an Abbott and Costello "Who's on first?" comedy routine. And usually finished by exchanging smiles. But not now. Clair and Helen were fighting for their lives and damn well knew it. If Bobby returned before they had a chance to escape...

Still, the simple exchange of an "I'm okay, you're okay" buoyed Helen and infused her with a gritty determination to break loose. No way was she going to let those bastards take down her family.

"What we need is a battering ram to roll across these parquet floors. If we can get something like that we can smash the door down." Clair hiked around the room, stepping over pieces of furniture and bric-a-brac until she found what she was looking for in a four-wheeled maintenance cart.

"This might do it."

"With that? It's too light."

"Not by itself. But with something heavy on it."

Helen pointed to the corner. "How about that credenza?"

Clair glanced around and nodded. "There's nothing else in this room big enough to do the job."

The heavy walnut credenza perched in a corner like a tank. It had to be seven-feet high and twelve feet wide. And weigh God knows what.

"Can we manage it?"

"I think so," Clair said, "if we can tip it onto the maintenance cart without breaking the cart."

"Let's try it, dear. I don't think we have much time."

"Are you up to this, Mom?"

"Do I have any choice?" Helen tried to grin but the

effort only twisted her mouth out of shape. The eye Werner had punched was shut and her nose was still puffed up.

She looked at the credenza. The task looked hopeless. Still, it was their best shot. They tilted the maintenance cart until an assortment of greasy nuts, bolts, pins, gears and hand tools toppled to the floor, then positioned the cart in front of the credenza. Clair got on one side of the credenza, Helen on the other.

"Ready, Mom?"

"Ready," Helen said, but to Clair she appeared weak, unsure.

"Okay, together now. Let's tip it over slowly."

Clair marshaled her strength and tugged on the credenza until it teetered. Helen strained; the cords in her neck stood out and her face turned a fiery red. The credenza shook a little and settled back in its upright position. Helen had to stop and sit down to catch her breath.

"Are you up to this, Mom?"

Helen nodded. "Have to be." Despite the air conditioning system pulsing cold blasts of air into the room, both women sweated freely. Helen wiped her brow.

They were ready to try again when a commotion outside their door made them stop. Clair ran to the door. "It's coming from the other side of the reception room. People yelling at each other to ... I can't quite hear it."

Helen dragged herself to the door and cocked an ear. "Sounds like they're yelling to get out fast."

Clair and Helen found each other's eyes. Fear spilled from them.

"Jesus, Mom, Bobby might be coming. Let's get moving."

They hustled back to the credenza. The urgency of

the moment gripped them.

"Ready now?" Clair said.

Helen took a few deep breaths, mumbled a silent prayer and nodded to Clair.

"Now!" Clair said. Both women tugged and pushed the credenza. Helen found the strength she needed and together, the two women tipped over the credenza. It crashed onto the cart and buckled the cart's heavy gauge angle iron legs.

"Thank the good Lord," Helen said and kneeled over to catch her breath.

"You did it, Mom, you did it!"

"Are the legs holding?" Helen asked, panting.

Clair bent over and examined the cart. "The wheels look okay. But the legs are damaged."

"Got to try it, anyway, and pray it holds," Helen said. "Let's clear the floor."

Together, they tugged the room's sofa and chairs and end tables and bric-a-brac to the sides, avoided looking at the sofa where Mr. Bones's body lay. When they finished there was a clear path from their improvised battering ram to the door of the reception room.

Clair gulped in air and tried to calm herself. Helen gathered her strength. The women crouched behind the credenza and grabbed hold of it.

"Ready?" Clair said.

"Yes."

"*Go!*"

The women dug their heels into the flooring and, grunting from the effort, shoved their improvised battering ram across the room. It thudded into the door and dented it; the frame cracked.

"Let's push it back fast and try again, Mom."

The women pushed the credenza-loaded cart back to its starting position.

"Ready?" Clair said.

"Ready."

"Let's go."

They shoved the ram as hard and as fast as their tired bodies would allow. It slammed into the door and the doorframe gave slightly. They rammed it again, and again. On the fourth try they splintered the door frame. On the fifth try, they knocked the door off its frame and both women reeled into the windowless reception room behind their battering ram, gasping for breath, their clothes sopping wet.

Helen immediately collapsed onto a chair. Clair careened around the room until she found what she was looking for. "Got it," she said triumphantly. She held a rifle over her head and grinned at her mother. Then plopped onto a sofa, exhausted. Helen depleted, prayed for time, knowing she would be too tired to resist should Bobby enter the room.

It wasn't to be. Moments later when her fatigued body was still screaming for rest Bobby broke down the door to the reception room and stormed in.

THIRTY-SEVEN

Clair

Clair pointed the rifle at Bobby. Terrified almost out of her mind. Terrified because this was the first time she had ever pointed a gun at anybody. Terrified because she knew nothing about firearms. Terrified because she didn't know if the safety was on or if the rifle held bullets. Terrified most of all because she didn't think she had the courage to pull the trigger.

Upon seeing the rifle in Clair's hands, Bobby stopped as if he had hit a brick wall. The speed of his reaction time startled Clair, alarmed her. Had she the courage to pull the trigger she knew Bobby would snatch the rifle out of her hands before she had a chance to fire it.

Bobby's face formed into a rictus of a smile, the kind that sends children shrieking and running to their mothers, the kind that provokes heart attacks in old ladies. The smile paralyzed Clair, immobilized her arms and legs. She swayed hypnotically, unable to tear her eyes away from Bobby's face.

Bobby dropped a large pink pillowcase stuffed with what appeared to be money. A few bills fluttered to the floor.

He turned his entire attention to Clair.

In slow motion Bobby reached over and slid his hand almost lovingly over the barrel of the rifle and gently tugged. Never once taking his eyes from Clair, his smile never once faltering.

Clair released the rifle and stepped back until she was flush against the wall with nowhere to run or hide. She felt the life force draining from her heart, lungs, brain, dribbling away to nothing on the floor.

"You don't want her, Bobby," Helen said in a surprisingly strong voice.

Bobby's head pivoted to Helen. "Your turn is comin', old lady. I'm gonna rip you to shreds. But first I'm gonna rape and kill your scumbag daughter while you watch." His malicious smile spread as he entertained the notion.

"What were you doing upstairs, Bobby?" Helen asked. Mother was buying time. *But for what?*

"Doin' what I shoulda done long ago. What I'm gonna do to you next." Bobby turned back to Clair. A look of pure venom flooded his eyes. Clair held her breath and cowered against the wall.

Helen pulled down her pants, exposing herself. She spread her legs. "You'll want some of this first." Bobby's eyes found Helen's bush and fixated on it. He couldn't seem to tear his gaze away. His pants tented again and he licked his lips.

"Mom! Don't!"

"Do what you have to do, Clair," Helen said, her voice trembling, touches of panic crowding in. "*What you must do.*" Meaning get out fast while Mom keeps Bobby occupied.

But Clair couldn't do it. Wouldn't do it. Not as long as her mother was in danger.

Helen's eyes slid away from Clair and she eased onto the floor, on her back, her face pale and strained, eyes feverish, body shivering.

Bobby grunted with satisfaction. He unzipped his pants, pulled his penis out and dropped to his knees in front of Helen.

"Run, Clair, run," Helen shouted with what strength she had left.

In the heat of the moment, Bobby paid no attention to Clair. He pounced on Helen, rammed his rigid penis into her. She screamed and clawed at Bobby's face. His thick glasses flew off his head and landed behind the sofa, out of sight.

"Dirty bitch," Bobby roared. He propped his body up on one hand, his penis still inside Helen, raised his other fist and walloped her with tremendous force. The blow landed on the side of Helen's neck and crushed the top of her spine. In her last fleeting moments of life Helen's eyes widened in surprise, then the light in them shriveled and died. She came to rest, her eyes still open, staring vacantly at the ceiling.

"*NO!*" Clair screamed. She leaped on Bobby's back and tore at his face, felt one of her fingernails rip a nostril. Bobby hollered and jumped to his feet, knocking Clair to the floor. He gingerly probed his injured nose, then snarled and dropped to the floor and crawled around, hands sweeping the carpet, searching for his glasses.

Clair grabbed his glasses from behind the sofa and, under the cover of surrounding chairs and end tables, silently crept away and hid behind the bar.

Frustrated, Bobby bounded to his feet, penis still hanging out of his pants. "Where are you, you son of a bitch?" he thundered. He moved forward, tripping over pieces of furniture, knocking them aside, using his hands to feel his way like a blind man. Snarling now and mouth frothing.

Abruptly, as if realizing that in his anger he might make a mistake and allow Clair to escape, Bobby stopped and collected himself. He resumed his hunt, this time more deliberately. He inched toward the bar, sweeping his arms in a wide arc before him. Clair would never be able to flank him and she knew it. Bobby's vision was still strong enough to detect rough movement and his speed and agility were unhampered.

Clair was trapped in a corner of the room, the bar the only barrier between her and an advancing Bobby.

Her pulse kicked into overdrive and she came close to outright panic. What could she do? An idea, hatched of desperation, flashed in her mind. Slowly and quietly she searched the shelves under the bar until she found what she was hunting for, a pair of ice tongs. She gripped them and took a deep breath, mouthed a silent prayer.

Then sprang out from the bar and grabbed Bobby's hanging penis with the tongs and jerked it with all her might.

Bobby, caught by surprise, screeched and jumped away. He tripped over a chair and landed with a thud on his back. The sudden action yanked the tongs from Clair's hand, but not before it tore a chunk of flesh from the head of Bobby's flaccid penis.

Bobby grabbed his bloody penis, bent over and cradled it in his hands. He started keening, a sound bringing to mind a dying German Shepherd Clair had seen shortly after the dog was hit by a car. The sound chilled her soul and drove her forward. Like a running back sprinting behind and around a guard, Clair circled Bobby and aimed for the doorway to the lobby.

But Bobby was too fast. He threw his arm to the side and grabbed Clair's thigh, not enough to hold her but enough to spin her around and disorient her.

Bobby rose and stood in front of the door, blocking it. Clair retreated until she came to the spot where the hunters had stored their weapons. She seized a revolver from the pile, the same revolver Mr. Bones had used to shatter Melissa's kneecap.

She pointed it at Bobby. "I've got a gun," she shrilled. "Stay away from me."

Bobby merely grunted. With tender, deliberate care he tucked his penis inside his pants and zipped up. A depraved smile made his face beam with pure malevolence. He took one tentative step toward Clair.

"Stop, you bastard, stop!" Clair sobbed. A steady flow of tears rolled down her cheeks.

"I got something special for you, bitch. I'm gonna eat you raw. Not like you think I mean it. I'll start with your ears, bite them off. Next, your tits. That's an appetizer. Next I'm gonna tear your chest open and eat your heart." He made slurping noises and rubbed his stomach.

"Stop it! Please stop it," Clair screamed.

"Not in a million fuckin' years." Bobby took another step toward her.

Clair grasped the handgun in both hands to keep them from trembling. Prayed that Bobby believed she'd shoot him, knew deep down she wasn't fooling him one bit.

As if reading her mind, Bobby smiled triumphantly at the visibly shaking revolver and reached forward to take it from her. Just as easily as he had taken the rifle from her earlier.

God save me, Clair prayed inwardly. Show me the way. The sweat poured from her, mingled with the tears on her face and dripped from her chin. Blood pounded in her ears.

Bobby shifted sideways and extended his arm and lightly stroked the revolver's barrel. In that exact instant, Clair saw the lifeless body of her mother lying on the floor, arms akimbo like a torn and discarded doll. Her throat welled and her soul cried out, *Goddamn it, you killed my mother. But you're not going to kill me.*

She scrunched her face and pulled the trigger with Bobby still holding onto the end of the barrel. The handgun thundered, sending a bullet plowing into Bobby's abdomen. The frightening noise made Clair's ears ring.

The confident smile dropped from Bobby's face

and he released his grip on the revolver's barrel, held his hand over the wound. He gazed stupidly at Clair, his eyes revealing disbelief, befuddlement.

"You shot me."

"Yes," she sobbed, "and I'm going to do it again." The next shot boomed and smashed into his chest.

Bobby staggered but remained on his feet. "You can't do this to—"

"Oh yes I can," Clair sobbed. She grit her teeth and emptied the clip. Two of the remaining three slugs tore into Bobby, the final slug smashing into his face and blowing off his nose. With each shot fired, Clair felt a colossal release, as if iron shackles were flying off her body.

Bobby collapsed in a heap at Clair's feet. She lowered the revolver and stood over his inert body. Without understanding why, she felt compelled to lean over and examine him as if what remained of Bobby was the most curious object she had ever run across in her lifetime. Mouth agape, she inspected every inch of his body.

Her eyes never leaving him, Clair dropped the handgun and probed Bobby's body with her foot. Her probing mutated to kicking. Soon she was dancing around the body kicking it and whimpering at the same time, small animal noises escaping her lips like spent air from a balloon. She felt an irresistible urge to beat her breastbone in the manner of her ancient relatives, an atavistic instinct she could no longer contain no matter how much she disdained it's senseless fury.

She could hold it in no longer. A savage cry tore from her throat and she threw her arms above her head, fists clenched, face raised to the heavens, in the universal sign of triumph. She screamed to God, demanding his attention, parading her conquest in the manner of ancient humans, the ageless celebration of life taken so life may continue.

Then she collapsed on the floor and crawled to her mother, held her lifeless body in her arms and rocked it, the tears flowing ceaselessly now, sobs wracking her throat, eyes swollen with sorrow.

Moments later Billy Ray and Marshall came charging into the room.

THIRTY-EIGHT

Clair and Billy Ray

Clair and Marshall sat on a sofa in the lobby and clung to each other. They paid scant attention to the small army of FBI and GBI investigators, state cops and sheriff's department deputies swarming over the Retreat.

Billy Ray exited the elevator and wended his way through the crowd. He plopped down onto a hardback chair opposite Clair and Marshall and sighed. "They're both dead."

"The Phesters?" Marshall asked.

Billy Ray nodded. "Gilbert and his mother. Bobby got them both. Mildred's body's is lying in a twisted heap in the penthouse suite. Gilbert Phester, or at least what's left of him, is splattered like a fried egg on the concrete apron around the pool."

Clair shuddered.

Billy Ray's face dropped. "Sorry, that wasn't real sensitive of me."

Clair managed a tremulous smile.

"Your mother was a courageous woman."

Both Marshall's and Clair's eyes filled with tears.

Billy Ray's cell phone rang. He listened and said. "Thanks, I'll let them know."

"They found your son, Mr. King. In the cave. He's alive and unhurt. Helicopter's bringing him back now."

"Marshall said, "Thank God."

Billy Ray wondered if Clair knew that Bobby had raped her brother. If not, he didn't envy Clair's father breaking the news to her. And he didn't envy Justin's task of moving beyond the rape. He guessed that the boy wasn't strong enough to overcome the horrible memory and his feelings of shame, would allow the incident to sour his life. Unless his father could turn him around.

"How about Heather?" Clair asked.

Billy Ray shrugged his shoulders. "The way the cops pieced it together, there was a Saudi Arabian buyer who bid pretty high to get her. A couple of attendants saw the Saudi leave the Retreat with Heather early this morning. She was pretty well drugged out."

Clair wept silently.

"I'll never forgive myself," Marshall said.

"If it'll help any, the authorities arrested every buyer and hunter they found wandering around in the woods."

"How many was that?" Marshall asked.

"Last I heard, about fifteen. Of the twenty-five or so who attended this auction and hunt."

"About half." Marshall's voice was bitter.

"And most of the Retreat's attendants. The ones they don't have now they'll soon find."

"Did all the attendants know about the white slavery business?" Marshall asked. "And the hunt?"

"They may claim they didn't know, but I don't think they'll get away with it. That's like being a sportswriter and being unaware of who won the World Series."

"How about that state police officer who turned us in?" Clair said.

"They got him. The GBI investigating officer in charge told me there may be a couple of others, as well as a sheriff's deputy or two, maybe even a couple of local politicians who Phester bought off."

"The doctor, the lady who drugged us?"

"Latest report is that she disappeared. Nobody knows where she is. If I was to guess, I'd say she skipped town. Lady was real savvy, on top of things. Knew what was going on around her."

"What's going to happen to you, Billy Ray?" Clair asked.

"Not sure. First thing, I guess, I have to answer for working as a lawman for Gilbert Phester. If I get through that without going to jail – and I'm not at all sure that I will – they'll take me back to Florence, Alabama. With any kind of luck I'll clear that trumped-up murder rap I told you about. After that, who knows?"

"Will I see you again?"

Billy Ray dropped into silence. "I sure hope so. But to tell you the truth, I'll probably serve time for working here."

Clair touched his arm. "Maybe it won't be for long." She wanted to see Billy Ray again but knew the odds were stacked against it. They came from totally opposite backgrounds. And of course, there was his drinking and his impending arrest. Still, who knows? Clair had faith that people could change, recognized that the traumatic experiences of the last few days had altered her perception of the world with breathtaking swiftness. She would never again face life without looking over her shoulder. So maybe Billy Ray could change, too. In his case, for the better.

Marshall patted Clair's hand and rose and shuffled off to the restroom.

Clair, watching her father, said, "I worry about him."

"No need to. He was very brave to return to the Retreat to rescue you and your mother. Most men would have kept running."

Clair had a faraway look in her eyes. "I guess Dad and I have a fresh opportunity to get to know each other."

Billy Ray said, "Maybe this isn't a good time, but do you mind if I ask you a question?"

"Go ahead."

"A minute or so before I ran into the reception room where Bobby ... well, where you and your mom were, I heard this blood curdling scream, like something out of the wild. Can't quite describe it. Maybe like a caveman who just fought and killed a thousand-pound bear with a spear, you know thumping his chest, screaming his victory to the high heavens. Truth is, it was so fierce it put me on edge. It didn't sound like Bobby, pitch was too high, but I guess the way you wounded him, it had to be." He stopped and gazed deep into her eyes. "It was Bobby, wasn't it?"

A sly smile crept along Clair's mouth and her eyes sparkled. "Sure, who else could it be?"

About the Author

Zane Smith is a pen name for Martin Smith, a retired company president who writes about business and management issues, when he's not writing novels. He is the author of sixteen nonfiction books and six published novels, two of which were optioned for film. He can be reached at zanesmith1956@gmail.com

NewPulpPress.com

www.ingramcontent.com/pod-product-compliance
Lightning Source LLC
Chambersburg PA
CBHW070553260626
47161CB00002B/594